DROWNING IN BEAUTY

the neo-decadent anthology

edited by

JUSTIN ISIS and DANIEL CORRICK

CONTENTS

INTRODUCTION

Daniel Corrick

Although we have been flying the Neo-Decadent flag for a number of years, the task of providing a set definition of it provoked an ongoing three-way debate amongst the architects of this project, with representatives from London, Tokyo and Santa Fe each emphasising differing aspects. We were however united on what Neo-Decadence is not: self-conscious stories of Parisian dandies and Crowleyan grave robbers set in locations the author knew of only from an hour's reading of another's work. Many attempts at Decadent writing in this scene have failed because the authors have merely attempted to imitate the prose and setting of an historical writer, Wilde, say, or Huysmans, rather than tailoring their style to suit the nature of the work at hand.

What then is Neo-Decadence? If we are to take the term literally we might assume it to be the content of the "original" Decadence updated to a contemporary setting and tackling or at least incorporating modern preoccupations. Yet this understanding, though broadly true, would leave us with the task of giving the meaning of Decadence itself, but a Decadence pried free from the era and locale in which it was first christened as such, the hyper-elegant London of the 1890s with its atmosphere of Occultism and veiled aristocratic perversion, and the licentious, turbulent Paris in the decades following the Second Empire—drenched in perfume and powder and rotting with lust, face flecked with gold, the rich incense of Catholicism still lingering behind it.

Maybe the best way to begin is to look at the prior literary tradition from which Decadence emerged and to which, for many, it proved the antithesis. I refer, of course, to the Naturalism of Zola and Flaubert. This movement with its emphasis on photographic realism and human psychology was one of the first forms of literature to attempt a primarily descriptive analysis of reality; that did not of course mean that Naturalist writers did not have a moral point to make—often they did—or that no judgement was passed on their characters, but that the world they chose to depict was indifferent to moral concerns. What's more, in their attempt at "unflinching realism"—intended to expose and scarify their audience with the hypocrisy of the bourgeois class—the psychological situations and character traits they tended to focus on were overwhelmingly negative: perversity, cruelty, greed and mania being but a few of their favourite themes. Ironically the "literature of beauty" was to be conceived through a fascination with squalor and ugliness.

What links the two movements together is the strong element of anti-consumerism they share. Although many Naturalist authors were in the thrall of a messianic positivism, in which Science was soon to provide a panacea for all social ills, the general implication of Naturalist literature was that humanity were becoming more venial and self-serving, and that the modern urban environment provided a perfect outlet for these vices; the same idea would return a century later with 60's writers such as J.G. Ballard claiming that the mod-

ern city was a breeding ground for perversion and un-
healthy fetishism. Ballard perceived that literary depic-
tions of the new patterns of behaviour created by our
technological society, the more outré yet accurate in-
stances of which were still being seen as fringe SF or ex-
perimental provocation, were in fact the new Realism.
Unwilling to accept this, "serious" mainstream literature has limped along with its eyes closed ever since,
like an aged matron acting out a hideous burlesque of
"the way we live now," occasionally borrowing the devices of more radical writers whilst still secretly attired
in its moth-eaten humanist props. In this it has been
aided by a vast system of academic approbation and
the demands of commercial publishing houses desperate for "relevant" new "masterpieces" on which indus-
try awards can be pinned. These inbred show ponies
have done much to cripple the direction of true art. On
the other, equally dubious hand, new commercial genre
fads continue to sprout up and quickly devolve into
mannerism, attracting fewer and fewer well-read and
well-travelled writers—profitably aided all the while,
of course, by conventions, Writers Workshops and
other braces for real creativity. However Bizarre, Weird
or provocative they might claim to be, most end up as
cul-de-sacs flooded with dross. Perhaps sensing where
things were headed, Naturalism was, for all its melior-
istic ardour, unable to refrain from giving voice to the
jaundice that must come upon a person of awareness
and refined sensibilities living in such a vulgar world.

Such 'boredom of disgust' opened up a new vantage
point from which to see the world, an aerial view from
which it was no longer possible to descend back into
the prosperous valleys of Naturalism. If the life of the
common man, be he bourgeois or proletarian, really

was so tedious and vulgar, why dedicate one's time to reading of it let alone writing about it? This shift in literary mood constituted a Luciferian revolt against the Utilitarian socio-civic values of Naturalism. Only that which transcended the normal, that which was against Nature as the former movement knew it, possessed the power to lift the reader out of the drab commercial world. This exploration of ecstasy in extremes is at the root of central Decadent concerns. In morality only great corruption and great virtue are of psychological interest: the shift away from social outcomes and towards alienated, solitary interiority meant that these characteristics soon ceased to be treated as matters of social imbalance and pathology and were increasingly spoken of in the quasi-theological language of sin and holiness, an otherworldly focus which only enhanced their appeal to those weary of earthly life. In Aesthetics the experience of beauty, contributing nothing to crude survival value, became the primary goal, both in terms of subject matter and the form of the artwork itself.

Decadence, then, involves a shift in aesthetic consciousness, an altered mental state which temporarily negates our awareness of whatever Utilitarian social purposes an object or person might serve. Exploration of beauty and its meaning becomes the aim of consciousness—whether it be the glimmer of the Godhead through earthly things or a narcotic to temporally dull the meaningless burden of existence, the beautiful serves as the vehicle of transcendence. Art and the inner lives of those dedicated to creating it become a central object of fascination; even more so than Romanticism, Decadence is art about the idea of art. The duality of lush, ornate style and extreme content lent the movement's disciples a new way of expressing their elevation over vulgar tastes; instead of celebrating beauty in the manifest sublime, many writers sought to find it in distorted situations, scenarios where human flourishing is put aside for some great extreme. According to this way of thinking, the mere scribbler can show beauty in a pastoral scene, whereas it takes a master artist to celebrate that quality in the sight of flesh succumbing to leprosy.

Ecstasy in extremes, art about art and the artist, hidden beauty; these are the defining features of Decadence, far more integral to it than the potpourri tropes—orchids, absinthe and satyrs—Weird fiction writers employ when they attempt to give their stories a yellow flourish. Neo-Decadence will look backward and forward: forward to where life in the 21st century is moving and backwards over the decades post-Sexual Revolution which shaped modernity. During the last eighty years world culture has seen an explosion of popular aesthetics, art-forms and movements associated with them: clothing, trends in fashion, tattoos, recreational drugs, musical sub-cultures, cosmetics, photography—all these can be the subject of obsessions, damnations and salvations. For the future, technological growth has greatly facilitated mass communication and material comfort, but it has also increased our capacity for distraction, for losing ourselves in profitless, obscure entertainment. Devices and formats, initially vulgar, are worshipped, only to be forgotten by all but the few initiates who, through their maniacal fixations, manage to uncover their hidden allure.

As has been mentioned, the creation of Decadent art often constituted its own subject-matter; a sizable amount of Decadent fiction was about the late 19th century art scene itself, either explicitly or implicitly.

Understandably, contemporary writers captivated by a Decadent ideal followed suit, something which though not necessarily detrimental to the individuals' stories, prevented Neo-Decadence from otherwise developing further. The varying contemporary art and fashion scenes present an inexhaustible supply of eccentric personalities and scenarios—to be involved in and with such would be of far greater value to one with a Neo-Decadent eye than any number of *fin de siècle* homages. It need not be Fine Art: fandom and counter-culture too are havens of the aesthetic extreme.

The stories that follow, then, are but a few attempts to apply the Decadent consciousness to these ready targets. Here in this volume the reader will encounter auto-pederastic time travel, cynical Japanese bar hostesses seeking a better world through the climax of nail ornamentation, fading love and sehnsucht amidst members of the Berlin music scene, antediluvian psychoactives and the artist's trials before the doors of Purgatory. Neo-Decadence sees a way out of various literary dead-ends through something like the realisation of Huysmans' dream of a Spiritual Naturalism which reaches backward and forward in time, encompassing historical fiction, fairy tales, contemporary street-level aesthetics and even glimpses of the future, fixated all the while on transcendence through style. The stench of the gutter is here, as well as the aromas of incense from exalted realms of beauty. The massive overcrowding and compartmentalisation of contemporary reality into specialised areas of concern is not ignored, but neither does it completely determine the course of the work or otherwise overpower the writers' selective skills. The accumulation of literary techniques over the course of the 19th and 20th centuries, with their vast experimentation, has been distilled down to an arsenal of weaponry. Neo-Decadent writers recognise that "Sincerity" and "Authenticity" are just outdated masks worn by the see-through stylists of the past, threadbare and useless. In their place is a focus on the apprehension of metaphysical sensations that more timid and respectable literature wouldn't dare touch. It is difficult to imagine an Occult-infused exploration of the retro video-gaming scene executed with languorously textured prose, but Damian Murphy's "A Mansion of Sapphire" manages it. Similarly, the jagged Futurist and Neo-Realist themes threaded through Brendan Connell's "Molten Rage" distil earlier movements with hyper-evolved concision.

Simultaneously steely and ethereal, this is a literature whose alchemical fusion of opposites gives it the dynamic push of the New. The Neo-Decadent stories and novels of the future have yet to be written, but the present volume presents numerous avenues for exploration. Decadence old and new is not only a style but a mode of consciousness, dying, decaying, growing and mutating as its objects do. Here, ahead, is its newest manifestation.

DROWNING IN BEAUTY

FIRST MANIFESTO OF NEO-DECADENCE

Brendan Connell

1. Words are only words, a somewhat artificial simulation of nature, and should not be given too much importance. Slick writing should be tossed out like men with sweaty hands, mass-produced objects, and food in Styrofoam cups.

2. Never imitate yourself. The writing should be artificial and shallow, without contrived emotions. Then maybe something will be realised. There is already enough sadness in life. Soak the book in gasoline if it must be soaked in something.

3. Character development is synthetic. It should be resorted to only with a certain amount of shame.

4. If it be political let it lurch to the left, burrow underground so that tall buildings tumble off their hinges.

5. Story arcs should only be used to hang oneself with. Nothing is ever resolved. Nothing progresses.

6. Syntax should be dredged out of old books, trimmed off of far-away planets, stripped from dreams. Trivial things should be said in a grandiose manner meant to disgust collegiate scribblers and make the lips of pseudo-great novelists twist in anger.

7. Kublai Khan was a modern. Things fell apart a long time ago. We are already living in the ruins of civilisation. There's nothing to celebrate. When you toast, make sure you smash your glasses together. This kind of writing should be the same. Harmony is overrated.

8. Forget about the sound of cars, missiles, clever machines and originality, since nothing is less original. There are enough monsters and demons in the real world without needing to look elsewhere.

9. Great developments don't come about by listlessly trying to please the crowd. They'll forget in a minute. If the only thing left is a fragment, it better be good. If you're lucky, you'll end up like some choliambic poet.

10. There's nothing wrong with writing a lousy book. Just make sure it's really lousy. There is nothing worse than competence.

11. Neo-Decadent writers will honour the fragmented, the contorted, the unfinished, the unpublished. Realising there is no glory, no reward, no lavish sup-

pers or dancing on tables. Living in obscure lanes and remote canyons, things will be written in unread languages or translated from the language of lizards and snakes, plagiarised from deep wells and signed with hands wet with the dew of rotting fruit.

12. Nothing comes to an end. Let a little light shine through the darkness and remember that when the universe collapses in on itself you can read the novel back to front.

October 17th, 2010

SECOND MANIFESTO OF NEO-DECADENCE

Justin Isis

1. A goat wanders at random, putting things in its mouth.

2. NO SUSTAINABILITY.

3. The kidneys are the prime organs of Neo-Decadence. The pink Gemini. Filtering. Most educated people have equally educated kidneys, which means they try to tell stories instead of pissing when needed. Keep an eye out for these creatures and their awards.

4. No precedence is given to the Decadent writers of the 19th century, their modes or milieu. Neo-Decadence is more likely to cross 1990s video game dialogue with the structure of a 16th century picaresque to discuss a drug deal in present day Mongolia. Fealty and earnestness can only hold back progress. We do not have saints, and we consume our idols.

5. Literature is not a guild system. Academies and workshops: a parade of inbred dogs with each generation more unfit than the last.

6. Writing can be neither sincere nor authentic; these are the clichés of the ranks of the dead. Style is a mute scream in symbols—that's all.

7. There is nothing to learn, but much to steal.

January 10th, 2017

MOLTEN RAGE

Brendan Connell

I.

Smelted. Molten carrion crucible whirring sound. The machine moved the ladle, an enormous metal bucket, forward on the end of a chain. They guided it with their hands.

"Stop!" the foreman cried.

Two rows of large, cylindrical moulds were lined up on the floor.

Massimo was short, with broad shoulders, a thick neck and the eyes of a villain. He had previously worked at an industrial foundry where they made grey and ductile iron castings, but had been fired;—had often arrived late; insubordination to the tune of alumino-silicates and dedusted stuccos.

Now he worked at Fonderia Artistica Bausani.

He loved to see it as it poured. Copper, 10% tin, trace of zinc. They tipped the ladle. Hot lucent orange mud flowed into the opening of a cylindrical block, filling it until its blazing tongue drooled over the top.

They moved from one to the next, down the line, filling them with the liquid bronze.

"I like fat women."

"The capitalist can live longer without the worker than the worker can live without the capitalist."

"The bodies of those beasts, whose blood is brought into the sanctuary by the high priest for sin, are burned without the camp," said Ugo, the patina man.

Each one spoke his own thoughts, without paying the least attention to what the others had to say.

At 6:30 the work was over.

Massimo got in his car, started the engine and drove.

The foundry was located in one of the ugliest areas in the world—on the outskirts of Milan. Huge factories and industrial complexes dominated the landscape, filled the air with an almost unbearable stink. The roads were strewn with nests of small billboards, the skyline perforated by the hooked necks of machinery cranes. Huge smokestacks rose up into the cement-coloured sky and new, shoddily constructed buildings sprang up from great furrows of upturned earth.

It was Friday. He did not want to go back to the lonely squalor of his apartment, so toward the city centre; manipulated his little vehicle through the oozing sludge of traffic: trucks roared by like angry rhinos, coughing out clouds of black diesel smoke, scooters buzzing around them like flies, wind inflated the shirt of a young man, streets a river of strange monsters—great engines encased in husks of metal—slobbering black oil over the corrupt pavement and filling the air with their shrieks. Indeed, the entire human race seemed enslaved by an insatiable mechanical hunger—men willing to kill, not only each other, but babies, old men and women, in order to feed these creatures in whose bellies they perched like half-digested herring.

⚘

Up and down narrow streets, maddening search for two square metres of pavement to leave the heap of rubber and screws, no parking so he did so illegally (he already had plenty of unpaid tickets anyhow).

Feeling hunger, he went and ate fried polenta smothered with meat sauce.

His manners were often raw. He was habitually sulky. Without proper reason, he thought himself superior—even as good as the founder of the Christian religion, though his mother, a cleaning woman of southern origins, was certainly no Madonna.

And then darkness swallowed up the meagre day.

He walked along the streets, gaze lowered, the fingers of his hands sheathed in his pockets, a cigarette protruding from his lips. The sidewalks were congested with people—their tongues clicking against the roofs of their mouths. His eyes dove and soared; he nudged his beak through the rising tide of fully developed but more often adolescent flesh which flushed out onto the roadsides on Friday evenings; bleach-dyed jeans; prematurely corrupt faces.

A hand, tapping on the glass from inside a restaurant, attracted his attention. He approached, stared through the pane of more or less transparent silicates, saw his friend Delio, a poet of odious free verse, a little, unshaven man with large lips who had the shifting, neurotic demeanour of a thief or drug addict (his writing had a mephitic tang to it, like sewage).

Massimo went inside. Delio was sitting with another man.

"This is Klaus," he said. "He is German but speaks Italian better than I do!"

Klaus had the beard of a mystic—wispy, pointy—and a thin, long face out of which protruded a huge nose like the beak of a bird of prey. His fingers, which he made constantly apparent with lavish gestures, tapered at the ends, were prehensile, and this added to his attitude of a raptor.

Massimo joined the two men and ordered a beer.

"I was just telling Klaus about my latest project," Delio said. "La Società Delle Poetiche Arrabbiate wants to publish a piece of mine in their yearly calendar."

"Brilliant."

"Yes, my poem begins:

   I sucked the lubricant from her plastic eyes
   Cut her face in half with my tongue . . ."

"No wonder women are attracted to writers," Klaus murmured as he plunged his fork into the last segment of beefsteak on his plate.

"They are partial to deep men."

"No—like animals," Massimo said, taking a sip of his beer, "they rut according to season."

"Speaking of seasons," said Delio, looking at his watch, "I have to go. There's a Nigerian girl I am supposed to meet in twenty minutes."

Delio left. The waiter came and took Klaus's plate away. Massimo finished his beer and ordered another.

"So Delio is a friend of yours," Klaus said.

"He is an acquaintance."

"You are a poet also?"

"No, I work for a living."

"A worker. Earning his monthly bread."

"Have to eat."

"Yes, but if you become too much part of the system . . ." Klaus poured a thread of wine into his glass. "The hardest-working slaves are those who consider themselves free."

"Well, if you want to philosophise . . ."

"I do." He filled the air with nebulous ideas. "First off, you have to accept the social revolution as the end to capitalism. The downfall of the corporations. The machinery of government is controlled by the corporate god. Violence is simply a means—to end the state. The code of established morality is another prison. Morality is injustice. Every day 40,000 children die as a result of poverty. Reform isn't enough. The right to vote is a mockery, serving only to consolidate the power of the corporate entity. Action is required—not just words, but complete destruction. Madman, fanatic. Great thinkers are initially misunderstood. A man must fulfil his individual potential."

"So," Massimo asked, "you belong to some sort of organisation?"

"No. I belong to a tactic."

He lifted his glass of wine to his lips and sipped it carefully, as if it were blood.

Upon parting, Klaus handed Massimo some pamphlets and a scrap of paper on which was scribbled his phone number.

"Call me if you ever want to meet . . . for a coffee," he said.

Massimo arrived back at his car, but it was booted. He shrugged his shoulders and threw his car keys into the gutter. He boarded the subway at Cairoli, took the Linea Rossa; looked at faces: distorted, shapeless as clods of earth. The passengers sat hunched on their seats—eyes hollow, lips set tight in tense depression. Yes, Klaus was right. These people were simply slaves of some great corporate entity, an entity which they worshipped without even knowing it. Massimo, under the influence of a subtle egoistic intoxication, felt as if he could knock the human race over with a word, destroy it with a few blows of his fist.

At Amendola two young men got on. One held an accordion, the other a guitar. They began to play, stubbornly, somewhat clumsily. Then the beggar's cup went round. A woman dropped a valueless coin in— and then they debarked, at Lotto. Massimo himself got off a few stops later at Uruguay.

He lived in the Quarto Oggiaro. Sinister activities, homicides, violence of every genre.

On the street, darkness, gliding shadows. He had a good walk, as the stop was far from his home. He passed by a group of Albanian prostitutes. That area of town was full of women either exploited or exploiting themselves. They lurked under the street lamps, flitted along the sidewalks like bats.

Gentle boiling red, painful veins desire sacred whore submit to sterilized fecundation.

Finally he was there. He made his way through the entrails of the building—up stairs—through halls;— then, arriving at his door, he realised that, when he had thrown away his car keys, he had also thrown away the key to his apartment. He rammed the rectangle of wood with his body, hurt his shoulder, forced the lock.

His apartment had a stale smell. Furniture crammed into two small, high-ceilinged rooms. He threw himself on his bed and slept.

II.

He lived amongst the constant roar of machines, grinding of metal, shouts and spray of sparks. The place was crowded with sculptures in various states; wrecked plaster busts, abhorrent nudes of bronze, monumental mythological themes and questionable contemporary retro-futurist pieces, post-apocalyptic-tribalism which might make one dream of the mating of invertebrates. Then the wax room: full of red figures, some minute, some gigantic, stuck full of nails—sprues—bizarre— more than vaguely masochistic—many resembling huge humanoid candles.

An artist in a white apron—like those worn by surgeons or dentists—stood atop a chair and worked on the wax of his sculpture—a massive male form, vaguely reminiscent of an elongated toad.

Massimo was touching up a figure of Padre Pio, taking the seams out of the wax.

Ugo came striding in, looking for some tool or other. His grey hair had turned green due to all the cupric nitrate and liver of sulphur he used in giving patinas to the sculptures. Stopping, he gazed with admiration at the piece Massimo was working on.

"Do you like what you see?"

"Ah, Padre Pio . . . he was a real saint . . . The stigmata you know," Ugo said, showing the palms of his hands. "He had them fresh and bleeding for fifty years!"

"*Stigmata del culo.*"

"Hey don't talk that way!"

"If it wasn't for you religious maniacs we would be living in a paradise."

"If you call the flames of hell a paradise, my dear!"

"Idiot!"

"Filth!"
"Faccia di merda!"
"Ruffiano!"
"Faccia da blatta!"
"Facciakkkallaa-ah!"

Ugo thrust his hands against Massimo's chest. The latter bunched his fingers together and began to swing—plunging his fists, one after the other, into Ugo's face. Then both men grappled, hugged each other like frenzied lovers, and flew backwards.

A scream, like that of some wild animal, went up. It was the artist. Ugo and Massimo had bumped into the wax of his sculpture, knocked it over, and it had broken to pieces. The strange, somewhat amphibian head rolled under a table. There were pieces of shoulder, a hand, the giant torso broken in three;—all of this bright red—like body parts after some especially heinous crime.

III.

Unemployed.

Filaments of rain descended from the sky.

New Revolutionary Techniques; The Necessity for Violence; Militant Disobedience. These were the names of the tracts that Klaus had given him, and he read them with ardour, his imagination infused with the smell of smoke, the chaos of crowds and the wailing of sirens. He hated. The emotion pushed itself out from within, like a pus-filled boil, demanded expression—in acts of aggression, violence, burning rage. He wanted to destroy—property, people—taste the pain of industrial society as its flesh was burnt smoking black.

A knock at the door stirred him from his reverie. It was Delio.

"I thought you could use some company."

"Why?"

"Why not!"

Massimo lit a cigarette and began to prepare coffee in a little aluminium espresso pot.

"Last of the coffee," he murmured as he emptied out the dark-brown, almost black powder.

"Hey, do you want to have some fun?"

"I don't want to visit your Nigerian prostitute if that's what you mean."

"No, I mean this."

He held up a can of gold spray paint.

"What's that for?"

Delio laughed uneasily.

"I see," Massimo said.

The coffee boiled. He poured it into two small, white cups.

"Ah," Delio murmured as he stirred a spoonful of sugar into his espresso, "you act like an anarchist, but really you are full of . . . middle-class prejudices."

"*Che cazzo vai dicendo!*" Massimo blurted.

"OK."

The poet pulled a somewhat dirty-looking rag out of his pocket, soaked it full of the paint and held it up to his nose and mouth, inhaling vigorously.

Massimo followed suit. The hiss of the paint can, like a snake;—flit of paranoia aching eyelids peeled back drinking melted fig red scorpion genitals of desert sparks. She. Prototype industrial woman, a golden female oozing out of a can: wrapped herself around his feet, as if in obeisance. And he could feel his body changing, becoming mighty, deified, snorting smoke, blazing eyes rolled back in sphere-shaped head. He glanced at Delio. The latter was transformed into a strange batrachian-like creature with tiny glittering eyes and the quivering antennae of a moth.

Massimo opened the window and began to crawl out.

"Are you crazy!" Delio cried, and flung himself on Massimo's back, clung there, the latter on the sill a vast sweep of molten air before him in aching strange red-gold tumble.

Together strength of deity of drug of hate (through Massimo's power) they began to float out and over the city, which boiled below, he soared above, the air around him hot as fire. Sucked up bodies spewed out ground corpses sprayed city slippery red muck blue steam sooty steam.

A giant serpent was curled up in the clouds.

"I am Tyrrhenian Sea Dragon," it said. "And what deity are you?"

"At the moment Gold Vapour God!"

The next morning Massimo awoke with a terrible headache. He opened his eyes and looked over at the clock, but it seemed incredibly distant, as if it were miles away. His body manipulated itself out of bed, made its way to the kitchen; hands fumbled with the coffee tin . . . Empty . . . He pulled on some jeans and left the place, to walk to a café. The streets seemed to be strewn with small pools, red, as if they were pools of blood.

IV.

He began to meet Klaus regularly in town, at the restaurant, and the latter, in his cultured voice, the voice of a professor delivering a lecture, would set forth the philosophy of violence, the working man's revenge on the great corporate machine. Sometimes he would fall into a sudden whisper and then deliver some very specific tit-bit, some morsel of information that his listener might draw on if he wished to make himself useful to the cause. And Massimo, nodding his head gravely, furrowing his brow, smoking cigarette after cigarette, lapped up this revolutionary talk as if it were water and he a thirsty dog. Ah yes! He was all for destruction. Let the whole world burn, so that the brightly feathered phoenix of the future could rise out of its ashes!

V.

"You are in love?"

"No. She is meat."

Delio had a rash around his nose and mouth. His whole person smelled of solvents.

The two men were in the city centre. They walked past the statue of Vittorio Emanuele II. An African in a huge yellow t-shirt, seated before the rearing heap of cast metal, motioned to Delio, but the latter ignored him. The Duomo, that largest of Gothic cathedrals, was there before them.

"Shall we go in?" Delio asked casually.

"What for?"

"Don't you like churches?

"No. I hate them."

"Ah, it is morbid inside . . . inspiration for poetry."

Through the huge bronze doors. Into the cool interior. The dark forest of the immense stone pillars. The large crucifix suspended about the chancel contained a nail from Christ's cross.

They wandered around, gazed dumbly at the vast stained-glass windows. Massimo's repugnance was mixed with a gloomy fascination. The place was incredibly grand, dreary, filled with the perfume of incense and the flicker of candles—a place where people suffered and murmured mushes of prayers through n-shaped mouths to the god they would never realise.

Then the two men found themselves at the entrance to the staircase which led to the roof. Delio took out his wallet and, with shaking hands, paid the entrance fee.

"Come on, to the top."

Massimo shrugged his shoulders and followed his friend.

They climbed the steps, were soon there, on the roof of that great church looking out over the smoke-stained city. Ranks of spires jutted up hungrily around them, each one dizzily capped by the statue of a saint, the highest of them crowned by the Madonnina, her body coated in gold. Whole quarries of marble had been expended to form this structure of which they stood atop, with no other company than a family of Spanish tourists whose lisps added a disturbing electricity to the environment.

The roof was bordered by a carved stone railing. The city was there, spread out like a map and Massimo, gazing over it, felt the power of a superior being swell up within him.

The family of Spanish tourists left, could be heard laughing, talking loudly as they descended the stairs.

Delio stepped over the railing. "Follow me," he said.

"But why? Are you crazy?"

"It is interesting."

Massimo followed. Up amidst the masses of marble, the expressive stone saints. He looked down, at the flying buttresses and then the piazza, dotted with people, small spots of colour; then splashes of pigeons, which looked like ash dropped from a cigarette. Their position was incredibly precarious; and he did feel a vague sense of satisfaction, like Zeus looking down from Olympus.

"Imagine jumping off of here," Delio said.

"Imagine."

Delio took a pack of Suzy Longs from his pocket, lit one, and then offered the pack to Massimo, but the latter shook his head.

The poet, the paint sniffer, dragged at his cigarette, looking intently at his companion.

"Go on, do it," he said.

"Do what?"

"Fly—like you did before." He had a wild, unsettled look in his eyes, began tugging at Massimo's shirt sleeve, motioning the latter out into the abyss. "Fly."

"Get away from me, or I'll smash you and toss your flimsy body off here."

Ten minutes later they were back on the piazza, both pale and silent. They walked along the Via Torino. Massimo was angry, queasy, disturbed; felt as if he were being watched and looked behind him, at the African in the large shirt, the same who had been seated before the statue, but who was now following them, accompanied by two other men.

The Italians turned onto one of the small side streets that lead indirectly towards the Corso Magenta. The Nigerians advanced rapidly, caught up with them.

"*Ciao* Bem," Delio murmured.

"Mama said you wouldn't pay Eliza."

"I'm going to pay her."

"She said you were rough with Eliza."

"I wasn't. Not at all."

"Let's see your wallet *ragazzo*."

"There's nothing in it."

"Wallet *ragazzo*. Let's see the wallet."

"Massimo . . ." Delio gurgled.

One of the Nigerians looked at Massimo. "You want trouble?"

Massimo frowned. "No," he said, turned and walked off, behind him could hear the high-pitched cries of the paint sniffer poet, as the latter was throttled, kicked and finally stabbed.

VI.

He spent his time lying on his bed, smoking cigarettes, envisioning acts of grand destruction: glass flying through the air, fountains of flame roaring skyward. A shrine of beer bottles accumulated in the kitchen. He formed vague plans for poisoning the city's water supply with LSD, for assassinating the prime minister and destroying the seats of government through violent means. His mind floated off, plunged itself into the bowels of the earth where it heard the tortured screams of the damned, gazed on lakes of molten brass and lava. He imagined himself as god, created a mentally generated body: with dark-blue skin, four arms, the head of a camel. He rose into the air and stroked the moon.

After all, even slime-minded Delio had known he had power.

Massimo perceived two selves: the one a man—worm with bones, a piece of red meat garnished with cognitive faculties; the other a being of great strength.

Issuing out onto the street, he saw the citizens not as sentient human beings to be loved and cherished, but as walking skeletons—skeletons covered with so many pounds of flesh, veins filled with so many litres of blood. When a beautiful woman smiled at him, he saw not her plump, cherry-like lips, but her skull filled with a wet and barely functioning brain—of little more value than an oyster in its shell. But what agitated him the most, what made his teeth grind and his armpits sweat, was the sight of rich gentlemen in suits. These he wanted to grind up, blow up, douse with acid, turn to dust. One day he even went so far as to assault one of these gentleman on the street—for no reason—simply in a mood of anguished rage . . . After pummelling the man for five minutes he turned and stalked off, thinking mountains of bones would not be adequate to satisfy his gnawing hunger.

"The people should worship me," he thought, "offer me garlands of cop flesh. Skewer themselves on giant blades at my feet—for my pleasure . . . Swallow bombs and let me see them blow themselves to shreds."

Volleys of fury; lashed by amethyst thunder.

VII.

Klaus leaned back in his chair, gravely stroking his beard.

"The static misery of today's electro-mechanical civilization . . . because there is always a surplus population, to be used as fodder for wars—a population which is daily being reduced to the powerful chemico-gelatine which feeds the Machine."

"The question really is what to do."

"The world has to be destroyed before it can be rebuilt."

"We will see. I will go to Genoa."

The German lit a cigarette and gazed, through the window, onto the street, with far-away eyes.

VIII.

He wrapped a black bandanna around his face and walked with the crowd. Officers, a wall of riot shields banged by batons, advanced down a side street off the Via Giuseppe Casareggi. Clouds of tear gas; bottles hurled in counter-attack. Stun grenades. The panicked shriek savage demolition spat star-shaped forward bricks a stink human vapour tangled joy in wads of angry meat. One man took a pole and shoved it through a window, others smashed up shops, howled like dogs. A woman was seen kneeling by a lamp post, her face buried in her hands. Cars overturned and set to flame amidst howls of frightened and angry glee, paving stones ripped up and tossed at *carabinieri*.

"Avanti! Avanti!"

He hurled a Molotov cocktail at an armoured police transport. It smashed against it, spreading out into a sheet of flame.

Blood-stained pavement, sobs, the patter of running feet.

Next thing he knew he was struck—a massive blow of a truncheon to the back of his head;—grabbed and violently pushed to the asphalt. Two policemen dragged him over railway lines towards a signal box.

"Sono Dio!" Massimo screamed. "I am God!"

The officers kicked him and beat him with their batons while he, instinctively, curled up into a foetal position for self-protection. Finally a group of protesters, throwing stones at the police, managed to free him. He stood up, not even fully conscious, his face painted with blood, and stumbled away.

IX.

In Milan. Evicted from his apartment, he squatted in an abandoned building in Gratosoglio, now a creature who lived in dark places, like a centipede. Tired, impoverished, gloomy, he went unshaven, lurked around the train station, that nest of vice and criminal misdeed, magnet for human leeches.

He scratched himself, peeled back his eyelids and gazed at the passers-by: huge maggots wrapped up in cotton, shod in leather, draped in synthetic fibres. He walked, lifting his leaden feet; stared at the ground like a man searching for treasure;—a stinking cigarette butt, some small coin, riches of the gutter.

On the corner of the Via Vittor Pisani and the Via Napo Torriani, that busy intersection at the Piazzale Duca D'Aosta, he noticed a man waiting for the stoplight. He was well dressed, with the wispy, pointy beard of a mystic.

It was Klaus and he approached him.

"Ah, it's you," the German said. "You look horrible—filthy . . . You must be living outside the capitalist system. Surviving off its refuse like a famished rat." He ran his hand through his beard. "I would join you if I could, but unfortunately I am a political animal. You can eat away at its exterior, I will burrow inside like a worm . . . Yes, we are both, each in his own way, despised creatures, seeking revenge on the monopolic giants who have chained us."

And his voice, that of the professional lecturer, droned on, vaguely delineating the man's philosophy and morals.

Massimo, who had eaten nothing but garbage for the last three days, had difficulty listening. He felt his stomach churn; asked for a handout.

Klaus looked slightly astonished. "Give you money? I am afraid I can't. It is against my principles to give only for the sake of charity. Private property is not yet abolished and . . ."

His words were lost in the roar of a truck engine. The next moment he was waving goodbye and crossing the street.

Massimo shifted his way along the sidewalk; fell into the shade of an alley, removed from his pocket a can of spray paint not yet empty, and proceeded to let the golden girl rape him.

Vishnu had once descended to earth and lived his life contentedly as a pig. Massimo was the new Avatar—drowning in the waste and crime of the city—feeding off filth and drinking industrial piss. God, revolution, love, prosperity: words for him as empty as the monotonous tone of a bell drifting through space.

THE QUEST FOR NAIL ART

Justin Isis

Erina, stage name Rumika (formerly known as Seika, Saeka, and, during her period of employment at Club Camus in Kabukicho, Suzuka) awoke at noon on her day off and almost immediately felt an irrational craving for instant ramen. Her diet prohibited everything but vegetables, popsicles and alcohol, but the desire remained and, over the course of the next hour, as she removed the makeup she had fallen asleep in, transmuted itself into thoughts of even more restricted foods—pork dumplings, sukiyaki, soba noodles in oil—until at last she found herself smoking a Marlboro menthol on the balcony while imagining a chocolate croissant from St. Marc's Cafe, the flaky crust crumbling as she pulled it from the orange wrapper. Ahead of her the towers of Shinjuku rose in moth-colored light, dull and silk-soft. Her freshly scrubbed face felt clean.

While Rumika had slept, her four phones, each a little universe of conversations and photographs, a little external organ, had given birth to messages: Work Phone One, a black Softbank iPhone 4S encrusted with alternating rows of black and pink rhinestones, displayed a message from Kurihara at the Emerald Club requesting an extra shift on Sunday; Work Phone Two, a dark silver Docomo Galaxy with a silver crystal faceplate and a pink and silver My Melody character accessory, recorded three missed calls from Nami at the Himawari Girls Bar and three missed calls from Boyfriend Four Hidemitsu; Private Phone One, a white AU iPhone 5 encrusted with a leopard print pattern of black and yellow rhinestones showed, alongside the ongoing Line app conversation amongst herself, Maho, and Mitsuho, stage name Kirari—the torrent of icons and one-line status updates interspersed with photos of clothes, cakes and small dogs that functioned as an aimless and interminable but obscurely reassuring electronic telepathy—two messages from Boyfriend Three Ryuji, a missed call from Boyfriend Five Keisuke, stage name Tsubasa, and two missed calls from Boyfriend Six Takuya; while Private Phone Two, an old pink Willcom mobile with chipped paint and a cracked screen, was filled with her brother's requests for money, which Rumika, as always, ignored. Boyfriend One Gou had not mailed her. Rumika took Work Phone Two and began drafting a message to Nami when a call from Boyfriend Four Hidemitsu interrupted her.

"Seika, finally. I called you four times."

"Stop calling me Seika. I'm Rumika now."

"Well, whatever. Did you get my mails from last night? I'm off work today and I thought we could go to dinner."

"I'm sick," Rumika said. "I caught a cold. Could you bring me a croissant?"

"What?"

"I want a chocolate croissant from St. Marc's. Could you bring me one?"

Hidemitsu paused for only a moment before answering.

"I'm in Shinjuku now, so I don't see why not. We can meet now and go to dinner later. How about Oak Door in the Hills?"

"Okay," Rumika said, and hung up. She imagined another tedious dinner in Roppongi with this customer-turned-patron who had fallen from Boyfriend Three to Boyfriend Four as a result of the steadily decreasing value of his gifts, the existence of his wife and the possibility of replacing him with an older, wealthier and less desperate patron, perhaps Nomura from Mizuho Bank, or Hayakawa the advertising executive, whose wallet could help transition her wardrobe to exclusively high-end brands—a process of critical importance, given her impending birthday.

The thought of turning twenty-two filled her with an almost convulsive disgust, as if the years were physically accumulating inside her, pushing her organs further and further apart, until solid chunks of time would break through her skin (she thought of them as a different kind of fat, slick and stiff, like the silicon implants Kotomi from the Butterfly Room had received from a fifty-three-year old pachinko parlour owner). At her advanced age she would have to begin shopping in Minami Aoyama and Omotesando Hills, buying Prada, Hermès and Dior instead of their derivatives at Lumine and Shibuya 109. But she regretted transferring to the Emerald Club, since there were few older prospects there who were not tainted with vulgarity. Even upon the receipt of a new handbag or shoes, she retained a childish shame at being seen in public with a customer whose suit did not fit properly, whose hairline had receded to a certain point and been left unattended, or whose skin had taken on the peculiar patchy look common to the indifferently tanned.

Rumika returned to her half-completed message and paused, unable to finish it. The mental blankness induced by hunger, usually remedied with coffee, cigarettes and energy drinks, now overcame her. Her immediate perception was softened at all times by a constant drift of thoughts like low-lying clouds, the hundred menial tasks clamouring for attention: laundry to be washed and folded, bills to be paid, text messages to be answered, calls to be made. But now the afternoon hours devoid of commitments stretched before her like the purest form of luxury: no one, today, would make her do anything. As she looked from one phone to the next her mind emptied of all thoughts, until the phones became only objects in her hands, and then the hands themselves absorbed her attention. Her fingers were long and slender, the nails medium-length, pointed, painted: glossed matte-black topcoats overlaid with fine white dots which at first suggested dominoes but broke down under scrutiny into a subtle asymmetry, the cuticle of each forefinger studded with a single false diamond.

On Private Phone Two Rumika kept an image folder of girls she considered more beautiful than herself. The folder was updated very rarely; all the girls it contained were absolute exceptions. Among them were several well-known models and television personalities, but most were photos she had taken herself of former co-workers and acquaintances. Of great prominence was Yurina, stage name Ageha, her mentor at Club Camus—now married to a customer and living a life of moneyed indolence, her ambition sublimated into self-maintenance, the all-day drift between department store floors and the doors of health spas and aesthetic salons—whose posture and natural confidence conveyed as much as her perfectly rounded eyes and the hair piled high on her head. Then there was Natsumi Shibata, her old enemy at the Hanabira Girls Bar; Rumika did not allow her detestation of this girl's personality to interfere with the consideration of her high nasal bridge and thin, elegant lips. Another was an astonishing half-Spanish dancer she had met at a party in Nishi-Azabu; a single photograph displayed her lithe figure draped in a black silk dress and her long neck, flat chest (Rumika, though an E-cup herself, disdained large breasts), strange green eyes and the jet-black hair she wore pulled back tightly in a bun. Cigar in hand, she regarded the camera with an indulgent smile; though they had exchanged only a few brief words, Rumika still consulted this photo for years after. The folder was the only form of masochism she allowed herself, its images worthless as a spur to action, since nothing could be done to raise herself to their level; even the temptations of plastic surgery offered little more than vulgar approximations. But the thought remained that, although the faces and bodies of the girls she admired were unobtainable, their nail art could be equalled and even surpassed.

Private Phone One went off in her hand with a call from Mamika, stage name Kirika, who began one of her usual abrupt monologues as soon as Rumika answered.

"Erina! So I was with Haruna and Emi yesterday but we couldn't find that store in Shinagawa you mentioned. It's closer to the West Exit, right? We ended up going to Daikanyama instead. Haruna got this black Rienda belt and I got a vine-red jacket from Vanquish, it looks pretty autumn. Where should we meet in Ebisu this afternoon, you are coming right?"

"I don't know," Rumika said.

"Okay, well, you should come! Anyway, so I forgot to mention, I was with Naoki on Thursday and we went to dinner and then to this love hotel in Gotanda, I wanted to go back to his apartment but he has a roommate who's some kind of student and he's always up. It was one of those hotels that looks like an office from thirty years ago, I mean there weren't even any cute pillowcases or little lamps or anything and the bathroom was really small, but I'm really in love with him recently so I didn't care. We bought these matching necklaces, they're waterproof and everything so we can wear them all the time, mine is an N for Naoki and his is M for Mamika. I felt kind of bad because I couldn't come, it's probably my fault but I think I told you before, his penis is kind of weird . . . I mean it curves up and down like an S, I know it sounds strange but I can't really explain it. Anyway right after we finished there was this knock on the door, we thought it was the cleaner or someone who'd gotten the wrong room by mistake, but actually—"

"It's not acceptable to have an S-shaped penis," Rumika interrupted. "You should probably break up with him."

"What? I don't care or anything, it's just . . . different."

"You should probably break up with him," Rumika said.

Kirika paused, not so much deflated as unwilling to address the suggestion in the way her ingrained deference demanded.

"Well . . . I mean, really? It doesn't seem that bad, but . . . anyway, do you want me to finish the story? We were lying in bed and—"

"I'm busy now, I'll get back to you later," Rumika said, and hung up.

Silence resumed, and she glanced from her hands to the open balcony screen and back until the clouds across her awareness dispersed. Slowly a great emptiness revealed itself, a mental vista larger than any suspected, until all that remained, like a single grain of gold, was a dull, irreducible desire for a more advanced and elegant form of nail art, one that would avoid the childish excesses of her contemporaries while retaining its expressive potential. Her concept of nail art was subtractive—the abyss of forms adorning most girls' hands overflowed with tiresome conventions, so that super cute nail art could be attained only through a complete removal, a detachment from the decade's worth of exhausted designs.

She considered sharing her thoughts with Boyfriend One Gou, but decided to wait for him to contact her first; an instinctive reserve cautioned her never to take the initiative, never to give away more of herself than needed. She thought back to the nearly terminal recriminations of last week's phone conversation, which had given way, after several protracted silences and tentative gestures, to what Rumika thought of as a new phase in their relationship, one capable of withstanding their temperamental differences, frequent separations and the opposition of Gou's parents.

"Anyone who loves me has to understand my problems," she had said. "I can't love anyone whose heart isn't big enough to understand me."

"I've talked to my mother," Gou said. "She still doesn't approve of your hair colour and nails, but she's moving in the right direction. She's at least willing to acknowledge you exist . . . at least in some sense."

This twenty-eight-year-old worked in a trading company and took frequent business trips to Thailand and the Philippines; his career seemed capable of enough upward momentum for Rumika to take him seriously as something other than a temporary convenience. He had the cleanliness, both physical and mental, that she associated with the inhabitants of Minato Ward. She had first noticed boys of this sort while riding the train as a young girl: the starched white shirts of their uniforms looked freshly pressed, unlike the grubby beige collars of the boys at her junior high school in Adachi with their pock-marked faces and hideous cropped haircuts, the dropouts and circle members who had first fucked her in karaoke rooms and the cramped cubes of manga cafes. She remembered the remote faces and shining black hair of these unobtainable boys during her first meeting with Gou, not only because he resembled an older version of them, but because the encounter had taken place on a train. On her way home from late night shopping in Shibuya, her hands filled with bags, she had ascended to the Yamanote Line platform and watched as the commuters formed into neat, tight ranks that pressed her in on every side. As the train doors opened and the crowd pushed her forward, the spike of her black Ferragamo high heel caught in the gap and she stumbled, sending her bags sprawling. Gou, who was seated by the door, stood up and helped collect her belongings as the throng of passengers scrambled for seats.

"Busy day at the stores?" he said, handing her a makeup case that had fallen from her handbag. She looked at him and nodded her thanks. He was wearing a cheap Takeo Kikuchi suit—not necessarily a disqualification, since a certain frugality, even austerity, was attractive in the kind of young office worker who placed advancement over appearance. An old man had taken his seat, so he remained standing next to Rumika, gripping the overhead rail. Eleven seconds passed before he spoke again.

"I'm sorry," he said. "This is pretty forward, but do you live around here? I could swear I saw you the other week outside the spider statue in Roppongi Hills."

Rumika, who had experienced every conceivable approach including an actual serenade from a studio musician who had brought his acoustic guitar to the Emerald Club, decided that Gou's interest was at least thirty percent less mechanical than average, although his tone was not precisely relaxed or direct enough to gain her unqualified approval; anything other than serene, absolute confidence connoted poor character. She plotted a mental graph composed of two axes, sincerity and directness, which, as they crossed into the negative, became cheapness and hesitation. In spite of the points deducted for his eleven-second lag and initially uncertain tone, Gou's approach still scored in the upper right quadrant, and Rumika awarded bonus points for his impressive posture: he did not slouch or otherwise incline his body towards her as he spoke, remaining somewhat removed, intriguingly formal.

"I live in Shinjuku," she said.

"Oh. It could have been someone else, but I remember that hair clip you're wearing. I cross through the square every morning. I don't suppose you work around there too?"

Rumika ignored the question and only looked at him, smiling; then she glanced at the train monitor to remind him she would soon depart. Gou took her meaning without any undue show of recognition.

"Listen," he said, "we're both busy now, but I'd like to talk to you more when we have the time. If it's all right, why don't we exchange numbers?"

He took out his phone. Rumika looked at the clean lines of his face and his thick but neatly trimmed hair. As the train pulled into Shinjuku she recited her number, then walked briskly onto the platform and down the stairs, her bags balanced in each hand.

The flat drone of the doorbell startled her out of her thoughts. She ignored it but the drone continued, and at last she stood and went to the entrance. Keeping the latch on, she opened the door and glanced out from an angle, careful not to show her unmade-up face.

"It's me," a man's voice said.

"Who?"

"Kenji. We met at ALIFE last month. You know, the event with Mayu-mi-X and DJ Kentaro. And then we came back here and . . . well, in the morning we had this long conversation about taking a trip to Shizuoka together. I've been calling you for weeks. I wasn't sure if this was the right apartment but I remembered it was a three at the end and not a two."

She supposed the events the man described had taken place, but she had no immediate memory of them, and he seemed too irrelevant to bother with for long. She did not sense that his heart was big enough to understand her, and his shoes, which were unduly scuffed around the toes, appeared to have been bought at ABC Mart or one of the other discount stores. She closed the door, went to her bed and lay back on the purple satin pillows. Soon the doorbell began droning again, so she connected her headphones to Private Phone One and put on the Kana Nishino album she had recently downloaded, then took Work Phone One and sent a message to Yurie, stage name Rimi:

Hi Yurie, how are you?

Misako told me that you went to some kind of Korean buffet in Shin-Okubo. I've also noticed that your face has looked a lot rounder recently. I don't mean to criticise you, but don't you think you should control yourself a bit more? It's only being considerate to your older sisters. Thanks!

She attached several smiling emoji and sent the message. Bullying the younger hostesses was necessary for business, but it was also a moderate pleasure equivalent to eating a single bite of Pino, the individually packaged ice cream nuggets which came in vanilla, chocolate and, in summer, mango flavours . . . she reminded herself not to think about food or ice cream by smoking a cigarette and putting it out on her wrist. If she made Rimi and Misako hate each other, it would weaken the alliance supporting Saki, stage name Riona—her current rival, who had reached the Number One position through over-flattery of the customers and the simpering facade of sympathy she projected to her juniors. However popular this made her, any hostess whose allies quarrelled amongst themselves could not remain at the top for long; therefore Rumika's method would be just as successful as attacking her directly.

She went to her bureau and returned with various issues of *Nail Max* and *Nail Venus*. Flipping through the brightly colored pages, she found little that met her approval—only the same absence of inspiration afflicting the nail salons of Shinjuku, Shibuya and Ikebukuro. As a teenager Rumika, like most of her friends, had fallen under the influence of the Carry Salon, with its extravagant designs and *Egg* model clientele, changing her nails to reflect any passing interest, requesting pierced acrylic nails with dangling chains and rings; pointed gel nails with gold and silver foils, water decals and butterfly stencils; leopard, zebra and Dalmatian-patterned nails with tiny hearts and stars; transparent oval nails with galaxies of glitter dusting their crystal finish; square-cut nails with teardrop jewels and flower gems forming tiny opalescent gardens; and water-marbled nails with orange and green swirls like neon cream in psychedelic coffee. But now these designs had lost their novelty, and Carry bored her as much as the high-end salons in Roppongi and Azabu-Juban. First in her mental inventory of errors were themed nails: Minnie Mouse accessories atop Disney castle decals, or miniature Christmas ornaments on red and green base coats; next was the other extreme, nails with no coherent order, only a riot of competing decorations: rings of rainbow beads and pearls encircling Swarovski crystals, or inset panels with poems traced in lacquered letters; finally there were nails too unexceptional to merit attention, the cheap painted press-ons and French-tipped cliches marring the hands of schoolgirls and indifferent office workers. Rumika had not fallen to these depths in years, but neither had she perfectly upheld her own standards: her current nails were cute and certainly inoffensive, but not super cute in a definitive way that would place them beyond criticism.

Work Phone One emitted a garbled burst of sound, a compressed version of the opening bars of the Ayumi Hamasaki ballad "Voyage," which signalled an incoming message from Boyfriend Two Hiroyuki, stage name Hakuei (formerly known as Taiga, Shiena, and, during his rise to fame at Stylish Lounge Miyabi, Ayumu):

> *Hello. Tired from work. Can't meet on Wednesday.*

Rumika, who had not suggested any meeting, interpreted this play at rejection as a veiled expression of concern. No communication had passed between them for a week, but this was not unusual; silence and terseness informed every period of their long association. Her dates with Hakuei were minimalist exercises in which the two of them regarded each other silently across a table, the host's mannered indifference a match for her own. Instead of speaking he would reapply his eyebrows with a brown pencil or examine the downward sweep of his hair in a hand mirror while Rumika played with her phones and only occasionally glanced up at him: magnets of like charge, they remained frozen at the same fixed distance, held apart and in place by their auras. Equally exhausted from the demands of work, neither was willing to extend their interest—although there was something else behind Hakuei's detachment, a fear that Rumika was better looking than him, not from any base sexual perspective, but in purely geometric terms of proportion, order, neatness and complexity. His interest in her, ostensibly sparked by her position in their shared social circle, was at root an extension of this refined jealousy, her gender merely an acceptable screen. Rumika recognized this, but she also knew that their underlying similarity prevented them from separating cleanly, no matter how far apart they drifted. He was too well known to discard, and demanded next to nothing, only the chance to resent her at close range, calmly. She would reply, but only when the impulse struck her.

The droning of the doorbell resumed, now interspersed with knocking. Rumika was about to turn up her music when Work Phone Two went off with a call from Boyfriend Four Hidemitsu. She counted to ten before answering.

"Answer the door! I've been out here for ten minutes," Hidemitsu said, punctuating the statement with a single loud knock which made Rumika instantly hate him. She compressed this hatred into a thin, girlish voice, high and fluted, full of surface innocence and airy regret.

"I caught a cold," she said. "I don't think I can come out today . . ."

"It can't be that bad, can it? Let me at least come in and give you the croissant."

"The what?"

"The croissant, you said you wanted a croissant, remember? You wouldn't believe how long I had to wait, it seemed like half of Shinjuku was lining up."

"I'll get it next time," Rumika said. "I'm feeling really sick."

"Can I at least see you?"

"I don't want you catching my cold."

"I don't care, I just want to see you."

"I couldn't stand it if you got sick," Rumika said. "You have to keep working hard."

Hidemitsu paused, and when he spoke again the irritation in his voice had shifted to petulance.

"I haven't seen you for weeks."

"I'll send you a picture later," Rumika said. "Now I want to sleep."

When he at last left, Rumika went to the bureau and took out a plastic tray containing small pots of gold and silver glitter, decals, angled brushes, striping tape and a dotting tool. Then she thought: what remained of nail art when everything unnecessary was removed? Would it be possible to reduce her nails to their barest formal elements without resorting to tired and obvious designs? It was not a question of materials, but one of sensibility, as she did not hope to appeal to the thoughtless customers and insipid juniors at work; only others like herself could appreciate technical advances in design. A vague panic overcame her, a fear of being seen in public with inferior nails by salon staff in the shops or train: a much worse fear than that of being caught without proper hair and makeup.

She thought back to her interview at the Crescent Salon in Ebisu six months ago. For weeks she had laboured over her portfolio, designing nails for her friends, experimenting in what little free time her multiple jobs allowed. She had heard of the opening from Maho, and was convinced that Crescent—a less well-known but competitive salon catering to high-end hostesses— would appreciate her attempts at innovation. She arrived at Ebisu Station wearing a charcoal-gray suit and skirt from Rakuten, the double-buttoned blazer worn over a cream-colored mandarin-collar dress shirt. She had opted for tasteful black heels, and her nails were simple white base coats with sapphire-hued Swarovski crystals and a high-gloss finish. On the ten-minute walk to the salon she was approached three times, first by a teenage boy outside the station who invited her to karaoke, next by a black-suited scout for a club she'd never heard of, and finally by a bored-looking host who gave up immediately after she ignored his greeting. After passing through Ebisu Garden Palace she detoured down a side street, walked two blocks and eventually spotted Crescent on the third floor of a narrow brick building, its name traced across the broad glass window in elaborately flowing English cursive.

Stepping out of the tiny elevator and into the salon, Rumika was greeted by one of the staff, who introduced herself as Kurumi. She was tall, around the same height as Rumika, and sported a white suit jacket, matching miniskirt and brown leather knee-high boots. Though it was late summer her skin was immaculately pale, and her chestnut-coloured hair hung down to the small of her back, enhanced by a system of plaited extensions. The impression was at once both princess and businesswoman. Behind her, other technicians were seated at the benches attending to customers, framed by the curved metal necks of UV lamps. The salon had been decorated entirely in white, giving it a smooth, enamelled look, featureless and modern, yet comforting in its almost medical cleanness.

"It's Erina, right? Satomi said you'd come. Do you have your certificate?"

Rumika produced a photocopy of her correspondence course certificate and a recommendation letter from Hiroko at the Nozomi Salon in Shin-Otsuka.

"Oh . . . Erina Sakurazawa? You used to be in Pink Diamond, right?"

The mention of her former circle irritated her; all of that now seemed childish and depraved. The scrounging for money, multiple abortions, rapes by club owners. For the girl she had been, not pity; only disgust at weakness.

"I have some friends in it, but I was never actually a member."

"What's your job now?"

"Night."

"Hostess, or Girls Bar?"

"Both."

"Oh. I do part-time sometimes at a club in Meguro. So, can I see your portfolio?"

Rumika handed her a plastic folder containing high resolution photos of assorted gel and acrylic nails. She had selected them to demonstrate the full extent of her talents, which ranged from complex decorative themes to more restrained adult designs. The final pages displayed her latest ideas: clear reflective jewels and metallic lacquers united in spare, geometric patterns, offset occasionally by contrasting foil strips. Kurumi flipped through the folder and stopped at the last page, which showed Rumika's current favourite: mid-length pointed acrylics with silver tips and white opal base coats. She had searched for weeks for the precise opal shade and eventually mixed two different kinds of polish to achieve the desired iridescence.

"This nail art is . . . kind of cute, isn't it?"

The qualification "kind of" presented an insult so thorough and penetrating that Rumika had to press her nail points into her palms to keep from speaking. She fingered the cigarette scars along her wrist, feeling calmness flow from their smooth surface, and forced herself to smile.

"Well, why don't you come back and do a demonstration?"

Kurumi led her to the back of the salon and called over one of the junior technicians, a frail-looking teenager with short blonde hair who sat down at a bench across from Rumika and, smiling shyly, extended her hands. Kurumi went to a shelf on the wall and returned with a case containing brushes and supplies.

"Why don't you try something for autumn? How about a leaf pattern, we've got lots of beads and accessories."

Rumika was not morally opposed to seasonal nails, but she considered their more obvious manifestations—cherry blossom decals, plastic snowflakes—to be juvenile at best. It was enough to evoke the expressive power of colour, pastel pink and palace blue in spring, mint green and lavender grey in winter: cliched 3D accessories seemed beneath the salon's dignity. She took the technician's hands—still those of a child, with thin fingers and tiny, square-shaped nails—and decided on a simple pattern that would highlight their inherent fragility. Over the next hour she applied yellow, orange and red base coats, topping them sparsely with emerald green rhinestones suggestive of a still-verdant foliage, the colours darkening on each successive nail so that autumn seemed to progress towards the little finger of her left hand, crystallising as a single silhouetted leaf, dark crimson, almost black. She concluded with the customary hand massage and exchanged remarks with the technician, who was leaning back and admiring her new nails.

"Wow, those are really pretty," Kurumi said, returning from the other side of the room. "Satomi, come look at these nails." She gestured to one of the staff, then turned back to Rumika. "Okay, could you wait outside for a moment?"

Rumika retreated to the waiting area and paged through a recent issue of *Nail Up*, stopping occasionally to check her phones for messages. Eventually she looked up and saw Kurumi walking towards her, the heels of her brown boots clacking across the uncarpeted floor. Her face wore a conciliatory smile: professional, impenetrable.

"Okay, we've talked it over. Your certificate is fine and the designs are cute, but we don't feel you've worked long enough. We're looking for a real professional standard, mainly because of, you know, who our customers are . . . but we'd be happy to recommend you to the Yamazaki Salon in Kamata. Emika there is looking for staff right now."

If Kurumi had declared war on Rumika's entire nature, this suggestion could have served as the critical strike. Servicing convenience store clerks and office ladies from Kawasaki at a backwater salon in Kamata was little better than prostituting herself in the street.

"One other thing that Maina mentioned. Your hand massage . . . well, it was a bit lacking in empathy. The firmness was fine, but we're known for our extreme empathy."

Rumika imagined a rat biting tiny, precise holes in Kurumi's face until it was a ragged tissue of blood and string. She willed not only immediate death but also sudden and irreversible weight gain, sterility, a ruined complexion and sexual assaults by foreigners. She thanked Kurumi for her time and promised to recommend Crescent to her friends.

On her way back to the station she stopped at the smoking area outside Lawson and lit a cigarette, then took out Work Phone Two and Private Phone One and messaged Nami, Kirari, Kotomi, Ageha, Kirika, Rimi, Reina, Ryoka, Nanaho, Midoriko, DJ Sonomi, Kayachan, Amicoro from JEWEL, Airi and Honoka from Pink Diamond, Mayu Koike the *Ranzuki* model also known as "Chinpan," Hikaru from Black Diamond also known as "Piichan," and Mayumi the pimp from Oak Door:

Hey have you been to the Crescent Salon in Ebisu? Just went there and the service was awful! Really dirty and doubt the technicians wash their hands . . . watch out for bacterial infections!

On the train ride home she sent a similar message to another thirty-seven girls.

As she returned to her bed with the design materials, an incoming call replaced the music from Private Phone One with the insistent, outdated house beat she had assigned to Kaoru, stage name Junna, her junior at the Emerald Club.

"Erina-sempai? I'm sorry . . . you're not busy now are you?"

"I'm busy," Rumika said.

"I'm sorry, I was just wondering if you wanted to come to Yoyogi today, they're having this cultural festival with food stalls, Middle Eastern I think. Rie and Shiho are coming too, we might go to Shibuya after . . ."

"No," Rumika said.

"Okay! Well, I'll let you know how it goes. What are you doing today? I was hanging out with Kana on Monday and I went to Disney Sea yesterday with Satoru, I'm really into him right now. He's coming today too, we're meeting in two hours, think he's at Yoshinoya now having a beef rice bowl or whatever. We went on that Whirlpool thing with the spinning cups, I thought it was going to be okay but I ate a chicken sandwich from Lotteria before going and I started feeling sick . . . I threw up in my mouth a little . . . I don't think Satoru noticed but I was really worried!"

"You should definitely break up with him," Rumika said.

"Why?"

"Guys who eat at Yoshinoya always cheat. If you'd said he was getting the beef rice bowl from Nakau or Matsuya, fine. But Yoshinoya . . . right now he's probably fucking a Chinese hooker in West Ikebukuro since he's too poor to afford quality Delivery Health. I hope you like incurable Chinese AIDS."

"When I was going out with Masa he ate at Yoshinoya and he never cheated on me."

"Incorrect," Rumika said. "He cheated on you with Misako, we just didn't tell you."

"What? I don't believe that, but even if it's true, Satoru wouldn't do something like that. He's not like Masa, he said he loves me. You really think I should break up with him?"

Rumika hung up, disgusted with Junna's naivety, permissible perhaps in a twelve-year-old, but not in someone almost seventeen. She turned her music back on and took her design materials from the plastic tray. Turning the tools over in her hands, she let her gaze pass over the glitter pots and bags of beads; then she looked down at her nails and imagined them blank, awaiting decoration. She considered floral patterns, lacework stems, roses blooming between her fingers. She considered colour gradations, arctic sunsets, light pink fading to darker coral. She considered butterflies, fanned-out rainbows, a wing's stained-glass symmetry. She considered darkness, clotted ink, obsidian foils, shiny liquorice. Everything seemed worn and worthless, the tools in her hands incapable of producing novelty.

Something was missing.

She needed a new fan brush.

She would have to leave the apartment, descend to the street below. But before that she would have to become herself. In the bathroom she examined the face that was not her face, the canvas on which her real face was painted. Its intrinsic beauty, if any existed, resulted from the contrast between the youthfulness of the skin and the inherently angular features, the severe cheekbones and thin nose suggestive of a much older woman. The small mouth and downturned lips formed a somewhat dour base expression, interpreted by her customers as regally aloof. As she applied foundation and bronzer and lined her eyes in white, the heavy makeup enhanced rather than softened the austerity of her features. Gradually her real face took shape, an expressive mask dominated by her green contacts and heavy false eyelashes. Her full, straight shoulders completed the imposing facade.

She put on a navy blue satin "Glittering Rose" dress from Dazzy with a high waist and open back, tied with a belt of golden rings. The white straps of her high heels matched the white D&G handbag into which she bundled her four phones. Before leaving the apartment she put on the first piece of her armour, the enormous Bvlgari sunglasses which covered most of her face. Her juniors sometimes made the mistake of going out intentionally dishevelled, taking to the streets in track pants, cold masks covering their unmade faces. But this was a beginner's error. The experienced scouts easily spotted off-work hostesses and targeted them with extreme persistence, so that by contrast going out in full makeup gave the impression of going to work. Headphones, the second piece of armour, further reduced approaches.

Approaching Kabukicho from the north, she passed through empty streets filled with love hotels. At first there were gaudy themed entrances—storybook castles, tropical jungles—but as she moved along these gave way to simple doors and elevators marked by sleek, minimal lettering. Host and hostess clubs replaced them after another block. Promoters stood at the entrances to soap lands, blow job parlours and pink salons. Everywhere neon signs flickered dully in the daylight. As she came closer to the station, the shops and businesses pressed in on each other more tightly with more of them concentrated in the same block, like toy bricks that a child had jammed together at random: cramped rooms rented by Chinese massage girls packed above pet shops with puppies imprisoned in plastic cages; costume stores selling school uniforms, animal masks and leather bodysuits; arcades with purikura machines and UFO catchers adjoining video stores with plastic crates full of old game cartridges; karaoke rooms; izakayas and grimy noodle houses; cheap nail salons; obscure pharmacies and men's clinics; transvestite clubs and Filipina pubs; capsule hotels; net cafes.

Rumika advanced with a quick steady stride, facing straight ahead and taking no notice of her surroundings. She passed by an old man standing in front of an enormous spread of manga volumes laid out on canvas. Another vendor stood by the opposite wall with watches and cheap jewellery. As she turned the corner and started up the hill towards the station a long-haired man in a baseball cap approached her, followed by two scouts in leopard print V-necks. The younger one followed along silently as his partner monologued.

"Hey, older sister! What are you doing today? It's hot, isn't it. Is that dress from Diage? I thought you were Shizuka Muto at first, you look exactly like her. Used to know her before she got big. Anyway—do you want to make some extra money?"

She thought of them as flies, these low-level scouts, easily deflected from her awareness. Unlike her juniors and even some of the more experienced hostesses she knew, Rumika retained perfect composure while ignoring approaches, not even breaking into the brief sprints some girls used to escape persistent monologues. As she crossed into view of the smoking area facing the East Exit, scouts and hosts followed on from each other in quick succession, most barely waiting for the last to finish before rushing in with their lines.

"Hey, older sister, have you ever modelled before? There's a show on next month . . ."

"Think I saw you at AXXCIS last Friday? No? You look familiar. Listen, wherever you're working now, I know a better club. Competitive, and you'll be making double what you are now. Listen . . ."

"Just started this job so I don't really know what to say, but have you done AV before? Adult video, yeah . . . could put you in touch with a really dynamic new company. It's mostly straight-up fucking but there's some pissing and lesbian shit sometimes too. Fifty thousand yen just for the interview. Hard to believe right? Hey, just a moment . . ."

"Hey girl . . ."

"Hey older sister . . ."

"Excuse me . . ."

Rumika took out Private Phone One and called Mitsuho, stage name Kirari, who answered after a single ring. The two girls often called each other in public to repel approaches, so that even when there was nothing to say they remained on the line, breaking the silence with whatever came to mind.

"I just got a pink beret for Catherine, but she still isn't feeling well," Kirari said. "She's more pale than usual, so the pink makes her look washed-out. I'm going to get some vitamins for her tomorrow, I think."

"All the chihuahuas are getting sick," Rumika said, referring to a recent incident that had caused extreme distress in their circle. Remi, stage name Midoriko, had brought her chihuahua Jonathan to Saizeriya during her lunch break. All day Jonathan had had a congested look, but Midoriko, preoccupied with work, had thought nothing of it. But as she took a seat at the back of the restaurant and waited for her chicken carbonara to arrive, she noticed that Jonathan was shivering uncontrollably. That morning she had dressed him in a forest-green jerkin with a tiny Robin Hood cap between his ears, and beneath it his skin seemed stretched across his skull more tightly than usual, giving his features a pinched, batlike frailty. His luminous wet eyes glanced over Midoriko's shoulder and froze, as if he had sighted some sudden horror. Then he sneezed three times and a vein burst in his eye, a crimson flare rupturing the terrified white. Midoriko turned but saw only the outline of Saizeriya, the familiar collection of young girls crouched over cheap plates of pasta, attending to their mobile phones or examining purikura photos. No one had noticed Jonathan dying in her arms, so she made a loud whimper, then attempted something like a scream, which at last attracted a waiter's attention. A brief scene followed, ending with a trip to the animal hospital.

"An extreme form of atherosclerosis, resulting in sudden embolism," Dr. Nakamura explained. "Spontaneous deaths like this are unusual, but not unheard of. You say you fed him Kentucky Fried Chicken and Wendy's hamburgers instead of dog food? The Big Bacon Classic isn't healthy . . . isn't good for these small dogs. I'm afraid there's nothing we can do."

Midoriko became traumatised, missed time at work and was downgraded in the hostess club rankings. Rumika, who had been considering buying a chihuahua herself, decided against it, although she remained tempted by the thought of dressing a dog in colourful outfits subtly coordinated with her own.

"It's definitely going around," Kirari said. "Shiho said Jessica has canine leukemia and isn't eating anything. I hope it's not contagious."

Rumika was about to respond when the phone began beeping with an incoming call from Junna. She promised to call Kirari back later and switched over.

"Erina-sempai? I'm sorry . . . is it okay to talk now?"

"What is it?"

"I just broke up with Satoru like you said. Now I don't have a boyfriend. What should I do?"

"Just go outside, someone will show up," Rumika said. "Talk to you later."

She hung up moments before stepping through the doors of Alta. On the fifth floor she found the brush she was looking for and bought it along with several cheap decals whose Celtic knot patterns interested her. While walking back to the elevator she noticed two of her juniors browsing in Liz Lisa and hurried past to avoid them.

Evening had fallen by the time she arrived home. She sat in front of the television, smoking a cigarette and watching a drama with the sound turned off. The faces of the actors moved in front of her, moulding themselves into exaggerated expressions of surprise and shame, relief and resentment. Rumika took a carton of shochu from the shelf, filled a glass with ice cubes and began to drink. Two hours and five glasses later she felt drunkenness settling over her. Now and then her phones beeped with messages, but she ignored them and played with the fan brush, idly running it over her nails. No ideas came to her.

Private Phone One went off with the DJ Yoji remix of G-Sigh's "Remo-Con," which let her know Boyfriend Three Ryuji was calling her. Immediately an image came to her of Ryuji, on amphetamines, driving around in his white van with the same remix playing, bronze hair blowing in the wind, sunglasses fixed to his face. After serving a year-long sentence for stealing building materials from the construction site where he worked, he had spent his first week of freedom searching the city for meth.

"You're home? I'm coming over."

Rumika could hear blaring music and the rush of wind past a window; her mental image had not been wrong.

"I'm sick," she said. "I caught a cold."

"No, I'm coming over! I'm just about there."

"Fuck off! I'm tired."

Ryuji began the incongruous, high-pitched laugh that served as an all-purpose defence against opinions conflicting with his own. "Are you drinking now? I'm pretty fucked already."

"I've got some time on Thursday," Rumika said. "We can meet then, maybe."

"Are you on your period?"

"Yeah."

"I left my towel there right? We can use that."

"Don't fucking come here!"

"See you soon," he said, and hung up.

Rumika finished her seventh glass of shochu and looked around the room, which now seemed blurred and unreal. She thought of getting up to see if she had locked the door, but the effort was beyond her. After lighting a fresh cigarette she scrolled past the record of Ryuji's call on Private Phone One to the mails and Line messages that had piled up over the past few hours. Amidst the usual status updates and event invitations was a text from Junna, punctuated by so many emoji that its sentences had distended into fragmented phrases, clumps of words immured by musical notes and lightning bolts, rainbow flourishes, sparkling blossoms, pulsing hearts:

> *Erina-sempai! I just got a new boyfriend, it's Taka from Relaxing Bar Orchid in Shinagawa. I think you were right about Satoru. I didn't really know if I could trust him, right? Taka is a lot more honest. I'm feeling much better now. Thank you for always helping me!*

Rumika deleted the message just as Private Phone Two began its familiar chiming vibration. It was a relic, so old that it could not even configure individual ring tones; the same twinkling MIDI melody accompanied every call. But there were only five contacts on it, and she had some idea of who it was.

"Mr. Okada?"

"Erina. It's been a long time, hasn't it. I hope you've been well." The voice, low and tarry, spoke its clipped stock phrases with relaxed conviction.

"I've been very busy," Rumika said.

"Oh? I hope you're taking care of yourself. I've been travelling for work, as I told you before. Now . . . I have some time, and I've brought you some presents from Hiroshima. Chocolates and maple leaf bean jam cakes.

I have some sake, too. I'd like to share a drink with you."

"Of course," Rumika said. "It's just . . ."

"Yes?"

"No, it should be fine," Rumika said. "Mr. Okada, I hope you've been well."

A sepulchral laugh passed through the phone. "I'm still very healthy. I'm in Shinjuku now. I'll be up soon."

The phone went dead. Rumika crushed out her cigarette and stood, feeling the room flowing past her in sickly slow motion. She could leave, or feign illness, but Okada was not a Boyfriend: he was a Presence, and could not be refused. To survive a drinking session with him she would have to vomit whatever alcohol remained in her system. On her way to the bathroom Private Phone One began blasting out its trance beat, and before long she heard Ryuji banging on the door. She ignored him and shoved her fingers down her throat but couldn't concentrate enough to bring on the sickness.

The door opened a crack and caught on the latch. She heard Ryuji's voice enter the room.

"Oi! Open up, I'm here."

She went to the door and peered out at him. His face caught the sliver of hers visible through the opening, and he held up the black plastic bag he was carrying. Several other bags had been tightly bunched around each other inside it, obscuring their contents.

"I've got some coke. And some snacks."

Ryuji carried his body as if it were moving in front of him, as if, abstracted by pride, he were regarding himself in the third person, contemplating the gym-thickened muscles displayed by his white sleeveless shirt, the tan equal parts salon and outdoor labor, the ruddy

face lit by shining teeth whitened monthly at a clinic
Rumika herself had recommended. When fucking her
he focused on a point somewhere over her left shoulder
and went cross-eyed as the climax approached, forgetting she was there at all, erasing her in his awareness of
himself. She felt herself being ground into the mattress,
buried beneath his protrusive chest. When they were
alone he desired her only for this private vanishing act:
outside, with his friends, she was an ornament.

"I'm tired," Rumika said.

"Got some snacks too."

She ignored him and returned to the couch, walking slowly to steady herself. She could see the fan
brush resting on the table, and next to it, the decals.
Unconsciously she found herself tracing the curves of
the Celtic knots. Ryuji continued banging on the door
and calling out to her. She was reaching for her headphones when she heard him go quiet, and another voice
came from outside. This one was low and restrained,
and she could not make out its words.

She pulled herself to her feet and stumbled back to
the door. Another man stood behind Ryuji: compact,
not tall, but standing firmly upright, a briefcase held in
his left hand.

To the casual observer Okada looked not only
harmless but irrelevant. He resembled a grandfather
from the countryside attending some fixed ritual—a
tax enquiry or funeral—some impersonal accounting,
formal, final. His occasional smile of yellow and irregu-
lar teeth had a disarming, childish openness, while his
suits were clean and well-pressed but outdated and un-
noticeable. The body these suits concealed had taken
Rumika by surprise as, she supposed, it had done to so
many others over the years. His skin was a bright, age-

less white, his limbs dense but angular, like a roughly sanded statue. Needlework tattoos covered him from the neck down. The Seven Gods of Good Fortune cavorted across his chest and stomach, while a dragon wreathed in flames rose over the expanse of his back. Pale, watery-blue carp swam across his legs, giving the impression that he was standing knee deep in a pond. But the mass of scars covering his skin overwhelmed these images. Most were old and faded, but some held more colour than the rest, a flushed pink at the heart of their beige outlines. Okada's rigid musculature concentrated itself in these scars, as if some force inside him were attempting a constant explosion but, held in place by the inked, stone-hard skin, had managed only brief pink ruptures. Rumika had kissed these wounds, lying naked with him in the outdoor bath of a private hot spring in Ibaraki, and knew that none of them had stopped him for long.

As she moved her face to the door, both men turned and looked at her. Rumika moved her eyes from one to the other, then looked at the bare wall between them.

"He's bothering me," she said, to both and neither of them. Then she closed the door and eased herself to the ground. The room in front of her seemed impossibly distant; she would rest for a while.

Her eyes flashed open; she had not noticed the darkness settling over her. She heard voices, first level, then raised, finally breaking into shouts: doglike sounds, clipped barks. Something heavy thudded into the door, knocking her forward. There was a brief yell, and she heard another noise of impact. A muffled sound followed, a kind of choking, then nothing.

She got to her feet and made it back to the couch. First she stared at the muted television, its flood of faces, then she looked at the light fixture overhead. She had replaced the bulb yesterday, and now pure white light shone down on her, calm and steady. When she looked away white spots danced in front of her eyes, contrasting with the dark at the corners of the room, lingering at the centre of her vision and resolving themselves into tiny white faces, angelic, alien. She thought of nail art and imagined two colours, silver and white: mirror fragments, the moon and stars. She would make nails with tiny white faces, anthropomorphic stars whose expressions conveyed an ambivalent, minimalist expectancy both conceptual and super cute.

She rose and rushed to the bathroom, feeling the sickness coming for her at last, the faces following ahead of her but fading now, present only in her mind. Someone knocked at the door but she barely heard them, as she was thinking now of what she would make and who she would be: someone sound of body, never giving in to anger but always smiling quietly within, someone who eats nothing and gains no weight, who drinks without vomiting and never feels sick, someone who learns by watching and listening to others but never places their needs above her own . . . she would live in an enormous furnished apartment in Ginza and if a rival stood against her she would crush her. Someone never known as a dreamer and always praised: thinner; ascendant over Riona; receiving the love of friends and patrons; not yielding to old men, young men or any other customers; minimal; more complex; cuter: she imagined herself with better nail art, more beautiful, richer, stronger, in the future.

A MANSION OF SAPPHIRE

Damian Murphy

"God places the soul in His own mansion which is in
the very centre of the soul itself."
—St. Teresa of Ávila

Two crows perched like defrocked priests upon the rail
of a stairway bathed in shadow. Stella watched them
through the window as she lay in bed, not yet ready
to relinquish the easy indulgence of her bedroom. She
amused herself by imagining that they conspired to
perform a heist. Indeed, they seemed to take a marked
interest in the jewellery shop that resided in the building next to hers. One of them spread its wings above
its body while the other hopped spasmodically along
the surface of the rail. Their stratagems eluded her attempts to comprehend them.

She turned herself around and swung her legs over
the edge of the mattress. Vicious beams of sunlight
streamed in through the window on the adjacent wall,
creating enigmatic patterns of light and shadow against
the bookshelves on the further side of the room. Dust
motes drifted like stale clouds of incense in cabalistic
arcs before an intricate armoire. Stella indulged herself
with a brief, if unfocused examination of the spines
of her most cherished volumes. Aside from a handful

of grammatical handbooks which sat upon her work desk, and an abundance of instruction manuals in boxes in the other room, these were the only books that she kept in her apartment. Her eye was drawn to a series of vaguely pornographic manga which she'd ordered from Osaka, a book on wilful acts of sabotage in the European workplace, and a slender volume of journal entries from the latter days of a nineteenth-century priest who had suffered the excruciating effects of spinal tuberculosis. The piercing cry of one of the crows outside drew her attention elsewhere. According to the clock upon her nightstand, it was nearly 4pm. She hadn't the slightest idea how long she'd slept.

She rose and dressed herself, neglecting, as if in observance of some obscure religious rite, to tend to the essential tasks of hygiene and decorum. The hazy memory of having worked until the sun came up resided at the threshold of her consciousness. She couldn't quite remember if she'd finished her translation. One way or the other, it would still be waiting for her later in the evening. She reveled in the luxury of not having to care about it for the moment.

Taking leave of her bedroom, she proceeded through the only other proper room in her apartment. One half of the room was dominated by a space enclosed by bookcases of dark black lacquer. Upon their shelves were found an exquisite selection of treasures, each worth more, at least to Stella, than the sacred heart of St. Camillus. Between them, on a simple wooden stand against the back wall, was found a reasonably antiquated television. In the centre of the enclosure, before a low table, stood a bench adorned with silk upholstery of crimson and iridescent gold. Temptation seethed in all of its satanic majesty within her heart, yet she resisted, determined to wait until after she'd returned to submit herself once more to her insatiable desires.

She passed through her front door, walked down a dilapidated stairway, and stepped outside into a quiet street suffused with the pleasurable stink of the distant harbour. The odious emanations were known, on occasion, to waft up through the alleyways of the lower city and permeate her neighbourhood like an infiltrating army. By the time she reached the gentle slope of the descending stairs, the crows had taken their nefarious devices elsewhere. She walked past several thick black doors, their surrounding arches embellished by the extravagant flourishes of the local graffiti artists. At length she emerged from the protection of the shadows and into the embrace of an oblivious and unrelenting sun.

Several minutes later, she'd returned again, a half-filled cup of coffee in one hand and a white bag containing a day-old Danish in the other. She sat herself on the bench and placed her acquisitions on the low table before her. On one side of the table was the most cherished among her few possessions: a ZX Spectrum game system in more or less pristine condition. The immaculate machine was an original model, produced by Sinclair Research Ltd. in the early 1980s. Several cheaper imitations could be had by way of various grey markets in every corner of the world, but Stella would settle for nothing less than authenticity. She had fallen in love with the device several years before. She'd started with an emulator on her PC, yet precious little time had passed before she yearned to possess the artefact itself. Between her initial infatuation and the present day, she'd become an ardent devotee of the Mysteries that Spectrum gaming had to offer.

She was currently immersed in a long-playing ex-
ploration-based platformer that spanned both sides of
twelve cassettes, the first of which was currently in the
tape deck. The device itself was attached to the game
machine via a stereo-to-mono cable. When the tape
was played, it could be heard to emit a series of high-
pitched pulses. These were transmuted into a stream of
raw data by the processor of the machine, which was
then parsed into a series of commands. From the latter arose a prodigious variety of rich and intoxicating
masterpieces.

A typical program, being no larger than 48K, took
roughly five minutes to load from the magnetic tape.
The resulting diversions were the very definition of
exquisite: compact, brightly coloured, and suffused
with an impeccable atmosphere. That the graphics
were extremely primitive could not be denied, though
their simplicity, in modern times, was an asset in the
hands of a true artist. Stella's obsession had grown increasingly puritanical over the years. She eschewed the
slick releases created by commercial outfits. Nostalgia
meant nothing to her, as she had been far too young
to play the classic games at the time that they were released. She turned instead to independent creations,
submerging herself in a culture maintained by hobby-
ists and savants. The underground retro-gaming scene
was nothing if not prolific. She had contacts throughout
Russia, Spain, the UK, and several Eastern European
countries.

The title of her current fascination, *A Mansion of
Sapphire*, did little to convey the game's extraordinary
depth. It had been passed around in retro-gaming circles over the course of several months, having been designed by a notorious misanthrope in Novi Sad. Little

was known about the reclusive developer. The game was neither accompanied by an instruction manual nor the ostentatious packaging that was typical of underground releases. The beguiling arrangement of mystery and colour seemed to exist entirely without context.

Stella ejected the cassette from the tape deck and flipped it over, rewinding back to the beginning so that she might start the game anew. *A Mansion of Sapphire* was a multi-load game: each side of each cassette contained three distinct divisions, while each of these in turn contained the data needed to render a particular area within the game world. What was more, the game was not sequential; if the player wished to pass from one space to another, they had to locate the precise section on the required cassette and feed the data into the machine before they could proceed.

This was, at best, a tedious and agonizing process, involving a continual exercise in fast-forwarding and rewinding until a brief gap between sections of noise had been found. If the tape had been advanced too far or not far enough, or if a different section of data than the one expected had been cued, the cantankerous machine would respond with the dreaded "R Tape Loading Error, 0:1". This message was anathema to the ZX Spectrum operator, leaving the hapless victim with no recourse but to start the game over from scratch, losing whatever headway they had painstakingly gained. Saving one's progress in a game as complex as *A Mansion of Sapphire* was far beyond the capacity of such an antiquated system.

Stella wasn't deterred by the agonies attendant to her passion. The deficiencies of the machine only made the process more enticing. The very presence of magnetic tape excited her. She was certain that the device exerted a tangible force. The fluctuations of the signal seemed to saturate her own etheric field, penetrating deep into the interstices of her subtle anatomy. Whatever gains she made within the game, so she considered, must have their analog in the exalted regions of the soul.

By the time Stella finished her Danish, the cassette had been rewound and the first section of the game was loaded into memory. She would have to retrace her steps, as she had so many times before, until she'd reached the furthest point to which she'd previously ventured. From there, she would engage in a fervid search for spaces that had yet to be explored, keeping watch for clues and patterns which might enable her to proceed ever further into the entrails of the mansion. A black Moleskine notebook lay on the low table before her. Any new areas or items found within the game would be meticulously logged within its pages. She removed the keyboard from the table and placed it in her lap. Her fingers fit perfectly within the shallow depressions on the tops of the rubber keys. Several among them had lost a certain portion of their surface beneath the prolonged abrasion of her skin. She cherished their welcoming embraces, gently nudging them back and forth within the confines of their casing.

A pleasurable feeling spread like morphine through Stella's limbs as the opening screen appeared before her. No title announced itself at the game's inception. Not a single option other than to simply play the game was made available to her. The action commenced in the foyer of what was presumably the titular mansion. Stella's avatar was simple enough: an androgynous figure attired in a greatcoat and button-up vest. She imagined, apropos of nothing, that the character was none other than Séraphîta, having escaped into the unlikely environment of the game from the pages of Balzac's masterpiece.

The opening room was nothing short of immaculate in its conception. Brickwork of sapphire and dark azure provided a garish contrast, not unusual for Spectrum games, with a series of rich golden archways that led on to other sections of the manor. Three high balconies were interspersed by hanging lamps encased in gilded cages. Much closer to her, on a low mezzanine, partially concealed by a balustrade, appeared a portrait of a pyramid engulfed in flame. A brief description of the icon had comprised the initial entry in Stella's notebook. It struck her as a fitting image for the underlying principle behind everything that she'd encountered in the mansion. After a moment of hesitation, she set off along a route that was well familiar to her, amassing a collection of items along the way which would allow her to explore the house to the limits of her current knowledge.

She passed through lavish parlours and elaborate boudoirs as the crimson rays of jeweled chandeliers washed over and through her like a scintillating tide. An upraised hand of delicate crystal was found upon a torch-lit stage. A ruby placed into a niche within its palm gave passage to a catwalk drenched in shadow. She ascended an ivory stairway into a powder room of coral and alabaster, its intricate ornamentation bathed in the shimmering light of two candelabra. A cut-glass washbowl, half-filled with water, resided on a decorative stand. Below, on a narrow shelf of rich, dark wood, was found a modest collection of patens and ciboria, censers, and communion cups, all arranged around an elaborate monstrance topped with the supremacy of the cross.

At the far end of the chamber stood a heavy door of pure white marble. She was certain that the space beyond contained the item she'd been looking for, and yet the door was impassable, it refused to open to her touch. She'd stood amid the intimate décor of the washroom several times before, pondering the rich array of accoutrements as if her concentrated gaze alone might force them to reveal their secrets. As far as she could ascertain, the furnishings were perfectly inert, though it was possible that they might be brought to life given the proper stimulus.

With her eyes upon the washbowl, she removed a recent acquisition from her inventory. She'd found the item on one of the floors below. Several lifelike statues were distributed throughout the manor; between twin archways, inside of niches in the corridors, beneath the flames of hanging lamps found in the lavish confines of smoking rooms and wine cellars. Their military uniforms and the similarity among their faces was suggestive of a connection between them. Stella harboured several theories as to their overall function within the house, yet thus far her experiments had yielded nothing. One of them was far more weathered than the others, a slightly shorter gentleman that resided in a quiet parlour bathed in darkness. Parts of the stonework had crumbled altogether, three fingers of one hand were missing, and the exterior was riddled with cracks. A light touch upon its surface was all it took to send the weathered statue sliding toward one corner. While she was disappointed to find no trace of a secret passage concealed behind the sculpted effigy, her efforts did not go entirely unrewarded. Lying on the floor beneath, in a place which had been covered by the statue's base, was a rough square of cloth soaked through with dark, red liquid. It was as if the life's blood of the unfortunate figure had slowly seeped out through the soles of its feet as it decayed within the shadows.

She dropped the soiled item into the pristine waters of the glass bowl before her. Almost immediately was the blood diffused into the water, turning it bright pink while the rag was bleached as white as bone. Stella was delighted to see the marble door swing open. She placed the now white cloth back into her inventory and proceeded, for the first time in her current session, into a place that she had yet to explore.

The room beyond was lit by pale wax tapers on tall golden stands, their flames like iridescent peacock feathers dipped in molten copper. As Stella advanced from one end to the other, vibrant bars of colour passed over her head and shoulders: chartreuse and magenta, teal and cyan. A low table draped in scarlet satin resided at the far end of the room. Upon its surface was found a silver serving dish, precisely in the centre of which had been placed an item that resembled a small, white sugar cube. A single candle stood behind the dish, the radiance of the flame bathing the display in a soft golden halo. The ivory cube, though minute in size, comprised the focal point of the entire chamber. It was a pixelated Eucharist, consecrated and infused with the exalted essence of the house. Stella consumed the sacred object without a second thought, encouraging its subtle fires to transmute her very substance. Something of the manor was now a part of her. Whatever secrets lay in store for her, she felt, would entail a degree of intimacy which far surpassed that of any other game in her collection.

She set the keyboard down next to her upon the bench, the rich patterns in the silk upholstery nearly swallowing the black casing with its rainbow stripe logo. The image of the game on the screen of her television remained frozen but for the monotonous flickering of the candle flames. She retrieved the black Moleskine notebook and the pen from the table before her, appending a substantial entry to what was already a lengthy and detailed record. By the time she finished her analysis, she had come to understand what must be done. For the first time in her gaming life, she would break one of her own cardinal rules. She would leave the program loaded into memory between sessions, thus abrogating the necessity to start again from the beginning the next time that the game was played.

The fact that player death, so far as she knew, was not a feature of *A Mansion of Sapphire* should enable her to play to the end of the game without having to retrace the ground she'd already covered. There was a long way left to go. She'd only reached the A-side of the second of the twelve cassettes, and she knew that there were previous areas that still hadn't been fully explored. Finishing the game, assuming it were even possible, would require several weeks at least. Playing any other game in the meantime would be out of the question. And yet, she knew, without the slightest trace of doubt, that she could not consume the Eucharist a second time. The changes that it brought to bear upon her avatar could simply never be reversed.

Night had fallen. The pallid glow of moonlight had established its dominion over the surface of the writing desk before the windows. Stella became cognizant of the fact that she hadn't eaten for several hours. A quick inspection of the documents that lay upon the desk confirmed that the translation she'd been working on was still unfinished. The luxury of self-employment allowed her to work during the quiet hours of the night. She transcribed user guides, data sheets, white papers, and technical documents for a variety of different clients. Her current job involved a treatise on the relative merits of Lean Manufacturing for a munitions company that maintained a handful of facilities overseas. She often amused herself, knowing that few would read her handiwork, by slipping linguistic ambiguities, absurdly detailed descriptions, unintuitive turns of phrase, and blatant contradictions into her translations. She would have little time to spare, however, with the document at hand. Several hours of meticulous work lay yet before her. Stella stepped outside to find a bite to eat. When she returned, she'd find a suitable disc to place upon the record player, adjust the lighting so as to create a tiny island of illumination around the front of her apartment, and dedicate the remainder of her evening to the more unfortunate necessities of her existence.

Little more than an hour had passed before Stella rose from her work desk. She was restless, irritable, unable to focus on the task before her. The needle of her record player had reached the innermost groove of the disc she'd chosen. The faint sound of the naked surface of the vinyl through the amplifier enticed her nearly as much as did the music itself. She lifted the needle and slipped the record back into its paper sleeve before returning the album to its place upon the shelf. So pleased was she with the image displayed upon the cover that she kept the record at the front of her modest collection. Both sides of the packaging were saturated with a vibrant shade of vermilion. A black and white image appeared near the bottom, a photograph of a scantily clad woman peering through a large cassette reel, a cat perched between her bare, arched feet. The title of both artist and record were displayed in gentle curves of black and pink along the borders of the design.

The LP in question, to which she had listened in reverse, the B-side preceding the A-side, was titled *Danses Organiques*, by the French composer Luc Ferrari. The music, if it could be called such, had been described as a "strange meeting between two women and a tape recorder". A session had been arranged in a recording studio, to which two young women who had not been introduced to one another were invited. The recording captured an affectionate conversation between them which quickly escalated into a sensual unfolding of mutual desire. To this was added a haunting backdrop of tape effects and reverb underscored with a novel approach to percussion. The result was a surreal soundtrack that evoked an undeniable sense of intimacy yet in no way came across as pornographic. Stella usually found its soothing ministrations to be an invaluable asset to her work. The spoken sections had a tendency to ward off the soporific effect so often imparted by dry, over-technical texts. In the present instance, however, it did nothing for her flagging concentration.

Upon again adjusting the lighting, she was pleasantly surprised to find that the remainder of her dinner was still waiting for her on the table. She had entirely forgotten about the delicacy, and had just been wondering what she might do to sate her appetite. Her apartment had no kitchen, and the icebox was perpetually empty. One slice of pumpernickel topped with sardine salad remained for her. She sat down on her bench beneath the soft golden luminescence of the overhead lamps and admired her collection as she picked at a wilted slice of tomato.

Her shelves were stocked with seven years' worth of tireless collecting. She had amassed a distinguished selection of enticing works of art; a rich array of games designed for several different gaming systems. Her favoured treasures were artfully arranged so as to create a colourful and elegant tableau. They displayed themselves like houris in entrancing configurations, some of them adorned with artwork while others strove for a more minimal approach. She never shied away from culling when and where it was needed. It was essential that the display retained its visual appeal. Too large of a selection would make the apartment appear cluttered, giving the impression of a hoarder rather than an aesthete. Nor did she allow herself to keep anything packed away or otherwise out of sight. Her possessions were not to be treated as an archive; they were to be taken together as a work of art, an altar for the worship of exotic gods, a single magnificent jewel with multiple facets.

A series of boxes stood lined up in a row upon one of the upper shelves, their ornamentation presenting a minimal, yet consistent, arc of aesthetic and design. Greyscale was peppered with traces of dark ruby and sapphire. Austere white fonts intruded upon grainy photographic film stills. The boxes contained diskettes for her beloved Commodore 64. They'd been created, by a woman and her husband in Montpellier, as an homage to the cinema of the French New Wave. *Ascenseur pour l'échafaud* was followed by *Pépé le Moko* and *À bout de souffle*. The latter half of the series contained a selection of gems from earlier eras, thus *Les Diaboliques* shared space with tributes to the *Judex* of Franju and the *Vampires* of Feuillade. The shelf below contained a stack of cartridges for the Philips Videopac G7000, that most unwieldy of beasts which spectacularly flopped in the wake of the almighty Intellivision. The games contained thereon, based on classic Zen koans, proved impossibly difficult to play and were notorious for crashing the machine.

Another shelf was entirely devoted to a display of great intricacy and splendour. Inside of a replica of the Basilica of San Clemente was found a VIC-20 cartridge encased in pristine white plastic. *Glória in excélsis Deo* had been programmed, if the creator's weblog was to be believed, by a heretic of the Church of Rome. The simulation was said to contain all of the secrets of the Mass.

On the opposing row of bookshelves, near the north side of the apartment, resided a modest selection of historical anomalies. Only rarely did Stella harbour the slightest affection for commercial releases. There were, however, certain exceptions. She was particularly drawn to items imbued with a degree of notoriety. The crown jewel of her collection was a faithful rendition of Pasolini's final cinematic masterpiece. The cartridge, for the humble Atari 2600, provoked the ire of concerned parents throughout the Western world, a scandal which was only to be eclipsed the following year with the release of the infamous *Custer's Revenge*. Proudly displayed on one of the outermost shelves was an Amstrad CPC cassette entitled *The Obligatory Bond of Suffering*. This, too, had been an officially sanctioned release. By way of elegant design and complex, yet subtle, gameplay, it allowed the player to explore the lost art of pre-anaesthetic surgery from the perspective of both doctor and patient.

Other games on other shelves housed splendours scarcely known to man. A collective of young women from Bucharest had crafted a handful of cassettes for the BBC Micro based on classic Italian comics such as *Kriminal* and *Satanik*; Катакомба, an outfit based in the Ukraine, had managed to translate Céline's *Journey to the End of the Night* into a fairly enjoyable survival horror campaign; text adventures based on the webwork novels of Harry Stephen Keeler vied with pornographic rogue-like slogs rendered in monochromatic ASCII-vision. Among Stella's long-standing obsessions was a series of 28 floppy disks, each containing a series of simple logic puzzles intended to initiate the player into the subtle mysteries of *The Zohar*.

Of all of the diversions that glorified Stella's shelf, none had ever enraptured her quite so much as *A Mansion of Sapphire*. It alone compelled the full extent of her imagination. It seemed to speak to her in an exalted tongue, a continual prayer which promised untold ecstasies if she could only find her way into the next concealed chamber. It was not so much a game as it was a work of art, a revelation, a holy sacrament. It embodied for her the very archetype of independent retro-gaming.

Stella resolved to finish her translation the following morning. She would explore the intricacies of the mansion until the sun came up, allowing herself a brief nap before rising again to tend to her work. She pushed the last, soggy remnants of the pumpernickel to one side and switched on her TV. The chamber in which she'd left her avatar appeared again before her, the candles dancing above the empty serving dish like holy men enflamed in prayer. Her character's appearance seemed subtly to have changed. The colours of the uniform had grown brighter, the contours more defined. The face betrayed a trace of cunning that had not been present before. The resemblance to Séraphîta had given way to something altogether more ignoble. Stella felt an unexpected rapport with her onscreen persona. The secrets that they bore between them smouldered in a place that was not entirely known to her.

Her fingers found their way back to the long-familiar keys. She left the chamber through the same door by which she'd come in, traversing the short space of the powder room and rushing down the stairs. She passed through bright sepulchres and long glass corridors, stepped lightly past a row of jeweled guillotines, crept above a prayer room teeming with cloistered monks, and made her way down a spiralling tower that resided beneath a statue of a goddess. Her movements were imbued with an uncanny decorum known only to connoisseurs of an obsolete technology. At last she reached an antechamber illuminated by the dim effusion of a single hanging lamp. Behind a modest wooden door lay the crimson pews and elaborate stonework of a chapel located in the heart of the manor.

The ivory tiles of the holy sanctuary lay drenched in shades of violet and vibrant blue. The sculpted bodies of forgotten saints stood poised in rounded niches in the nave, their lifeless gazes regarding the intruder with unconcealed derision. Impeccable stone columns stood to either side of an extravagant altar carved from pure white marble, its surface lined with candlesticks of radiant gold. A concentrated ray of light, stained deep red by several panes of coloured glass, shone down through a broad, circular window above. The image that appeared in the stained glass was nearly identical to that of the portrait found behind the mezzanine in the game's opening room, though here the blazing pyramid had been rendered by a far more sensuous hand. The image, all of a single colour, bespoke a pious longing to be consumed, as if the flames provided solace to the ancient stones that had long since been abandoned by the builders. The radiant shaft terminated in a disc of transparent scarlet on the floor before the wooden benches, the distorted form of the portentous icon appearing in its midst like a vision of the Holy Ghost.

Stella had bathed in the light's majestic rays many times before, always with the expectation that the action would unlock some secret mechanism within the chapel. Thus far, nothing had become of her experiments. The consumption of the Eucharist, so she suspected, may well have provided the key that had been missing during her previous attempts. She stepped without hesitation into the scarlet circle, allowing the effulgence of the vivid hue to bestow its influence upon her body like a swiftly working poison.

Of all of the idiosyncrasies of the ZX Spectrum system, the most notorious was the phenomena known as "colour clash". Due to limitations in the display memory of the machine, overlapping objects were forced to share a single colour scheme. While it was possible to work around the unfortunate constraint, many retro game developers chose rather to incorporate it into their designs. Thus, as Stella passed beneath the ray of light, her form inherited a ruby tint from its environment. She remained immersed in the luminous bath for upwards of a minute. Her anticipation slowly turned to disappointment as the layout of the holy place failed to change in any noticeable way.

Just as she'd begun to consider other avenues of exploration, the light changed from red to a vivid chartreuse. The transition seemed to impart a subtle shade of meaning, as if a minor mystery had been unveiled by the colour change alone. Stella felt as if a shift had taken place within her avatar as well. Again it had changed in appearance. Whereas before, the figure had appeared ambiguously gendered, now it bore the high cheek-bones and distinguished brow of a woman of considerable notoriety.

Again the ray of light changed colour, the taint of chartreuse giving way to a wash of royal violet. The degree to which the light had saturated the figure bespoke an influence that bordered on the erotic. It seemed to penetrate into her most secret abodes, transforming the very substance from which the pixels were composed. A bewildering sequence followed: violet turned to bright emerald, followed by ruby, deep sapphire, vermillion, lime, and scintillating amber. The colours shifted with increasing rapidity until they finally dissolved into a dazzling white. The cycle, in its entirety, had the impact of a fiery sermon, the true import of which, while opaque to the intellect, had been impressed upon her memory like a cipher.

At last, the light went out completely, leaving the chapel in darkness but for the torches in the nave. Stella was surprised to find that the window had disappeared. Behind the altar rose a stairway which would take her into the space beyond. She hesitated before passing through the portal, prolonging the tension of anticipation so that the rapture of attainment might consume her all the more. She was intoxicated by the prospect of the depths that lay before her. She had set her sights upon an acquisition that was impossible to attain. The ecstasy attendant to her approach would surely drown her long before she breached the final chamber.

As she passed through the aperture, Stella was prompted to load the next section of the game from the cassette. She placed the palms of her hands upon the surface of the bench, relishing the sensation of the silk upholstery beneath her fingertips. Her lips were numb, her eyes tense with strain; she had a tendency to lose herself within the splendour of the rich environments that played out on her screen. She rose and walked over to the window. A light drizzle gently licked the surrounding rooftops. The reflection of the streetlamps shimmered like drunken starlight on the cobblestones below. She considered stepping outside of her apartment, allowing the rain to run in streams and rivulets down the contours of her face. Her reverie was interrupted by the cessation of the loading noises which indicated that the tape had reached the end of the datastream. Quickly, she darted back to her machine lest she let it run too far.

It took her very little time to re-immerse herself in the evocative atmosphere of the game world. The chapel now behind her, Stella stood upon the uppermost platform of a long, descending stairway. Its wide white marble steps were flanked by alabaster walls adorned with darkened niches, tiny windows, protruding lamps, and intricate traceries of stone. A subtle attraction seemed to compel her downward. She was certain that the treasures which awaited her below far exceeded anything she'd witnessed in the upper sections of the complex. Impassioned by the fervour of anticipation, she began her descent into the unexplored depths of the mansion.

She passed by elaborate doorways inset with jewels and bright red banners bearing indecipherable phrases. Ornate fountains overflowed their shallow basins, their waters coursing down the stairs beside her and running into iron drains set right into the marble. Flaming lamps illuminated statues which appeared to one side or another at regular intervals. The finely carved figures depicted women in long, flowing robes, their bodies twisted into excruciating poses of devotion and supplication. Their eyes blazed with the ecstasy of the god-intoxicated, their fingers locked into elaborate mudras in the air above their heads. While they were bound to one another by a certain likeness, each was imbued with distinguishing qualities all her own. They bore a striking similarity, both in style and in size, to their more militant counterparts above.

The windows which opened in the walls were far too petite to allow for ingress. They gave view, without exception, to claustrophobic chambers lit by undecorated and diminished candles. Stella occasionally passed beneath a fissure in the sloping ceiling. The flames of unseen torches in the rooms above cast distorted shadows on high walls of decorative tile. The shifting forms suggested swinging censers and bodies shuffling in circular procession, the figures rising and falling with entrancing regularity. Stella imagined that she could smell the fiery odour of the incense that they burned: mastic mixed with white copal and a hint of Siamese benzoin.

The downward passage continued for far longer than she had expected. After well over thirty minutes had passed, she was instructed to load the next section of the mansion from the tape. This she did without the slightest hesitation, her eyes remaining locked upon the screen throughout the tedious process. Twice more was she required to advance the cassette before she came to the end of her descent. Each instance was preceded by a long and ponderous plunge into increasingly decrepit terrain. Though there was much to admire in the surrounding décor, and the progressive decay of the scenery was rendered in meticulous detail, Stella encountered little opportunity for interaction. She drifted through the ruined passage like a ghost consigned to wander through the remnants of its former habitations, vaguely wondering if the remainder of the game would be entirely occupied by this single repetitive environment.

At long last the stairway reached its lower extreme, terminating before a slender arch which opened like a wound within a high wall of weathered stone. Tall, yellow candles enclosed in glass on either side of the portal caused the shadows to dance and undulate across the surface of the passage. Stepping through the arch, Stella passed into an intimate and tasteful chamber. The colours and arrangements which confronted her provided a striking contrast to those found in the upper reaches of the mansion. Anaemic lamps of frosted glass shed their understated radiance on painted walls of sensuous amber. Two tall armchairs of dark wood and rich upholstery resided in the shadows like a pair of furtive altar boys. A chestnut armoire appeared to one side of the entrance, its drawers inscribed with upright hands having keys in the hollows of their palms. A doorway opened in the wall between the armchairs. The unlit corridor beyond let onto other passages which themselves granted entrance to an extensive network of interconnected rooms.

She passed from one space to another, losing herself amidst a visual feast of colour and texture. The occasional bluebird winged overhead as she crept atop the tiles, emerging from a porthole and proceeding through an open doorway. Every location that she explored, along with each accessory and fixture, seemed to have been designed by a single, fastidious hand. The aesthetic could not have pleased her more if she had fashioned it herself.

She was aware, as she pressed further, of a particular vibration—a dim, yet steady pulse that seemed to saturate the atmosphere. Its reverberations seeped beneath the visible surface of her avatar, coursing through her bloodstream and inflaming the chambers of the heart. Following the summons, she continued to explore the mansion by way of mechanical levers and hidden switches, complex and elegant puzzles, cabalistic feats of navigation, and the subtle manipulation of magnetic currents.

As the minutes turned to hours, Stella found her way into the remoter abodes of the complex. By way of an ingenious strategy, she gained the patronage of seven women of great influence and determination. Each was engaged in a vicious campaign against the others, employing subterfuge and duplicity to shift the balance of power among the upper regions of the manor in her favour. Their machinations revolved around the rumour of a sleeping abbot, an inscrutable persona who oversaw a lineage of which Stella alone was the rightful heiress. She passed encoded missives back and forth between her benefactors and their advocates, nurtured pockets of dissent and conveyed concealed threats, assumed the mantle of diplomacy in a complex game of loyalty and betrayal; all the while, she sought to penetrate still further into the strata of a house whose revelations seemed to have no limit.

At length, having advanced nearly to the sixth of the game's twelve cassettes, Stella forced herself to break away from her obsession. Countless hours of play had ravaged her senses. She'd become estranged from everything that lay outside of the dominion of the mansion. She rose, placing the keyboard down beside her. The sun had long since risen and again begun its descent. Her apartment was suffused with the deep crimson radiance that had come to dominate the western skyline. Stepping over to her writing desk, she opened up the window as far as it would go, savouring the impression of the rough wood on her palm. Physical sensation gradually returned to her as she placed her hands upon the windowsill and leaned out over the street below. The rain had stopped, yet the surfaces of the surrounding buildings had been inundated by the deluge. The rank scent of the harbour brought fresh verve to her weary heart. She felt an urgent need to descend into the streets in order to re-adapt to the texture and physicality of the natural world.

She slipped out through her door and drifted down the stairs, emerging onto the rain-soaked stones like a lost cat in an abandoned city. A single crow scrutinized her from a desolate windowsill above. She imagined that it sought a means of ingress to some hidden place—a secret alcove into which to deposit a stolen coin, or a locked cabinet whose drawers concealed a fragment of a map. She couldn't help but think that every facet of her neighbourhood was connected by subtle threads of cause and effect. She started as a piercing caw resounded through the still night air, certain that some section of the city had been subtly altered by the cry.

She ascended a stairway which ran along the back wall of a sunken courtyard, tempted by the brightly lit rooms that were visible through the windows on the opposing side. Her fingers sought out hidden switches in the undersides of stone icons and beneath the windowsills of shops that had closed for the night. The monuments and statues of the city promised untold discoveries if only she could shift them from their places. Even the emerging stars appeared to harbour clues and portents in their inscrutable configurations.

Upon returning to her apartment, Stella succumbed to an overwhelming wave of fatigue. She allowed herself a brief respite, a refreshing dip into the waters of unconsciousness that she might return to the game refreshed. She slept upright, propped up in the chair before her writing desk. Lavish images of the interiors of the mansion danced and swayed within the pallid light of hypnagogia. Brief snippets of half-lucid dream revealed unexplored passages and corridors, statuettes with broken limbs, a ritual procession of painted birds, and a host of spinning chandeliers that floated like wayward angels from one exquisite chamber to the next. An enticing clue had just revealed itself within an altar room of gold damask as she surrendered to the soft embraces of oblivion.

Stella woke in her chair with her head leaning up against the wooden back, unsure how long she'd been asleep. Her limbs were stiff. Her stomach growled like a contentious beast. She cast a quick glance about the room before she rose, taking care to stand slowly lest she lose her balance. She leaned against the windowsill, her face bathed in moonlight, a gentle breeze caressing her arms which lay crossed, one over the other, atop her chest. She was sorely tempted to take herself into her bedroom and collapse into a long and restful sleep.

She sought only to gratify the immediate desires of her body, having given up all hope of finishing her translation before the official deadline had passed. She placed one hand on the edge of the open window, curling her fingers around the outer surface. The brisk night air upon her face brought an unexpected rush of pleasure. She felt that she could remain thus standing for an indefinite period. Crowds would pass by her on the street below, supposing she'd gone mad or had succumbed to paralysis. Her source of income would wither and vanish. Her rent would go unpaid. At length, she would be carted off and left to rot within a cell beneath a single hanging bulb. After a long moment of inactivity, the fantasy exhausted itself. She returned to the bench, took the keyboard in her hands, and abandoned herself once more to the demands of her insatiable muse.

Several cassettes' worth of data lay yet before her. It was absurd to suppose that she would reach the end of the game in a single sitting. The need to return to sleep would overpower her eventually, to say nothing of the urge to eat. She put these thoughts out of her head. Blind ambition would keep her going for a good while longer. The apotheosis that awaited her appeared before her inner eye, its revelations taunting her from deep within the heart of the impossible edifice. She beheld the radiance of the infernal throne, the central pivot around which every element of the game revolved. Its brutal majesty seduced her like a sacerdotal chorus of sirens. She knew that it was already a part of her, for she'd partaken of its essence in the upper levels of the mansion. At the centre of its brilliance lay a solitary pixel, an illimitable logos which contained, if only in potentia, every permutation of light and colour that the machine was capable of rendering.

Upon returning to the game, Stella crossed over a threshold into the vastness of a region that had yet to be explored. A convoluted series of ornately sculpted caves took her deep into the uncharted regions of the earth. The influence of the seven sibyls that resided above prevailed within the catacombs like the distant echoes of a whispered prayer. She came across a tremendous statue constructed in her likeness. Its body was fashioned from untarnished brass, its interior replete with garrisons and oratories, long, winding stairs, and decorative archways that opened onto uncovered balconies. Elaborate altars flamed unattended in the endless, subterranean night. Several spots on the metallic surface of the statue were struck like gongs by blind ascetics, giving rise to an entrancing rhythm which reverberated throughout the cavernous hollows. Undaunted, she pushed ever onward, striving to collect the scattered fragments of a document the existence of which was shrouded in myth and rumour. The object that she sought was no less than the deed to the manor itself. If obtained, so she had been led to believe, it would bestow upon her a crucial eminence which exceeded the splendour of the kings of the earth.

Abandoning her supplicants, she set out upon the ravages of a primitive, tellurian landscape. She witnessed monstrous aqueducts and cathedrals bathed in flame. She passed through furnaces and charnel houses, libraries and blackened archives, currying the favour of the gods of the depraved that she might advance ever further toward the heart of desolation. On occasion, she caught fleeting glimpses of the burning pyramid, its fiery form engulfed in sheaths of night and clouds of rolling fog. Several attempts to reach it ended only in disorientation. It seemed to be protected by forces and intelligences far beyond her understanding or control. She found herself at last upon the shores of an infernal ocean, unable to proceed further against the magnitude of the tide. The unrelenting waves rolled forth and broke on the stones before her, threatening to pull her into unfathomable depths beneath a seductive and uncompromising current. She fell to her knees before the untamed waters, her thoughts overwhelmed by her desire. She'd been stripped of all her resources, divested of the attainments that the mansion had bestowed upon her. All that remained was the ardor of her aspiration, flaring like a dying match-head in the vast abysses of obscurity.

ARNOLD OF OUR TIME

Yarrow Paisley

Arnold Addresses Congress

Arnold believed that there was much to separate Man from Animal: spatial and verbal intelligence; moral reasoning in collaboration with metaphysical critique of somatic illusions; and most critically, restraint of basal appetites in order to appease sacramental social obligations. Since he himself could not demonstrate facility with any of these means, he considered it his patriotic duty to vote for Representatives to Congress who embodied fulfilment of all his humanistic expectations.

Artistically, it was a simple matter of periodically colouring a box to ward off the demise of Democracy (that avatar of all that was best in Man); after that, his conscience spotless, he could devote himself without distraction to the Hawt Sauce in a Girl-Shaped Bottle of the Month Club.

When the first bottle arrived, Arnold dialled Club HQ Select Service in Abernethy, Arkansas to confirm his subscription immediately, indeed enthusiastically. It, the bottle, was, as promised, in the shape of a girl, and not just any girl . . . but Girly Singer, a well-known *chanteuse* of the first order, her impassioned melismas (charmingly inflected with a sincere, down-home twang) familiar to anyone who knew anythang (up to and including everythang).

Little wonder that Arnold began to sweat even before unscrewing her cap: between the erotic shapeliness of the glass and the promise of deep, exquisite heat within, a boy could not help but succumb to the sudors of Desire.

Without fail, in years to come, in spite of wars and blizzards, the Girl-Shaped Bottles arrived on time, month after month. It was exhilarating, indeed humbling, to know that something in life could be depended on; so reliably, in fact, did the Sauce arrive on the third day of every month that his gustatory rhythms adapted to the schedule, his craving for authentic Mexican cuisine swelling on the first and second days until it became a bloated blister of raw, needing hunger that only the figurative needle of Hawt Sauce from a punctual Girl-Shaped Bottle could adequately drain.

For stellar performance of duties, Arnold thanked the Postmaster General, who replied with a letter of acknowledgment bearing an official seal and a seemingly genuine signature; for Hawt Sauce, there was no one to thank . . . chalk it up to Survival of the Fittest.

For the Shape of Girls, of course, Arnold thanked Gawd.

Arnold Wears the Jersey

Arnold felt constrained by his natural propriety not to mention sensitive details of his altercation on the bus today within the hearing of his Grand Ma Ma. Not to suggest that she was "sensitive" or "hearing" . . . But reasonably, a man *is* entitled to his privacy, even in the presence of his Grand Ma Ma—a profound and ineluctable figure in the life of a man.

"I . . . there's not much to say about it, really," Arnold stammered. He picked his nose. She grimaced, reconfiguring her wrinkles into an arrangement no less unpleasant than the original one. She slapped him hard.

"You disgusting pig," she said, clarifying the subtext of the violence, should he have been at all in doubt. "But there's nothing to be done; a lout you've always been, and a lout you always will be. It doesn't matter, I suppose, and so I shall breathe a calming sigh and ask you kindly and gently why your shirt is soaked in some sort of blood-resembling ichor? And why you smell of an *abattoir*, seeing as how I'd only sent you out for milk?"

Arnold sank to his knees, his hands automatically seeking their customary, supplicatory station just below his chin.

"It wasn't my fault!" he cried. "It's not like I was asking for it!"

Where to start? Start with Chess Fan.

"Best freakin' Chess Match I ever freakin' witnessed, and I seen 'em all," said Chess Fan, who was seated beside Arnold on the bus. "Wear the jersey." He nudged Arnold in the ribs, and Arnold noticed that a bright blue team jersey had been tossed into his lap, "Queen" stamped across the back.

"I said 'Wear it'," said Chess Fan, "unless you're a Pawn or somethin'."

Beautiful Woman sat across the aisle, watching the pair of them intently, a mysterious smile lending a seductive shape to her lips. Arnold nodded, attempting and failing to catch her eye. Chess Fan chortled and snapped his arm hard across Arnold's chest, pinning him to the plastic seat-back. His heart commenced to bang desperately against the constricting limb. He struggled to breathe.

"I made myself clear yet? Or you need further encouragement?" asked Chess Fan, winking suggestively at Beautiful Woman as he reclaimed his arm to its former, pugnacious station on his thigh.

Arnold said, sneaking a glance at Beautiful Woman, "No. It ain't clear, Mr. Meanie." It started.

That Arnold threw the punch was, admittedly, out of character, thus straining this tale's credibility. His power, we must allow, was admirably lethal; however, his accuracy was not. His punch sailed past Chess Fan's face, and its continuing progress compelled Arnold's body to pursue its flight, leaving him sprawled across Chess Fan's lap. Slowly, savouring the glee, Chess Fan bore down hard and began to spank Arnold. He chortled and sputtered as he spanked. Gently, almost tenderly, he grew an erection into Arnold's soft belly.

In his mind, Arnold saw Beautiful Woman seeing him. It seemed that no matter what he did or how hard he tried . . . in the end, it would always come to this. A jock spanking him while the female of his dreams looked on with detached amusement.

"Is there any chance you'll let me off your lap?" asked Arnold.

"None," said Chess Fan. "So you gonna wear the jersey, or what?"

"I will," said Arnold. "I promise. All I need is a private place to get changed."

"I don't think so," said Beautiful Woman. "I've been looking forward to the striptease."

"Tell this maniac to let me go, and I'll do it," Arnold whimpered, defeated and aroused all at once.

"I knew you were a Queen," said Chess Fan triumphantly, releasing Arnold from his hold.

Arnold—with his gaze—caressed Beautiful Woman. He winked. And began to unbutton his shirt.

Still unbuttoning, he cantered back and forth in front of her, swinging his hips gracefully from side to side. By the time his shirt was off, Beautiful Woman was swooning, fanning herself with the edge of her hand. Many have tried, and many have failed . . . but in that moment, Arnold was a winner!

Arnold smooched the air between himself and Beautiful Woman. Their eyes locked passionately. He felt a swoon encroaching but maintained his composure.

The moment stretched. Secrets passed back and forth, *billets-doux* of consciousness, cherished missives stolen from the courier of time and savoured in the vault of sentiment. They existed outside of time, Arnold and Beautiful Woman, immune to Chess Fan's jeers. In fact, Arnold, in that moment, became a Man, the sort of Man that Women simply can't resist.

In illustration of this principle, Beautiful Woman, her smile fading, drew a pistol from her handbag and shot Chess Fan in the face at point blank range. "It was going to be you," she murmured thickly, a single tear streaking the rouge of her cheek, "but you showed me you're no Pawn." Then she turned the gun on herself and slumped with seductive languor against the window.

Wistful and dispirited, Arnold donned his shirt (inadvertently bloodied by the Tragic Love Event), mismatching the buttons with their corresponding holes.

✠

"There's only one solution," said Grand Ma Ma with a theatrical sigh upon the conclusion of Arnold's tale. "If I'm going to have reliable milk, I'll have to arrange for milk delivery. And you can go to your room, young man." Arnold threw her a questioning, but meek, glance, and Grand Ma Ma concocted one more sigh, this time more for pleasure than effect. "Don't," she intoned, "leave the bloody shirt in the hamper. Just throw it in the trash. Throw it away, be gone with it, there are always more where that one came from."

Arnold did as he was told, then retired to his bedroom and spent the day admiring himself in the mirror with his new sports jersey. He especially enjoyed the look produced when he held the gun in an authentic Gangsta stance, although the James Bond pose was also effective, albeit incongruous with the apparel.

Arnold Proposes an Alternative

Arnold contemplated the view through his bedroom window from time to time, supposing to himself that should a window have been situated just across, all these years, rather than a brick wall, in which Flirty Girl, for example, or perhaps even Giggly Slut, might occasionally have undressed her luscious body as it assumed a variety of imaginative and stimulative poses—unknowingly, yet also calculatedly, for his blissful benefit—then he would have passed a much happier and more fruitful adolescence.

In fact, theory did not preclude the possibility that the feminine gaze of his fenestral counterpart could in turn have studied his form with cognate carnal designs along the same eyeline; indeed, at times, perhaps their eyes would have crossed paths somewhere between the panes, midway, here or there, floating, circling each other shyly, buoyed up on shimmery clouds of Innocence, emboldening each other by the gentle acclimation of Desire simply to *let go* . . . yes, *to fall* . . . to fall in Love . . . and thus in Romance catch each other up from the hard landing of Perdition.

Everything is regret.

All hope—for the lack of a single window—had been lost to him:

Flirty Girl, it was well known, had been subdued by Heedless Jock; now she was known as *La Belle Dame Sans Merci*. Already, they owned a house together. Heedless Jock cheerfully manicured the graves in their backyard after his early-morning shifts at the Blight Insurance Agency.

Giggly Slut had relocated to NYC after high school and changed her name to Hipster Delite; she wore a red knit hat and a thin necktie on Social Media. Her firm yet waggly tongue tip and her bobbling cleavage were treasures now only to be appreciated in pixel renditions.

Grand Ma Ma alone timelessly perdured, bright star that she was.

Arnold Knows What Comes by Way of Night

Arnold had been known to experience erotically flavoured dreams featuring women he had encountered fleetingly in daylight; our subject hastens to assure the reader, however, that none of these occasional nocturnal scenarios were in any way pornographic or exploitative of the women, but very tasteful indeed, even sensible, sophisticated, and culturally *haute*, the sorts of productions that would garnish a distaff résumé with sprigs of undeniable class and respectability. Bach on keyboards, Mozart on drums.

Now, for example, his dream concerned Moll Scarlet, alluringly clad, posed, rouged, and lipsticked from her lowest toe to the tiptop of the sexpot. By day, Moll passed for a mostly meek (yet mildly cheeky) checkout clerk in a grocer's grimy mid-block bodega, but in Arnold's Nighttime Emporium of *Ooh la la*, Our Lady of Ginger ascended into the Body of Commerce itself, optimising the flow of goods and services through efficient, well-greased circulatory channels: arteries of naughty sex, veins of haughty shame.

Economic ejaculation is inevitable in any unregulated Market-driven system; the Market surges inexorably toward a fever dream of its own ideal form. In lack of dampening forces (some prefer baseball statistics, others concentrate on the photograph of Grand Ma Ma in a silver frame above the bureau), the Irrational Exuberance of the Crowd overflows into Madness . . . fantastical schemes and fanciful bubbles (such as postulation of Moll Scarlet's obsessive respect for Arnold's flawless poses of his sinewy, iron-toned physique) inflate then collapse in tragic cascades as clarity (expressed internally, for some reason, in the precise voice and intonation of Grand Ma Ma herself: "Nonsense! Your physique sickens all its witnesses") resumes in the minds of temporarily frivolous investors . . . *ergo* do they scurry in spermatazoic hordes to sink their funds into the more risk-absorbent instrument of a grimy towel haphazardly arrayed across a sweat-sogged, shamelessly distended belly.

A certain relaxation of traditionally stricter boundaries may attend such recessions of financial activity. The markets are always in flux, after all, and sometimes the Body of Torpor ascends to relieve for a time the Body of Commerce from her duties. Exhausted, grateful for this rare opportunity to seek some well-deserved R&R, she makes her way through evening crowds into Arnold's Dream Casino and flags down a drink, smooths her silken evening gown against alluring curves before slipping into a cushioned chair at the Baccarat Table, and allows the moustachioed grifter on her left flank to explore discreetly (and skilfully) the loamy lands among her loosened limbs while she backs the Bank to run and pays no attention whatsoever to the outlay of the cards.

Arnold Sees the Light

Arnold exercised himself to examine the World through his Grand Ma Ma's eyes: in the light by which she saw things, he saw that his own light had been wrong all along . . . completely *wrong*.

"Light," she informed him, "is a particle."

His light had been a wave, most likely the result of squinting, an indecorous and most unattractive habit, against which his Grand Ma Ma was forever warning him. With good reason, it turns out.

Arnold's cheek twitched to fend off a stray beam (composed of particles) from an imaginary Disco Ball (he dreamt often of disco, as so many have, as so many will).

Grand Ma Ma's cheek precisely replicated Arnold's twitch . . . incited by an unseen stimulus . . . not *necessarily* a disco beam . . . but seemingly *something* similar to one.

Like particles spin together: the quantum axis spans Creation to acquaint strangers in unforeseen intimacies, a truth well known to Science. But when it comes to Grand Ma Ma, who is by no means a stranger, nor galactically distant, one must be careful to avoid unfruitful hypotheses. If, however, for the sake of argument, an Arnold particle were to act spookily with a particle of Grand Ma Ma? A New Day for Science may even now be Dawning!

Arnold ventured, in the realm of subtle research, to scratch what itched. Grand Ma Ma, confirming Theory, delivered a twitchy finger to the cognate coordinate upon her own somatic continent.

His particles tingled all over (this New Physics was sensational): a shiver progressed through Arnold's masses. By an as yet untangled mechanism of Cause and Effect, a consonant shiver was observed to traverse all the bulk of Grand Ma Ma (while she observed her Daytime Programs).

"We are Intingled," Arnold averred.

Arnold embarked upon an expedition for Ice Cream. Theoretical Physics had exhausted his sugar stores.

He was an undiagnosed psychosomatic lactophilic hypoglycemic: onset induced by Emotional Torment or

Mental Effort . . . and now, it seemed, Intinglement. The only effective remedy, sad to say, was Ice Cream.

Grand Ma Ma held no warm opinion of Ice Cream, which, she allowed for broadcast, "delivers more Naughtiness per cubic ounce than any other substance known to Man. One must steer clear, my boy."

Early signs of Ice Cream deficiency, however, were manifestly present. Tremors in his Ice Cream zones. Address must be made, or consequences would be faced, even should Grand Ma Malian disapproval follow.

Arnold's Ice Cream sensors directed him to the most dissolute, disreputable Parlour in the city, Ice Cream Heaven. He spoke softly to Shy Counter-Girl, who daintily pivoted to fulfil his shameful request; the orchestra swelled, dominated by a rampant, ancient god of implacable rhythm. Shy Counter-Girl's sly hip captured, quelled, and domesticated the beat, converting sempiternal sonic wrath into temporal human grace.

The truth came clear soon enough: in Ice Cream Heaven, Disco was the Lord.

A complex interweaving of limbs, bodies, spirits, Ice Cream, and disco beams enmeshed young Arnold into a tapestry of forgetfulness. Leaving Self behind, he stepped out of his material prison into etheric ecstatic oneness, moved toward Universal synchrony, each arm triumphantly ascendant and bearing aloft an exultant pointer finger, even while his hip slid laterally, both supporting and subverting the dominant theme. Within the Groove of All Being, Arnold became a diamond stylus releasing Dance Pulsations from the vibrant matter in which they had been hitherto undetectably embedded. Partnered to Shy Counter-Girl, Arnold transcended the gulf between persons. No objective reality remained discernible but the coruscant infinity of the Disco Ball, its emanations demanding eternal and obedient adoration from the Visible.

Neither a wave nor a particle: light is disco.

As with Arnold, so with Grand Ma Ma.

When Arnold entered the Grand Maternal chambers, a vision of peak revelation shimmered before him. Intingled all along during Arnold's Disco Rhapsody—having matched him spin for spin, strut for strut, slide for slide, until her heart stopped—Grand Ma Ma was frozen dead in the iconic Staying Alive stance (a.k.a. Plato's Finger), upon all her features the stretchmarks of Rapture.

Another Disco Martyr.

FIRES HALFWAY

Ursula Pflug

Our first night in Berlin I went out with Katie, the German label's A and R woman, to a pub called Die Ruine, in a bombed-out building near the Brandenburg Gate, never restored since the war. The second storey, roofless, crumbled upwards into the night sky, while in the tiny, one-roomed club itself, a trio of young women looked like they were falling asleep from terminal boredom. I found myself staring and Katie nudged me. "They're junkies," she whispered. "Disgusting."

Still, I stared. I felt like I was in the bar at the end of time. In those days, before reunification, West Berlin residents received subsidies from the state, hence, all sorts were attracted here by the lure of easy living. And heroin was as popular with artists and musicians as among street people, unlike in Canada. So, of course, were Colours.

The bartender's name was Max; he wore a Western shirt and a flowered tie. He sported slicked-back hair and a handlebar moustache, looking like a character in the Wenders film, *The American Friend*. There was a record player of elderly but good vintage, and Max played us Velvet Underground and early Stones. Everyone was dressed in black and very thin. I watched an old gay derelict clean tables and empty ashtrays for a few minutes; Max pulled the man a pint in exchange for his trouble. He sat at a table alone after that, sipping beer, opening and eating a can of sardines with a clean fork he got out of his jacket pocket.

Katie and I were joined by one of her producer friends, but before we could be properly introduced a raven-haired woman extricated herself from the trio and offered to read our Tarot cards. Katie tried to get rid of her but she whined persistently, reeking of patchouli and layered in scarves. At last I gave in, making her promise that once she'd done my reading she'd leave us alone. Leni, for that was her name, agreed, laying out my hand after I'd shuffled. My question, which I didn't share, was whether Rudy's German tour would ensure greater success back home. In Canada to be famous you have to be famous somewhere else first.

Card fifteen, the Devil, came up. She asked me to re-shuffle, as if to want for me a kinder fate, but even when I did, there he was again, and the third time too. I thought Leni must be adept at sleight of hand, would promise to exorcize my devil for some large price, but instead she sighed, "What are you doing with him?"

I thought she knew I was Rudy's girlfriend. I was smug enough about his small-time fame to assume bar gossip had already labelled us his for-the-moment prince-less entourage, and told her truthfully: "Even back in high school, his music spoke to me more than any poetry ever had. I even changed my name to the same name as the girl in my favourite song. When we finally met last year I asked who Kim was and he told me she didn't exist; he'd made her up. I said I'd changed my name to Kim because of the song and he said he'd hoped someone would do that, become Kim for him."

I was so busy delivering my monologue I didn't at first notice Leni staring as if I were a little mad, and Katie glancing from one to the other of us, suppressing giggles. I could have gone on, but I shut up. Scotch and jet lag, what can I say?

"Who are you talking about?" Leni asked.

"Rudy Mix, of course."

She tossed her locks. "I've never heard of him. Does he play with Lou?"

Katie elbowed me, whispered, "She means Lou Reed. He lives here now."

"I've met Lou," Leni said. "I've read his cards. Here. Right at this table."

Canadian that I was, I unashamedly glanced around the room to see if Lou was there, if I might have to call Rudy, get him to cab over, meet his maker. He'd thank me forever. But no Lou. Just his music pouring out of the speakers, changing us forever just like the first time we'd heard it.

"Maybe he lied. Did you ever think of that?" Leni asked menacingly. "It would be a good way to get in your pants, yes? I bet you Kim is his first wife. It's your Rudy who's the devil, I see it now." Leni tossed her hair again.

"But the devil doesn't mean the devil personified," I said, explaining Leni's Tarot to her as if it was my profession and not hers. "It can mean addiction of the mind or body, any kind of enslavement."

"Precisely."

"I don't even believe in the devil," I said.

"No one said you had to," Leni said. "But you agree with me there exists real evil in the world?"

"Of course."

"Keep it symbolic then, if you prefer," Leni said.

I stubbornly kept defending my boyfriend. "Rudy's music is amazing. He's not rich but he is by my standards; I'd never have gotten to Europe on my own. What's devilish about any of that?"

"All the same," she said, peering at the rest of the layout, reading a meaning there that was, even with my superficial knowledge of the cards, completely opaque. "I see coming enslavement of a kind."

"How precise. You have real talent," Katie's friend sneered. I thought maybe he was trying to save face for our little group after I'd made us look like ingénues not knowing who they meant by Lou. Leni just shrugged him off, a piece of fluff, a beetle. Katie pushed several Deutschmarks in small denominations across the table, as if hoping once Leni had her money she'd find someone else to scam.

"He paid my airfare here," I said.

Katie looked alarmed; she hadn't thought I was taking this seriously. I hadn't thought so either. Scotch and jet lag, I told myself again, call it a night and get some sleep.

"That's worth your soul?"

"My soul isn't in danger," I pointed out, "it's my self-respect."

"How so?" Katie's sneering friend asked.

"I'm a fan, for God's sakes. I went backstage at a concert in Toronto and got him to autograph my programme—I gave him my number and he actually called. How pathetic is that?" I'd never seen myself as a groupie before then. I'd thought Rudy was in love too. "I should come up with an art of my own," I continued, "not just turn myself into a character in one of his songs."

"Don't be ridiculous," Katie said. "You'll do something worthwhile one day—or not. Not everyone should feel they have to. What's the point of it? And to be pretty and clever is more than most people ever get. Whether you worked for it or not you should enjoy what it brings you."

Katie's friend, whose named had turned out to be Hans, agreed. "If a handsome young musician asked me to keep him company on his US tour, you'd be sure I'd go. What if the chance only comes once?"

I nodded, trying to believe them. Leni reassembled her deck, wrapping it in a square of patterned blue silk with pretentious ritual. Katie and Hans rolled their eyes after she'd gone, slunk to another table to try her luck. The table was populated by regulars, not a rube like me among them, and she was waved away. Katie pointed and laughed at her as she sat down alone at the bar, nursing a glass of red wine and smoking; her friends had already left. Still, I said goodbye on our way out.

"It's through the wall for you then," she sighed with great import, and Katie laughed the entire taxi ride back to the hotel where she dropped me off.

I didn't see much more of Berlin.

Rudy hadn't practised at all but he'd already scored some Purple. Of course I did a few lines with him, even though I was exhausted and more than a little drunk. I thought it was laced with something else, because when we disrobed I saw his penis had turned into a pretty blue candle. It looked like a regular candle, just blue, not one of those penis-shaped candles they have in sex shops, thank heavens.

Of course I lit it and turned off the lights. Instead of having sex, we watched for hours, his penis's flame the only blue light in the dark room. Just before it burned to its end we blew it out together: one two three, blow.

I meant to go to sleep then, but Rudy asked, "Kim, are you ever afraid of going insane?"

"Yes," I answered truthfully, "but not here, not now."

"What do you mean?"

"It isn't my time to go crazy yet," I answered. "This is yours." I didn't know where the words came from. Blame it on the Purple.

And I was right too. The next day Rudy had to check out the club and run through a few songs with his band; I stayed in our room and slept. When he came home I wanted to go out for Schnitzel but he wanted to order from room service and do more of the new Purple. Somewhat reluctantly I agreed. I was here on his dime.

A brand new candle appeared almost immediately.

"Where are we, Kim?" Rudy asked. "Have we gone too far in this time?"

I have no idea where he got the Purple. I know he'd tried in Canada and hadn't been able to get any; we mostly had Green there, not the same animal at all. Maybe Katie got it for him—I wouldn't put it past her—or maybe he bumped into Lou on the street.

Who wouldn't take beautiful, exclusive, scary new drugs given to them by Lou Reed? I would have, then. I took them from Rudy, after all, not nearly so glamourous. I guess he was to me what Lou was to him; Rudy was my Lou. I have no one to blame but myself, that and my age; I was only twenty-two, if clever and sophisticated as Katie and Hans liked to point out.

Most of the time, I was pretty happy about my life, knowing, as Hans said, it would likely only come once. Only now and then did I fret I was a mere groupie as I had that night in Die Ruine, or that I'd wake at forty, lonely and alone, in need of a long stay in rehab.

Like what happened to Rudy.

To answer my question to Leni: Rudy's little West German tour was the height of his fame. With the exception of "Fires Halfway" his next album was awful, and the one after that bombed. His contract wasn't renewed, but he still had habits, and they are harder to kick even than memories of failure. I only know this from hearsay, because after I flew home alone I never saw him again.

I went to fashion school and now design upscale maternity clothes and am successful enough at it for my standards, admittedly not high, but I have my health and work I love, and that is a life blessed. And if you remember the seventies or early eighties you weren't there, but I didn't forget Rudy, and there he was last week at a gallery opening, Rudy whom I hadn't seen in years.

Rudy who? Everyone asked later as I tried to explain his career—he sells real estate now, or software or something—I'm afraid I've already forgotten. "Fires Halfway" was never more than a minor hit, but it's the one that got people to know who I meant. It's still in rotation. Its reputation has grown, if anything.

Isn't that enough to get him a new contract, you ask?

Well, no. Because he didn't actually write it.

Sometimes, I have to admit, I'm still pulled in by the past, by the hopeful love I felt for him that I wonder at now. Neither Rudy nor Lou died, neither there in 1982 in Berlin nor in the twenty years since, although not for lack of trying. And neither did I, or I wouldn't be telling you my story. But enough people have paid the final price, including Serge, one of Rudy's favourite drummers, who OD'd on heroin in a Paris hotel room. You'd think we'd all have seen enough by now, but it seems each new generation falls for the same dangerous lies, for the girl at the opening on Rudy's arm couldn't have been more than twenty-five, and her pupils were big as saucers.

"What's with her?" I remember whispering.

"Orange," he whispered back. "It's so good. Want some? Remember Fan?"

Maybe he should have died.

✖

"Halfway there," I muttered gloomily, watching his nightly candle. By the third night I felt seasoned, knew what to expect, almost tired of the inevitability.

The dead pull of Berlin. Out of time, out of space. I could stay here forever, I thought.

> *I could stay here forever*
> *Counting down*
> *And never get to zero*
> *I could stay here forever*
> *With you*

Rudy and I wrote a song that week. It ended up making him enough to pay cash for his Toronto house. We were already split up when he next recorded and it didn't occur to me to ask for a credit and he didn't offer me one. It was Hans who tracked me down and told me I should threaten to sue. Which I did, and Rudy sent me a large check worth, indeed, half the royalties. I didn't care about my name. He told me to buy rubber spike heels, thinking he was being cute, but at the time I was back in school and put it towards my loan.

We indulged heavily in room service. We didn't go out, unless he had a gig. His playing was less than memorable, but he looked beautiful. Giggling, we'd take a cab back to the hotel afterwards, refusing all invitations.

"We'll hate each other before it's over," I said, thinking I already did, a little. But I couldn't stop any more than him. We experimented with sex on the new Purple and discovered it was not just possible but fantastic, inexhaustibly compelling and inexhaustible every other way, until, at dawn, we'd both want to stop but seemingly couldn't. Sleep, when it came, was always a welcome respite. I felt like we had hormones in an IV drip. It was almost embarrassing.

One night when I was alone I turned on the radio and heard the fire song we'd written together a few nights earlier and had been singing together every day, as we cried or laughed at our plight, or more likely, just made strange love again.

Of course that was impossible; Rudy hadn't recorded it yet. The music was very beautiful. I wished I knew more of music so I could sing him the melody when he returned from seeing Lou (my euphemistic name for his Purple supplier, which I shared with him—he didn't get the joke) and he could write it down, because it was far better than the one he'd written.

But the words were the same, word for word.

What is time? What is creativity?

I felt like we'd been sent out on a space probe, the two of us, to bring back the unearthly answers to those portentous questions, but who could survive that?

Still, waiting for him to come back I tried to tap it out on the room's piano, but I have little ear for music and I never got it right. When he eventually got back he said, "That's the most beautiful thing I've ever heard you play; it captures so perfectly our eerie trajectory."

"It's a quarter of the original, if that, and many notes misheard. It's the melody to 'Fires Halfway'."

"'Fires Halfway' already has a different melody. What do you mean, the original?"

"This one's better. I heard it on the radio."

"You're a technology-based Coleridge," Rudy said. "I know you said you'd wanted to be Kim, and I said I'd be happy if you could, but now you're pushing it." Still he madly scribbled notes, and the lost portions he replaced with accessible poppy riffs, not nearly so frightening. It was a good collaboration, the one and only between ourselves and the Sirian extraterrestrials singing to me and only me from the radio. Or so I joked. Rudy winced. I could say things like that and still remember to pick up the dry cleaning; it was before Fan came. Rudy was concerned; he had a lighter grip that week than me. Kim, whom he'd conjured, strange, wise beauty, was turning out to be a little more than he could handle.

"How was your meeting with Lou?" I asked.

"Not very productive. Possibly a good thing as I have to play tomorrow night."

"They'll love you," I said. "I was going to go shopping with Katie to buy a dress. Want to go out? We haven't been out for days, except for shows. I'm kind of glad you couldn't get any more Purple."

"Where is there to go? We're past Pluto, Kim."

"You'll have to get back in time for your gig tomorrow."

"Yes," he sighed as if he didn't like it much. "I could spit on them and they'd love me. Why do people worship celebrities?"

"I don't know," I said, wondering whether he was ready to hear me say he wasn't much of a celebrity compared to Lou but thinkingI'd wait. "But I think we need to go out. We haven't been out for days except for gigs."

"Where is there to go? We're past Pluto, Kim," he said again. "And the bars have closed."

"Die Ruine's private and open all night."

"You're not kidding." Rudy laughed a little bitterly and took two dry-cleaned silk jackets off their hangers: one black, one mauve. At least the cuts were different.

A blonde with dark circles under her eyes told us she loved Rudy's song about Kim and introduced herself as Fan. I recognised her as part of Leni's group from the first night and when she asked us to join her we agreed; the place was standing room only. The three of us drank rye, which is odd as I generally hate it. We were glum and silent, maybe because of the whiskey.

I went to the bathroom, the atmosphere at our table was so claustrophobic I had to escape. There was a hole high in the crumbled wall; I stood on the toilet and looked through, saw two stars like eyes looking back at me, the eyes of God or perhaps the Devil as the tarot reader had said. One of them must be Sirius, I thought. My home planet. I half believed it; we were that far gone. It was an interstellar distance Rudy would have to take on stage tomorrow night but I figured it was almost a requirement in his profession; Lou had likely played from much farther out in space. I got back and told Fan and Rudy.

"There's a dark twin to the Dog Star," Fan said. "Want to go?"

"That's where we've been the last week, since we arrived," I replied.

"Ah. You must mean you have some of the new Purple. I'd like to join you," she said.

"We're lonely explorers. The arduousness of our journey through uncharted territory has caused us to go from love to hate in less than a week," Rudy said.

It was true I wanted more than anything to get away from him; the problem was Purple impelled us toward one another: tiny electric trains about to crash, derail, explode. It always seemed worth it until afterwards. When Fan reached over and fondled Rudy's thigh I was thrilled at the possibility of dumping him off on her but she had other plans for the three of us.

Two days later, waking up, curtains pulled against the glare, I glanced at my watch.

"Shit," I said, noticing the date, "we have three hours to catch our plane."

"You go," Rudy said, reaching over and cupping Fan's breast in his hand. "I think I am going to stay here, with Fan."

She nodded solemnly, extricated herself from his fondling, leaned over and submerged his unlit cock in her small mouth. Her long black hair veiled the act decoratively.

I put a few things into a suitcase, feeling neither jealousy nor even curiosity. I didn't remember when she'd arrived, or why, and wasn't sure I cared.

"Don't forget this," Rudy said, reaching over to the night table to pick up a silver choker we'd bought in an expensive jewellery shop on the Ku-Damm.

"Oh thanks, I almost did forget it." I popped it into the suitcase. What had we been doing for the last forty-eight hours? The memories came, a little at a time. More or less what Rudy and me had been up to, only there'd been three of us.

"Oh no," Fan said, "you should wear it." She got up, having finished her job, and clasped the choker behind my neck. "Zo baby, you don't think you will stay here with us?"

"No."

"Why not? You find me beautiful, no? You seem to like it with a girl. I could teach you . . ."

I looked from her to Rudy, a statue in repose. A naked prince. A young lion. Purple did little for my vocabulary. It had seemed a good thing, once. "I think maybe I have had enough of beauty for awhile, you know?"

"Ah," Fan said, "I never have enough of beauty. Never never never."

"I know," I said. "That's why you're a junkie and I'm not."

She laughed instead of taking offence, whispered in my ear. "I sense that you are a little bit tired of him and I understand. I have a girlfriend, Lucerne, who would be only too happy to take him off our hands. The thing is, we would have to take the credit card. You made him put it in your name too, didn't you?"

"No."

"But you can make his signature, yes? A girl could be a Rudy."

"His name's Rudolph," I said, giving away his worst secret.

She sighed. "No good. How much cash then? And of course, we could sell the dog collar for quite a bit, that is unless you're very fond of it." She was forgetting to lower her voice but Rudy didn't seem to hear, or maybe he didn't care.

"Well, I'm thinking it will make a great memento of this bizarre chapter."

"What? I do not always understand your Canadian English. I lived for a time in London but it is a much different accent."

"Not worth repeating."

"Between two women there is always all the time in the world."

"It's not personal."

Fan wasn't offended. In retrospect I'm not surprised. It was her job, after all, to understand such things. "You get sick even of the best sweets if you eat too many," she said by way of analysis. "Now when we do Purple it no longer fulfils each desire like liquid light."

"Did you write that down?" I asked Rudy. He didn't answer, paging through a magazine.

"I know," Fan continued, packing her own little patent leather case, "we get bored. Too much of the same is not good. There are many things I could teach you. Many different and new games you have not experienced before. We play to amuse ourselves."

"Like dolphins," I said, "or maybe dogs."

She didn't hear my sarcastic undertone, beamed widely. "Genau! Dolphins' sexuality is so spiritual, no? Like us."

I had to admit it had occasionally felt like that, playing like dolphins in a flooded old hotel room, sporting a baby grand and drawn mauve curtains. What is it about mauve? It was the only colour I wore then, if I wasn't wearing black.

Fan took off one of her many scarves and pulled it tightly around my breasts. I moaned, wondering whether dolphins ever moaned.

"Lie down," she whispered. "Just once more."

I complied.

Lying there, my eyes closed, I heard her charge Rudy two hundred and fifty dollars. "American," she whined. I heard her get up and fish through the wallet he'd left on the night table. "What is this? Don't tell me you don't have any American?"

My eyes slammed open. "You're paying for this?"

"Well, it's actually the first I've heard of it."

"Not true. You agreed to pay me before I came up, and you did pay me half last night, remember?" She winked at me. "It's been amazing. Think of it this way, it's half my regular rate because Ich finde Sie beide sehr cool, very beautiful. Beauty always pays a lower price, in all things."

Fan and her damn beauty obsession. She was slated for a lot of face lifts some year, that was for sure.

"Are you really going to go?" Rudy asked, looking forlorn. I covered him with a sheet.

"Get a grip, kid, you need it. Although I have to say it's been a ball. If a very strange ball, doesn't bounce like other balls, obeys physics from another dimension."

"It's not my fault, I didn't know. I thought she was a groovy pick-up, just like you did."

I figured him for a liar. And what was wrong with paying a groovy pick-up? Fan had a plane to catch today, just like I did, only hers was to Paris.

Still haven't been to Paris.

"You wouldn't have to pay if it was just you," she whispered, lasciviously. Rudy glowered at her, overhearing. "We could make a lot of money. We could go anywhere, travel the world. I have great connections."

"I'll bet." Watching her pack scarves. Would she wash them out in tonight's hotel room? Where did she live, and with whom? Do women like Fan 'live' anywhere? Do they have kitchens, or only restaurants? I'd buy her drinks and ask about her life but I knew I wouldn't get to hear her stories unless I joined in them. You hear the best gossip only when you give people something to gossip about. I'd have to earn her trust, she wouldn't give it away for free.

"Well, if you gotta go, go in style." She gave me her black lace shirt to wear, a rubber miniskirt and net stockings. They fit perfectly.

"I guess you'll be wearing my jeans and T-shirt out," I said, unzipping my suitcase to dig out clothes for her.

She took them and held them up against her long slim body, delighted. "They are a very nice jeans and T-shirt. They will remember you me always."

"Cool," I said and kissed her briefly on those soft soft lips. "Take care. Don't get hurt. There's some crazy people out there, some bad bad drugs."

She smiled, so happy I stopped to think she might be endangering herself. "I am the craziest," she said. "Is no one badder than me." She laughed delightedly, sharing me in her big secret, the one she depended on to keep her safe from harm. I hoped it would, even if she was the devil.

"No doubt," I said, glancing at Rudy before I left. He was asleep. Would they spend another few days together, Fan steadily emptying his wallet of traveller's checks, or was it over between them too? Who knew, and more importantly, who really cared?

※

Katie drove me to the airport, shrugged when I told her Rudy had changed his flight, would be staying on with Fan. When we got to Tegel I asked whether she'd supplied the Purple. Maybe there'd been a lot I'd missed. Maybe Fan and Katie had cooked it all up together, right from the beginning. She didn't reply, not really, and who could blame her? Katie was way too slick to ever implicate herself; in that way she and Fan were of a type. Instead she asked, "What's with the clothes?" Giving me the once over.

"I've been in Berlin," I said. "What do you think?"

"Did you go to the other side?"

"Yes."

"What was it like?" Katie asked.

"Strange. But good to see it, I guess. To know what's there."

"But you wouldn't want to live there, right?"

"No," I said. "But then, that's what everyone from this side says, don't they?"

She nodded, smiling. "The new song. No one will ever forget it."

SOMNII DRACONIS

Colby Smith

I go to the shore to think, even though it offers no insight nor does it inspire anything novel.

Here the world is achromatic. My provider isn't covered out here, so my smartphone can't vampirise my time. Huge rocks—scales shed from a gigantic reptile—litter the beach as if the limestone cliffs that veil the coast were struck by rockets. The water which performs cunnilingus on the continent is grey as roadside slush, showing its true age.

Gulls soar overhead but they do not cry out. Better kites than dinosaurs.

(Exponential frequency in reports of museum collections disemboweled by thieves.)

Lately, I've become sufficiently paranoid of media. My body blushes with extreme anxiety and sadness when an advertisement offers my wife or my daughter more things than I could ever offer them. All that I can offer them originates from the companies behind the advertisements. Any aspect of an advertisement has the potential to inflame my emotions: the general colour scheme; the absurdly hygienic bodies of the actors and actresses; the therapeutic and seductive tones in their voices; the jingles that my family memorizes instantaneously when they never bother to memorize equally inane Top 40's, or nursery rhymes, or folk songs, etc. Packaging can also elicit a response. For instance, when I go to the pharmacy to obtain my monthly refill of Prozac (40 mg. daily, a.m., taken with food) they wrap the bottles in cellophane embroidered with myriad cartoon hearts and a label on the front and back of the wrapper that reads WE CARE. I get depressed when I read it, because I know the manufacturers of that plastic wrap are feigning their concern for my well-being for the sake of profit through *argumentum ad cupiditatum.*

On one extremity of the beach I see a billboard—a dead windup key enjambed in the earth—advertising allegedly cheap rates for a Holiday Inn located 2.5 kilometers down the road. I begin to weep when I see the exclamation mark asserting the fairness of these deals.

(New black market hype derived from the ancient Chinese medicinal canon.)

I wipe my eyes and, from the polar extremity of the beach, the first human I have seen all morning approaches. In his hand, he clutches a dowsing rod. The instrument licks the air like a snake, searching out the warmth of beloved minerals. Every dozen paces or so, he picks up a rock, examines it, then feeds it to the ocean.

I approach him as he makes his seventh round. The folds of his black tweed coat applaud in the lapping wind. It is quite baggy on his bonsai frame. From his breast pocket shoots a cluster of dead yarrow; I suppose the bees don't bother him much as those plants are stiff as evil, but it is a shame that they must drive the butterflies away. He appears to be slightly over forty, glasses filthy, taut lips ready to speak the first canto of the Comedy whenever. His yam-colored hair, made wiry by the alkaline breath of the Atlantic, spills down his back and shoulders in gentle coils.

(In which farmers upturned dragon bones while ploughing fields.)

"Excuse me, what are you looking for, and why aren't you using a metal detector?"

The man squints like a vacuole and replies in a sleepy, viscous voice, as if his vocal cords were over-cranked or he was hearing every vowel and consonant echo against his elvish ears.

"You might suppose I am a prospector, but I do not prospect metals rare or common. I seek the sex of stones."

(The priests would then grind up the bones and employ their supposed properties against metaphysical ailments — chi imbalance, dimming souls, rotting spirits from old possessions.)

"I don't believe rocks have genitals."

The man thrust his face towards mine and pried open the lips of his right eye.

"You suppose you see straight, yes? When I consider your eyes, I see that your horizon is a horseshoe, and you will notice likewise with my horizon. When Schrödinger conceived the undead cat, he became a sage and discovered that Nature is not merely nature but the perpetual coupling of Nature and Unnature. Existence is essentially a parallax."

"What are you going on about?"

"Guitar strings."

(Toxicologists have determined that the effects of paleo are subject to what species is ingested by the user. Sauropod-eaters consistently report feeling immense and are often found with an exploded stomach from consuming copious amounts of vegetable matter. Mammoth-eaters sweat profusely and eventually dehydrate. Megaloceros-eaters experience incomparable migraines and tend to commit suicide

by gunshot or by traumatic impact. Smilodon-eaters teethed their canines on steel till their mouths are nests of bloody splinters, and they usually die by bacterial infection afflicting the torn gums. Theropod-eaters have been observed to form hunting parties, then proceed to stalk and cannibalize while intoxicated in the streets.)

The incoherent man resumed his mysterious work and grew deaf to my pleas and epithets. It is bizarre that I have become so angry towards this man, for he is the most interesting thing that the beach has revealed to me.

After about seven minutes he picked up a rock the size of a skull and beckoned me over.

(Popping tears of amber like birds harvesting gastroliths. The lenses in their eyes reproduce till the eyes resemble those of the arthropod prisoners in the gems. The kaleidoscope is too much.)

A trilobite was encased in the rock. It was a beautiful fossil despite the right flank being chipped off. The contrast was stark and the ridges of the segmented exoskeleton were prominent. The compound eyes, sandpapered by the fossilization process, bulged from the lateral sides of the head segment.

The man turned the rock in his hands, examining the specimen meticulously.

"Yes . . . probably genus *Calymene* . . . fat cephalon and tricadeca-segmentation a dead giveaway."

(Ravers who had ingested Carboniferous ferns were found standing dead in a christpose, exhaled continuously till their lungs gave out. Like a Roman roadside, a forensic investigator remarked.)

He set the rock back on the ground, stooped, and withdrew a mallet and chisel from his coat pockets. Jamming the tip of the chisel against a pressure point in the rock, he raised the mallet and struck the head of the chisel with the rhythm and dynamic of a beating heart. If he is a paleontologist, I should find out what institution he's allied with so his position can be revoked.

"The fuck!"

The man hammered the trilobite until it was reduced to rubble. Its remains looked like a pile of rotten teeth. He picked up a shard with his forefinger and thumb, then scrutinized it.

"Do you know how we know fossils respired before their tissues were mineralized?"

"You just destroyed . . ."

"Humanity has suspected that these sculptures are the remains of living things for a long time, but when that Danish Saint matched tonguestones with the teeth of a leviathan he dispelled any honest skepticism. Then we drew anatomical and inferred behavioural connections between the statuesque life of old and the fluid life of young; not only from the specimens themselves but from adjacent minutiae which suggested what sort of paleoclimate they inhabited. In a sense, they are still considered 'failed sketches' in the painting of creation, despite their individual aesthetic and compositional merit in the scheme of things. Much later, we detected residual biomolecules in the fossils—unfathomable organic wisdom entombed in the lithified dead, peace be upon all of the dead we know, do not know, will never know, have forgotten. This is what I meant by the sex of stones. I seek the vestigial memories locked in the fossils."

(Governments have discouraged gift shops the world over to continue selling authentic fossils as souvenirs, and some countries have already taken the initiative to defund natural history museums in the interest of public safety.)

He scooped up the Silurian splinters and rose.

"You look sick, sir."

My argument froze on my tongue.

(Paleontologists are pariahs. Mothers and fathers of dead sons and daughters marinate the airwaves with bitter rivulets, damning methodological naturalism back to the scarcely-methodological Aristotle. Creationism revives in the public sphere, so families can heal from the trauma.)

"Perhaps not sick . . . more like *exhausted*."

"Everything exhausts me, indeed."

"Things have become too complicated."

"Yes."

(SCIENCE IS NOT AN ILLICIT SUBSTANCE, read the picket signs.)

He places a shard of the fossil into my hand.

"Swallow it. No need to chew. It will cure you. On three."

I don't know what to say anymore.

"Ichi . . . ni . . . san!"

We toss the fragments towards the backs of our throats.

I feel my bones giving out—my limbs receding—my mouth shifting—my flesh oozing and calcifying—my torso segmenting—my pupils reproducing asexually rendering the world a blurry kaleidoscope.

Such vivid memories so unlike the blind artistry of humanity!

Two young boys found a pair of human buoys, curled up like pill bugs, bobbing against the dawn blazing on the water.

THE MEDDLERS

Colin Insole

A raw east wind rose that February afternoon, funnelling from the sea into the small market town. It curtailed the usual bonhomie of the dog walkers in the park and the lazy conviviality of parents collecting their children from the infant school. No one lingered to chat. They hurried home, hunched and taciturn, as flurries of snow grew thicker in the glow of the street lights.

As the town drew its curtains, the wind gathered strength in the darkness, probing and scouring. A layer of dirty sleet—more scum and filth than snow—was left in the porch of the church, creeping in under the gap of the huge wooden door. Its force ripped at the sparse layer of grass on the sand dunes—laying bare the soil, as if skinning a rabbit. Discarded objects, buried for centuries—broken clay pipes, bottles clogged with earth and lumps of metal, with tumours of rust, bubbled to the surface, like the overflow from a blocked drain. The wind offered these dingy little relics to the town but kept its wonders secret. In a sheltered cove, hidden from view, a chunk of earth dislodged by the violence of the gale slipped from the undercliff and dropped into the sea. And in the exposed rock, was the fossil of a prehistoric bird, the lines of its beak, claws and feathers, as clear as when it fell, millions of years ago.

Later, when the wind subsided, moonlight would catch and mirror its reflection, shimmering in seawater.

The church clock struck two. Muffled and distorted by the gale, it seemed more a warning siren than a marker of the hours. The wind now played with sound, teasing and mocking. It collected fragments from the radios of solitaries and insomniacs, flinging them into the dreams of those who turned and fretted in their sleep. It prised out things that should have been left undisturbed—picking at memories and collecting the rubbish of thoughts and dreams, to smear them over the town. And it discoloured and stained all that it touched, infecting the restless with an unwholesome energy.

The snow fell, barely settling, like flakes of ash or the soiled feathers from a torn and stinking pillow. From his window, in Leafy Manors, the clifftop nursing home, eighty-six-year-old Leslie Trelogan watched the flurries as they whirled and spiralled. All the familiar landmarks of his home town were blurred or curling at the edges. The sea, the cliffs and the minor road that snaked out past the sand dunes, to fields where sheep grazed, were warped together in a churning mass of wet grime. He was conscious, too, of his failing wits—how he could become lost and disorientated in once familiar places and how the faces of his family and friends seemed like masks, donned by strangers in a crowd to tease and baffle him.

The strongest gusts made the home's lights flicker and the sound of the wind became mixed with the shuffle of slippers and walking frames in the corridor and moans and whimpers from adjacent rooms. He had been woken by some nagging urgency—either from dream or a neglected task that required his immediate attention. And now, peering out into the cold, half-lit streets of a February night, where familiar things fragmented and realigned, lost images became vivid and clear again. Old routes and pathways, buried since childhood, were recalled and gave him the impetus to explore.

As clifftop, sand dunes, roads and buildings, lost their shapes and identities in the sleet, Leslie Trelogan negotiated the corridors and nursing stations, as a shadow might flicker through the dappled light of trees on a summer's day. Overcoming excruciating spasms in his hips and knees, he descended two flights of stairs—his stick seeming to stifle the heaviness of his gait and silence the creaking of the floorboards. The pain subsiding, he passed unnoticed, in plain sight, through the vigilance of the nurses' patrols and evaded the bulwark of the duty sister's desk, whose lamp shone like a searchlight on foyer and entrance hall. Blinking slightly, on the hinterland between the noise and light of the care home and the cold wet darkness of the street, he plunged into the blackness. As sure-footed now as an acrobat on a tightrope, he recalled doorways and gaps, his body moving with a fluid intuitive grace. All the confusions, blockages and dead ends of the encroaching dementia, that made modern life so alien and frightening, were dissolved. He walked now in an old landscape—its tracks, boltholes and sacred places, engrained from childhood lore.

The strict regime of surveillance and monitoring, practised at "Leafy Manors", discovered him missing within an hour. Vehicles screeched into the cold and search parties hastened out with torches to scour the lanes and bridleways that led to his old haunts. His history was well known to the nursing staff, for he was garrulous and anxious to share memories and pore over old photographs. Orphaned when his parents died in an air raid of 1941, he was adopted by his Uncle Bernard and Auntie Brenda—austere Baptist lay ministers. The transition from relaxed urban hedonism to strict puritanism, with all the added privations of the war, was an ordeal for the child. He had run away several times. But eventually he had adjusted, compromised and prospered— settling in the town and raising his own family.

The little sorties continued in vain until dawn. A frail, confused old man had eluded them all. The general consensus amongst the nurses and managers was that he had made for the sea—or 'a home run', in the gallowsbird humour of a handful of residents. There was a distinct hostility between staff and patients over breakfast, and a feeling on the part of the staff that Trelogan's cronies had colluded in the escape. Privileges and treats were withheld in punishment. The television and radio remained silent and cutlery was slammed and clattered. In response, a song rose—at first from a single table, but soon becoming a chorus of rebellion and mockery from the entire room.

> "Oh give me a dose of pentobarbitone
> And I'll give you trouble no more.
> I'll fade in the night, when the moon's shining
>   bright,
> And be gone, before the dawn comes a creeping."

Some understood the lyric but most hummed along in ignorance, pleased to cause a nuisance and upset the smooth efficiency of the institution. And when they had finished, they cheered, for outside the dining room, they could hear the rescue helicopter, as it flew low, searching the beach and the sand dunes for the truant.

He was not found until dusk. All day, the residents watched with growing amusement as the figures in uniform gesticulated and scurried—a mimed farce of incompetence, like a modern Keystone Cops. When news finally came, the street lamps were shining again and light gusts of frost blew across the empty turnip fields that bordered the care home.

Three teenage girls had discovered the body, hidden behind an evergreen hedge, in a snug little recess, backing onto the cliff face. The place was old and stretched back into the earth. An arch of dead wood formed a core, with roots and branches giving comfortable seating for three or four people. Hollow chambers had formed where the wood had withered, suggesting animal burrows.

The body was in rigor and could not be squeezed or wedged through the narrow entrance, without the foliage being cut away. Police Sergeant John Thringarth supervised the operation and took statements from the three girls. They had the air of tenants unfairly evicted from their home by bailiffs. One, in particular, had a forlorn look of panic, as if the secret hideaway, only discovered a day ago, had been a place of genuine sanctuary.

"At his age, he had no right to be here," she whined. "See how guilty he looks. He's ashamed to be caught here, at the Leckles."

Sergeant Thringarth studied the old man's face. The girl was right. There was a look of surprised contrition, as if his presence in the chamber was an act of sacrilege.

As the body was lifted clear, he noticed an old exercise book lying on the floor, which had probably fallen from the hands of the deceased. Alone in the confined space as twilight gathered, he took in the geography of the hideout and its pattern of twisted branches and roots. The girl had named it "The Leckles". Both the word and the images recalled a memory from his own childhood. For a few days, he too, had spent time here—fervently and intensely. And that was the name with which his group of friends had dubbed the place—maybe a corruption of "the nettles", which had abounded that summer. After less than a week, they had stopped coming and all recollection of their time here had been buried—perhaps deliberately and wisely, for its associations were painful and disturbing.

Sergeant Thringarth took the exercise book home, intending to forward it to the care home. It belonged originally to the long defunct County Grammar School and smelled of earth, leaf mould and wild garlic—the predominant hedgerow herb of the lane in early Spring. Coincidentally, the book was inscribed, "April 10th, 1944" and titled in spidery fountain-pen handwriting, "The Misadventures of Two Piejawing Hee-hawing Chumps—who diddled, dished and stitched me up like a kipper." Written over three days, it was an exuberant satire, vulgar and scatological, lampooning his two Baptist guardians. An early photograph of Nazi storm troopers, wearing baggy shorts and sporting bulging kneecaps, was superimposed with the heads of his aunt and uncle. There were parodies of advertisements from *Punch*.

"Well-turned out men flock to Uncle Bernard's grooming aids, passion suppressants, calf-leather trusses, nose tweezers and second-hand toothpicks. As seductive to the outdoor He-Man, as to the strictest hellfire preacher, the accessories of the Gentlemen's Disciplinary Rubberware Company are as masculine as pipes, guns and cross-country runs."

But the bulk of the book was filled with games of Consequences, where the thirteen-year-old Leslie Trelogan and three companions had compiled their stories—each entry written blind to the previous strand. The sergeant read the first one aloud.

"Jock Ribbentrop met Auntie Brenda at Stepney Public Baths. He wore nothing but his little stick of Blackpool rock. She wore the biggest aspidistra in the world. He said, 'Is this the queue for offal?' She said, 'Can I do you now, sir?' The consequence was that he pleasured her vigorously in the orangery. And the world said, 'Very very tasty, very very sweet.'"

Throughout those pages, Auntie Brenda capered and flirted. She mouthed the slogans and popular songs of the day and was invariably ravished by a succession of high-ranking Nazis, musical entertainers or local school masters. Uncle Bernard, in his turn, was depicted as a degenerate and prowling voyeur or pederast. A cartoon motif, modelled on the figure of Mister Chad and repeated throughout the book, showed him peering salaciously over a wall and dribbling the words, "Lovely, lovely, lovely."

Sergeant Thringarth dreamed of the clandestine group of four, that night—their smut, their jokes and their fits of uncontrollable giggling. But their experience, despite its banality and tackiness, had been cathartic—purging the young man of a festering hatred and bitterness towards his guardians that might otherwise have damaged them all. Leaving their den for the last time, the boy had dropped the exercise book into the hollow of the roots, almost as an offering to the spirit of the place.

Sergeant Thringarth woke and hurried to find the book. Its humour was infectious and there was a line he tried to recall. In the night, its pages had crumbled, flaking to dust and specks of ink. A draught blew, billowing the curtains and all trace of it was gone. But the dream memory of the boy's offering it to the trees of the den recalled his own experience, in June 1990, aged fourteen.

For five years, since his father had abandoned the family, he had lived in the flat, content and prospering, with his mother. But around Easter, her work colleague, Mr Jessup, was invited regularly for dinner, and the food seemed to taste of grey ash and sawdust. Soon, he moved in. An inherently decent man, with a painful willingness to empathise and understand the surly teenager, he followed John around the small flat, in an attempt to bond.

Escaping his clutches one Sunday, John met with two friends. Walking on the clifftop and hitting out at the bushes in frustration, the layers of evergreen had rippled away. They had discovered their hideaway. There, for three or four days, he vented his anger. Using a backing drum rhythm, whilst a friend beatboxed, he screamed incoherent abuse into a small tape recorder. When they played it back, its inadequacies, with waves of sound fuzzing and fading, suggested a furtive bootleg, captured at dawn—the drowsy culmination of a night's revels. It evoked the exhaustion of hours of dancing, the stained, acid colours of the improvised raves and parties, Lucozade and ice lollies. At school, during the lunch hour, the sixth-formers supervised sessions of loud music in the hall. Students were invited to bring their own tapes—invariably recorded from the radio or copied illegally. John had smuggled his offering into the pile. It was played and judged favourably, with much incredulity that the music was his own. Thereafter, his status within the school was redefined. Mr Jessup seemed smaller and less important and, in time, melted quietly from his life, when his mother grew bored of the cloying neediness.

The duplicate tapes that he had created were long destroyed or lost but he remembered the act of offering one to the bushes—the ritual had been observed and acknowledged by his friends. Into the mouth or eyes of the dead, the ancient Greeks placed coins to pay the ferryman, for the passage across the river, from this world into the next. And here too, it seemed, some token was demanded. Determined to retrieve his tape, he returned to the site. One of the girls who had discovered the old man's body was there, lingering on a corner, like a mother bird, deciding whether to return to a disturbed nest. With a gesture of despair on seeing him, she fled. Recalling the traumas of those teenage days, he realised how strange it was that no one had discovered them in the den. Their noise would have been heard on the edge of town. But not a single resident in this busy area, near the cliffs, where the aged population harry and chivvy the young, had complained.

The entrance to the den eluded him. Despite the sawing away of branches and vegetation, the hedge had seemed to close and enfold upon itself. Eventually brute force and anger uncovered the hole. Groping in the root cavity, he quickly located his tape. But his fingers also touched two more objects, which he pulled into the light.

The first was a 1969 copy of *Jackie*—the magazine for girls. The main picture story, of a burgeoning romance, had been heavily annotated with biro, changing the central characters. The two lovesick protagonists were now a pair of senior teachers—nicknamed "Wetleg" and "Miss Tizzbag", from the county grammar school. He remembered them from his own years there. They were martinets—two chaste, almost asexual bulwarks of discipline and regimentation. A mathematics teacher, Mr Bradstock's soubriquet was earned when he returned from the lavatory with one trouser leg soaking wet, either from water or urine. He was universally loathed. Even his gravestone was daubed, in later years, with the slogan "Drip on and Rust in Hell—Wetleg—You Dirty Squirt." They were absurdly incongruous lovers, as they oozed and gushed.

"Oh, Wetleg, you are my hunny-bunny. Please stay in my heart and I will stay in yours. I will buy you a car coat for Christmas. We will have matching coffee mugs in the staff room and practise our sums together."

"Oh, Miss Tizzbag, you are my sugar, my squishy pink dumpling. I will sponge the soup stains from your tweed tie. We can sit up in bed together and you can read me your own translations of Julius Caesar's campaigns in Gaul."

Sergeant Thringarth wondered about the identity of the young satirist. He found and recognised her name at the back of the magazine, alongside numerology that assessed her compatibility with the singer, Marc Bolan. Now a successful businesswoman and philanthropist, she also served as a school governor and Justice of the Peace.

From the magazine came the sweet smell of bubble-gum and orangeade. But the second object exuded a perfume that was sophisticated and enticing. It was a letter, postmarked from London in August 1920 and addressed to Polly Cushat, c/o Waltham Arms.

Sergeant Thringarth had made a study of the lost inns and pubs of his home town. The Americans had insisted on the closure of the Waltham Arms, in the spring of 1944, as an immoral house that was corrupting their troops. And of course, they had been right. It had always been an underworld pub. But oddly, that had been its front—a mask for something even more esoteric, known only to its habitués. There was a secret glamour about its history—stories of modern witchcraft, of doomed or ecstatic liaisons and a poetry that clung to the old photographs and engravings. At the end of the war, the town's suet-faced establishment had obliterated the site, razing every stone to the ground, as if performing an exorcism. The letter, in an odd mixture of polari and improvised London underworld slang, read:

"Marvelossa to vada you, Poll, last yadnus, my dorcas. I am neetneves today—a coopered dillo buor—with my macka Mog—miaow, miaow—a lickle yowler! Mulcho trade—heigh-ho—but enough gelt now for a flowery or even a bijou latty.

On the Mary Blaine to the Dilly—a fungus—all meese and meshigener—ogled me. A naff omi—nanti pots in the oven—all kennetseno—feeb and reeb breath—stains on his kaffies and red fambles. Full of glim, I say!

You should vada me now—how we should cackle—zhooshing our riah as we did yadnus—toppling over our willets, our luppers all over our thews. Alamo! Alamo!

I'll send the dinari when I have the latty—you must troll up, my dorcas—would be so bonaroo. I'll blag you from the station.

Oh and gratis for the aunt nell danglers at The Leckles.

Bona nochy for now

Muff"

Sergeant Thringarth no longer had the facilities to play cassette tapes and resolved to transfer his music to CD. He left the two documents on the floor of the den. From the 1920's, there was that curious folk memory of "The Leckles". He remembered, from his infancy, the proud independent figure of Elizabeth Cushat—novelist, poet and visionary. That afternoon, at the library, he consulted the set of her first editions and found the dedication in her most acclaimed volume of verse.

"To Muff—My Ariel and my Prospero"

He dreamed of the den that night. But he was a furtive visitor—a spy and interloper, peeping through the branches. The three girls, who had discovered Mr Trelogan, were comfortably in occupation, huddled together. Apart from the mobile phones they operated, their fingers racing, they might have been young witches or cunnings, solving their problems with spells and incantations. And finally, at peace with themselves, they prepared to abandon the site. From his own time, he knew it would be their last visit. Their leader, once the most troubled of the trio, now smiled and gently posted her phone into the hollow.

He woke with a consciousness of the depth and history of the den. He had merely examined the surface cracks, like an archaeologist drilling a tiny hole into a tomb and shining a candle into the aperture to expose a glimpse of wonders. The site had been occupied for three or four days in 1990, 1969, 1944 and 1920. There was a brief fervour every generation and then it was forgotten. It fell into a dream-like lethargy, as if its occupants had drunk the waters of Lethe. Forgetting the urgency of the three current inhabitants, he hurried there—his temper rising as he battled the branches to find the entrance. The colours in the teenage magazine had faded with unnatural speed and the ink on the letter was yellow. Thrusting his hand into the hollow, he retrieved some cloth. It was a piece of embroidery from a child's sampler. Stick-like caricatures in red cotton danced on crude little gallows. The stitching was rough and poorly executed but retained the verve and spirit of the artist, who had signed herself, "Louise Anne Parker 1864—Wheezy Anna". A notebook lay alongside the embroidery. From the 1880's, he had unearthed a boys' quarrel that simmered at their public school.

As he probed deeper, he twisted and broke the living wood of the hedge, heaving the snapped branches into the nearby ditch. Sap stained his arms and face and leaked onto the floor of the den. He had now passed beyond the years of common literacy. The objects spilled out in their hundreds. Many were locks of hair—the colours still intact and bright. They had been touched with perfumes of flowers, buds and grasses. There were rosettes of stringed meadow blooms—formally grouped together, to comprise a fitting bouquet for the spirit of the place. And pieces of wood or bark, some beautifully carved, represented people, animals or divine beings.

Some had left trinkets or curiosities of the natural world—a blue jay's feather or the skull of a stoat.

Each object seemed to have soaked up the character and world of the child who had offered it. For pictures raced through his mind as they passed quickly through his fingers. A few had scratched sketches or doodles, with knife or flint. Most were crude misrepresentations of people or animals. He noted a wolf pack, a shapeless bear and something with a flipper-like appendage that was either a seal or a beaver. But something from half-way down the pile, made the hairs on his neck stand up. It was the remains of a cuttlefish. Into the flaky white cartilage, someone had carved the letters, "Lech-Las", embellishing them with dyes. The symbols were surrounded by an arch of branches, resembling the exterior of the shelter.

He worked with a destructive stubborn energy—careless of any irreparable damage he might do to the fabric or soul of the site. There was no cathedral hush about the den to alert him—no stained glass or hymns to denote its sanctity. But nonetheless, it was a place of healing—not with solemn prayers or devotions but guffaws, sniggering, filth and ribaldry.

Winter sunlight burned into the hollow and the fibres of tendril and root cracked as he heaved and tugged at them. There was a fragility about the place. Once breached, it succumbed easily, like a tender plant exposed to frost.

At the centre of the hollow, now separated from the living tendrils and roots, was a circular knot of wood—the heart and bones of the place. He wrenched it into the light and noted its rings of blue, green and grey, like those of a tree trunk. There were over four hundred, and he realised that each represented a single generation. This place of sanctity and healing had existed since the ice sheets melted. He brushed his finger over one close to the centre and saw vividly the little tribe who inhabited the river estuary. Two girls, in early adolescence, were attracting the attentions of a shuffling, predatory older man. Both slipped unseen into the den and he witnessed their pantomime of mockery—the grunting, gurning and howling imitation of their suitor.

The two external rings of the wood were fluid, as if incomplete or subject to change. And he understood that they belonged to the generations of the living, who had visited most recently. A last, aborted strand had the appearance of a scrawny featherless bird, ejected from the nest—all raw pink and scraggy grey. And embedded in the timber, like a watermark, in the colours of earth, sky and river, were the letters, "Y Lech Las".

His exertions had wearied him and he fell asleep quickly that night, having carried the stump home as a trophy. He woke from a leaden dreamless slumber. His muscles ached and there was an angry red rash where his fingers had touched the rings of the wood. Covered in a mould-like dust, it had the appearance of bleached coral. Flakes had dropped, draining the colours of his carpet. In the night, the wind had risen again, flinging about the detritus of the town. His own windows were stained with leaves and some stray flowers.

He was not on duty that morning. But his colleagues were called to the town's railway station, where a teenage girl had flung herself under the fast train. Already bragging of "natural selection", her enemies and critics at school were gloating and celebrating on social media. And they were homing in now on her two friends, prompting and goading.

A package containing a CD arrived for Sergeant Thringarth and he settled down to listen to the music he had created in 1990, which evoked a landscape of communal dancing, love and fun. All was changed and distorted. A wind roared, menacing and wild. Far in the distance were faint cries, like lost souls drowning at sea. When the voices came, they made him jump for they were loud and threatening. They were the words spoken by both the past occupants of the den and their persecutors. But they seemed to have been filtered through something like a Punch and Judy showman's swazzle. Each word, however innocent, sounded malign and knowing.

"I'm in the house. I'm in the house. I'll be your hunny-bunny, if you will be mine. Gummy, what a chap—he's a downy bird. Vada the onk on that charpering omi. Don't brabble with me, you crossbiter. He's a cold fish—look at his corybungus—what a tooty-fruity! Turn your back, you saucy cat and say no more to me. Oh cornuto—he has the French marbles! What moonmen, tatterdemalions and jarkmen they are. Well stow you, stow you, I'm off to the trugging house." Many of the words were unknown to him. They came in ancient tongues—some guttural, some lyrical and some whose meaning he almost caught, before the phrases were lost. The commotion rose to a crescendo and died, leaving only the sound of the wind.

It seemed to catch the echo of the gale in the streets and mimic its gusts and flurries. The den was broken, its protecting branches hacked away and the piles of old offerings were scattered and flung into the streets. And the windows of the town were spattered with the sodden remains of summer flowers and garlands, shells from extinct molluscs and words of flame that flared briefly into life and were gone.

JACK

D.P. Watt

Jack was certain that some cunt had spiked his drink; he was absolutely mashed. He looked up at Kev, Damien and Susie and thought he saw little grins on each of their treacherous lips, wry little conspiratorial curls that revealed them for the deceitful pigs that they really were.

It was meant to be a friendly game of poker over a few beers, to catch up with Damien and Susie after they'd got back from their trip to Chile and before they went off again on another part of their world tour. Damien had won fifty grand on a scratch card and they seemed to have spent most of it already. They'd been virtually everywhere in Europe—their Facebook updates had been unbearable, especially when they headed to more exotic places and took selfies everywhere; India, Vietnam, Thailand, Malaysia, South Korea, Japan, New Zealand and Australia. Their three months in the States had been a relief really as they were too busy partying to send much out online. Jack wasn't jealous; he didn't want to see the world. The furthest from home he'd been was London and that was such a shithole he said he'd never go back. The odd night out over in Manchester was grand, but that was far enough for him. Good luck to them, he thought, it really isn't my bag at all. Jack had worked with Damien for five years at Matlock Motors. They'd been good mates then; things were changing now though—*Damien* had changed. *Susie* had changed him—yeah, she was fit enough, but really she was a posh bird. At least she knew how to spend Damien's money; he'd just have wasted it down the bookies.

Jack was sure it was Kev that had spiked him—he'd always been a little arsehole, ever since they were kids. It was probably a good whack of GHB. He'd done it before. And it had been his idea to have the poker game, like they always used to on Fridays, before Susie appeared on the scene. Yes, it was definitely sneaky old Kev that had done it. He was shit at cards and was also skint, so he'd probably planned to clean up a bit of Damien's money, and some of Jack's too. Poor old Damien was probably off his nuts too.

Jack looked up at them all again, his eyes—that had felt so suddenly leaden—were now alert and eager. Their faces were pale and strange. They looked like odd white statues, or bright new shop mannequins. The tatty green upholstery of the bar benches glowed brightly as though it were some kind of fluorescent algal bloom in a hidden cavern beneath the earth. The barmaid's teeth flared white as a wedding dress in a blizzard, behind lips as red as the dripping knife of the Ripper. The whole pub was aflame with colour, and each one enflamed his volatile emotions and his pounding heart. He felt his whole body quaking with the drug as the bubbles of his lager danced before him like mocking demons, intent on stealing his mind and torturing his soul. Fuck it, Jack thought, I'll play your little game, Kev. I can take the fucking lot.

He downed his pint and smiled at Kev. He felt as though his whole face was falling apart—as though a great tear had spread from the corners of his lips and had slid around to his ears in a huge slash. His face itched as though a scurrying plague of beetles had escaped from his skull and were devouring him. Still he smiled at Kev.

"What's wrong with you, you twat?" Kev said, with a sneer. "Play the fucking game, you dick, it's your hand now—what you doing? You need twenty quid just to stay in."

Jack looked down at his cards. The reds, blacks, yellows and whites swirled in an eddy of unreality—something else was edging its way into his vision, something violent and oppressive. The air about him shimmered and he could feel his body flushing with heat. His organs were on fire inside him and he gasped for air, which felt like cold water rushing down his throat. He heard the laughter of the guys up at the bar, like a jeering crowd at an execution. He was desperate now and had to get control back somehow. He closed his eyes and the darkest of darknesses suddenly opened to reveal another world entirely.

There was a great field, gleaming with greens and browns of tall grasses. It seemed to reach out forever into the distance. He turned to look at the horizon; it was bordered by seven great hills, upon one of which he now stood. He was at the edge of a wood, whose great oaks reached high above him into a thick canopy of leaves. Crows hopped eagerly between the branches, squawking and chattering. Buzzards wheeled and soared out into the warm, rising air and hung there, slowing time into the black focus of their eternal eyes. The hazy afternoon air was desperate with insects, their fragile wings urgently losing them in any direction, their minuscule brains irate to feed; a presentiment of death firing them with a frenzy to replicate their mechanical monstrosity. The silent trees itched with a million scuttling critters, burrowing and fidgeting through bark, chasing each other's flickering, chitinous tails. Nature was gathering to enact its everlasting exchange of costume.

Out in the field vast squares of silver shone in the decaying sun; great arcs of red and gold, blue and yellow were dotted here and there with patches of black, brown and white. It looked like a painted canvas of architectural forms; an abstract, geometric work constructed with the bodies of angry, violent men, desperate for murder, and the dark, flaring nostrils of pure-bred horses, keen for the charge—a work traced by the dancing curvature of proud flags and the gleam of sharp halberds, worked to razor's edges on the whetstones of proud fathers. It was also a raw, Fauvist image, screamed into existence with the quivering skin of terrified men on the brink of annihilation, and the braying of muddy pack mules, agonised by the day's final, tortuous push—an image darkly tinted by the feverish whisper of half-remembered prayers and the desperate clenching of crude folk charms fashioned by the cracked hands of tearful mothers.

Beside him stood a man in a puffed, red-velvet jacket, its edges trimmed with yellow and black braiding. He wore bright green leggings and had tall, black, leather boots. In his hands he carried a yellowed parchment that had been rolled up and tied with a green ribbon, with a large lead seal across it. The man's face was square, his chin protruding in a cartoonish fashion. He was clean shaven and his jet-black hair was cut in a similar square fringe, giving his face the effect of being framed like a small, close portrait. He looked down at himself; he was dressed identically, and also held another scroll, this one bound with red and black ribbons and sealed with a smaller black wax seal.

The man made his way down the hill. Jack felt compelled to follow. A loud trumpet sounded from the trees behind them, and then another. And then a chorus of blasts joined them in a constant, long drone.

They made their way down to the colourful field and, as they approached, a drumming of weapons upon shields sounded the beat of their step. Striding past the cavalry, the pikemen, the archers, and the bombardiers, they were soon out into the open space beyond the ranks, heading for the lines of blue and yellow.

Two other men, dressed in similar attire to themselves, but in those opposing colours, headed across the open ground towards them, each with a scroll in his hands.

They met in the middle as the sun began to turn the prophetic red of early evening.

They exchanged their missives and turned to their own lines.

A horseman broke from the enemy ranks, clad in a light coat of chain mail, his blue cloak streamed behind him like the midday sky torn from the heavens. His savage face was contorted in hate; his strong and brutal arm raised a thin sword high in the air.

On he charged at them. They began to run and yells of fury went up from their men. A volley of charge was lit and the cannons sent metal hell through the air above them towards the deceitful enemy.

Behind them they heard the swish of steel through the air, as though the world were being ripped in two.

The blade sliced through his companion's throat and his body sailed forward with an arc of dark blood trailing behind the spinning head.

An arrow dislodged the lone rider from his steed with a solid crack that sounded like an oak door being split asunder.

In a moment he was back with his men who were already moving forward into the evening's carnage.

❈

"So, what you doin' then, Jack?" Kev laughed. "I reckon our Jack's turned into a three-pint man, myself. Earth callin' Jack! Earth callin' Jack! D'ye want to go home to your bed, sleepy head?"

Jack stared at the cards. They tumbled with colour again. They tumbled like a decapitated head—all reds and blues and purples and oranges and yellows; all death and beauty, horror and power. They tumbled like the scattering of terrified rabbits in a field. They tumbled like cheap, bright party clothes in a launderette dryer.

"What's the ante again, Kev?" Jack slurred. "I can do you!—both for money and for drink, you little worm."

"Oooh! Big Jack's back, swinging his big package!" Kev laughed. "Fancy some crisps to soak up that half-o-shandy? My treat! Cheese and onion too strong for you—how about plain? It's twenty quid to stay in. . . *twenty* quid."

Jack flipped a red counter into the middle of the table, where he saw a pile of other counters heaped upon each other. The hand must have accrued a good thousand pounds, maybe more. What had he done? He only had a few counters left—maybe ninety quid. Everyone had put the money into a biscuit tin back at Damien's, to divvy up later.

Little, round game counters, from a card game pack Jack had got one Christmas. It came in a shite black plastic cover that never clipped together properly. They'd used it for years—first for pennies, then for pounds and now for twenties. They were big boys and girls now.

A big pile of counters on the table; a big pile of the past.

"Ok, then," said Susie, looking sheepishly at Damien. "I'll close all this down now and call you. There's *one*." She was clearly nervous that the game might be rumbled by the bar staff for the gambling it really was.

"Alright then, we're done," said Kev, his rotten-toothed grin darker and more foul than ever before. "Before we show, why don't I get us all another round in, or can't you go another one Jackie boy?"

There was a silence around the table. Damien looked awkwardly at Susie, and nodded his head sideways to the door. She agreed. Kev loomed over the table at Jack, his round head shorn of all hair, like an over-inflated red balloon of resentment, his flat, broken nose a dabble of blackheads and broken veins. He was a disease that seeped into the very air of the pub. Jack could see it flowing into the drinks and wafting up the noses of the weekend revellers, filling them with bile and misery. His stink fuelled the relentless chaos of the everyday. Kev was Armageddon—Ragnarok in stained jeans and a faded AC/DC t-shirt.

"Mine's a double whiskey and ice, you twat," said Jack. "And none of the cheap crap, either. . . something decent. About time I got a drink from you, you mean fucker."

Damien and Susie covered their drinks with their hands and shook their heads at Kev. They had flights to book and plans to make. They had lives to dream and mirrors to gaze longingly into.

Kev tottered to the bar, taking out his old Velcro wallet—with the skating graffiti on—the same one he'd had since he was a teenager. He ordered himself a draught bitter, and the sharp, high-pitched whoosh of the drink frothing into the glass surged into Jack's ears like a gallon of blood gushing from the freshly slit throat of a slaughtered pig.

The first morning light was upon the field. A fine drizzle coated everything with a sheen that looked like a rubbing of oil—a careless match might return the whole scene to the cinders it came from. The green was gone, the field was red. Red with the fine red livery of fallen knights and the red surcoats of light cavalry but also with the raggle-taggle red uniforms of the infantrymen who had done their best to demonstrate conformity and now lay as rich in red death as the noblemen splayed beside them. Occasional patches of blue showed the few places where the enemy had been slain. But between, and through, and below them all there ran rivulets of red, streams of red and rivers of red. The muddied ground was a brown-red mush that stuck to everything. There was a choking miasma of cannon smoke, sweat, horse shit and human piss, and in the background that sweet, haunting, mocking stench of life—blood.

The birds were at their work, strutting and plucking, cawing and cackling. The few bodies that still moved shooed them weakly away with the last strength they had; soon they would breathe no more and their flesh would be carrion.

Others were at the corpses too. Women, from the support caravans, wailed and screamed beside the bodies of their men; others surreptitiously looted, gathering the scrappy, worthless goods together in bundles of bloodied clothing.

Waggons were led about the field to remove the dead. They were attended by the powder boys, most of whom had survived. They swung the limp bodies into tottering towers of flesh and metal and trundled the steaming heaps slowly back to the remnants of the ruined camp where other survivors were digging trenches for the mass burial.

Up on one of the far hills the victors surveyed the massacre, arrogant with the vanity of their triumph; thankful to have deferred their own deaths for another day.

The whisky looked like dark, morning piss; the ice glinted like virgins' eyes, slowly melting into ripples of shimmering iridescence. It smelt like a thousand summer mornings. Jack downed it in one. It tasted like a thousand angry wasps in flight.

Kev laughed and laid his hand down, "Flush of clubs—beat that!"

Damien threw his cards down; a pair of kings and a pair of fives.

Jack looked up at the door to the pub just before he laid his cards down. A man had walked in in a red tracksuit. He was tall and very thin. He had a square face and a chiselled jaw. He looked about the pub and saw Jack. He smiled and came over to the table.

Jack laid his cards down—three jacks and two queens.

"I think you know that it is time to leave, my friend," the stranger said to Jack.

Susie flung down a feeble pair of tens.

"What! You bloody bastard, Jack," Kev raged, standing up and thumping the table. "Who's this sodding joker, too? Has he been feeding you our hands from over in the corner? I'd say that this hand was void. I want my money back."

Damien and Susie tried to calm Kev down.

Jack stood slowly and took his coat from the back of the chair.

"You can keep all the money, Kev," he said. "I don't think I'll be needing it."

Jack and his companion left the pub together and walked away through moonlit streets silvery with a fine, relentless rain.

GREAT SEIZERS' GHOSTS

Avalon Brantley

> Yet herein will I imitate the sun,
> Who doth permit the base contagious clouds
> To smother up his beauty from the world,
> That, when he please again to be himself,
> Being wanted, he may be more wonder'd at,
> By breaking through the foul and ugly mists
> Of vapours that did seem to strangle him.
> —Henry, Prince of Wales (Shakespeare, *Henry IV*, I:ii)

East of ancient Paris, high in the *donjon* of a grand white castle gleaming under the unspotted azure of a late-summer sky, young Henry V, King of England, lies abed. Though the worst throes of the bloody flux have subsided, he is wrung by the fever that for days has laid siege to his frame, leaving him as waterless as that pleasant blue expanse beyond the window. It is the thirty-fifth year of his life. He is dying.

Only moments before, his councillors and retainers were assembled in this chamber to attend their regent's final will and testament. Government of France and Normandy would be left to his brother John, Duke of Bedford; to Gloucester was bestowed the Regency of an England Henry would never see more; to the others, divers portions and responsibilities in the same merry green land across the channel, including the tutelage of his infant son Henry (to be the Sixth so coronated) and stewardship over the recently reconquered realms of Wales, the dying king's birthplace.

For so many years, thoughts of that Silurian land refired Henry's pride—not for his birth in that place, but for the reason that he counted it the first of lands he ever conquered. For such a prize did he advance at Shrewsbury amidst the knights of Bolingbroke, to prove himself not the slouch of repute, nor the swaggerer of a youth misspent in the uncouth company of John Oldcastle and his disreputable band of ruffians, outcasts and heretics. Henry was sixteen that day at Shrewsbury when he cut his teeth in battle against Owain Glyndŵr and his Gaelic warriors; there too, an arrow shot into his face cut *him* to the teeth, nigh slaying him. Yet so thirsty was he to prove the nobility of the blood even then flooding his own mouth and throat, Henry gritted those teeth and, with a hand that he willed to still from its shaking, the young knight snapped the shaft of the arrow in his face and fought on, less impeded by its presence. When the day of battle was done, his archrival Harry Hotspur lay cold on the field with the other enemy dead, and in the days that followed, the Royal Physician contrived a curious and delicate drill by means of which he secured anchorage upon the splintered arrow shaft in the prince's cheek, extracting the arrowhead, then healing the remaining wound by washing it with scalding spirits and soothing it with balms of honey sired of crimson roses. Damask returned to the dauphin's cheeks, which now bore too the irrefragable proofs of knightly fortitude in his valour-gotten scars. For this reason did that tall, warlike prince openly show his face in battle, fighting brazenly alongside his men-at-arms, letting them look full upon him, and long for their own wounds of honour.

But thoughts of all these things were far from Henry, now the courtly men had made their solemn departure from his chambers. Before they were gone one attendant had fallen to his knees at the king's bedside, begging Henry that he should consider his soul, "For it so seemeth to us, Highness, thou canst have not more than two hours left to life." Henry had nodded weakly, almost as if drifting again into dreams, but this was his tacit assent to have the confessor summoned.

Sleep stole over the king soon after.

Suddenly he opes his eyes to the room, peaceful in a sunlight-yellow glow, to espy a strange, smiling man in his attendance, and lingering near-hidden from sight in the shade-flocked corner. The man is clad humbly in garments of dusky hue, and his lank hair seems of itself unsure whether its strands be gold or grey.

"Who or what art thou?" the king rasps through dry lips, all his vocative flesh like a parchment to be over-written. There is a joyous air to the stranger's countenance, which Henry misapprehends for mockery; this villain has impudence not merely to smile over him, but to meet the gaze of the king with his own. No lowly subject would dare stare their monarch direct in the eye; the churl ought to set his eyes in the dust before the sight of his sovereign. Henry grew incensed; a leonine fury flashed in his eyes even as the last bright lashes of a flame will precede its expiration.

"Dost thou laugh at a dying king's bedside, sirrah? Art thou some agèd and impious jester, mayhap Court Madcap to Charles the Mad, from whom I retook our Gallic possessions? Wast thou wont to prance before his board in these very walls? Aye, I warrant he might have taught *thee* a merry jest, as no doubt he showed the Dauphin how to cross swords with battalions invisible to men of healthy senses![1] Pray, Jester: does Beloved Charles think me too made of glass,[2] that like himself I should shatter, wert thou to break into sudden song and sodden dance? Would he have me assassinated by thy asininity? And is thy apparition at my sickbed the same deposed and unfit king's mad means of ending me—that thou shouldst jab our person with japes, or assail our sad state by gambols? Come, then! where is thy motley? Where thy coxcomb? I will surrender: transport me with laughter even as thou indulge it thyself—or art thou so foolish in thy foolery that only thou knowest when time has come to laugh?"

"Time shall always come to laugh, Your Highness."

"Not at such weak wit as thine is, base Jester!"

"I have been rightly styled Fool, Sire, but no man's jester am I."

"And thou sayest so in pride? Play no word games with me—give thy meaning!"

"I would it were so simple for a man to give his meaning. But as well thou knowest, O King, thou art going out from this hard and hardened world and into another. Those in this Earthly life who live closest to truths beyond it appear ever as Fools in the eyes of the world. Thus is it that such 'fools' laugh when their fellows do not, thinking them knavish and mad, whilst vast unseen battalions do array themselves against us, and others assemble toward our defences, even as the

---

1 Henry's insult references an incident of some thirty years before when, whilst passing through a forest on campaign, the young King Charles VI (later 'the Mad') reputedly hallucinated—and in a fit of frenzy commenced to do battle with—a band of foes invisible to all others in his company.
2 He alludes to another of Charles' widely known delusions.

rest see mere emptiness in everything. Yet what could be more of madness or folly than to see Nothing in Everything?"

Henry's rage dimmed, and with it all irate strength in his voice. The stranger's philosophy was strange as he, and yet something in it spoke to the king. Weakly, Henry ventured: "Thou art a philosopher? Or a priest?"

The man merely smiled, almost as if toying with a façade of imbecility.

Henry grew restless, and worried. There was little time left for repentance.

"Art thou my confessor then?" The air of each word came with a burning, as though a long-dead Lollard tailor[1] were returned, still aflame, and writhed now as a torch at the back of Henry's throat. He choked as though through smoke: "I thirst . . ."

The stranger's smile was suddenly a kind of comfort—a sunray out of clouds to transmute storm-iron to silver, or yet loftier alchemies. He approached from the shadows with a cup held out to Henry.

"Here. This do in remembrance." His voice was mellifluous, marvellous, the words sounding in the surrounding air as unseen honeybees, or sweet midsummer breezes borne with madrigal strains. The king took the cup, and could drink again! And keep the drink! Warm ease filled his throat and belly, found his limbs, found him strength to speak the thanks that returned to him that increasingly familiar smile on the man's kind, round face.

And the drink *did* bring remembrance!

____

1 John Badby, whom Henry saw burnt for the Lollard heresy in 1409. [Arthur Machen made a simile of similar sort in his "Strange Story of a Red Jar".]

"Do I know thee, sirrah?" asked the king. Certainly he did look familiar, and his voice, so lilting and musical, that made him think of his mother: how she used to sing to him over the lute, softly, her voice low and warm as running honey. She was twenty-four when she died, and Henry only seven. He had not thought of her for so long a time. There was no sorrow now in the remembrance, nor even the feeling of reaching the mind back through the distance of years; he should not be surprised to see her emerge now, somehow, at the bedside beside this blessed man, smiling in the same old way, as though never gone, ever-young. The wine, whatever it was—some transcendent panacea—seemed to have gone not just to his head but to his soul, to quiet even that stormiest of places!

The visitant's eyes met Henry's still, warmly, and any concerns over impertinence scarce occurred to Henry now.

"I know thee . . ."

"Aye, once, if no longer," the humble man replied, his thin, enigmatic mouth hardly moving, and from the sight of the mouth a lost memory sparked at the king's eyes, transforming the stranger's face—for but a moment in his mind—into the face of a child he knew once in Wales: Llacheu MacInburn, son of the nurse tasked with watching over him ("wee Hal") then, in those long-ago days at Monmouth Castle. Young Llacheu could scarce mutter the King's English for his alacritous Celtic tongue, ever-tripping, so like a caged bird behind his little teeth; yet he'd ever had ways of making his mind comprehended, of somehow showing things outside of all speech, all words.

So too did all that overwhelming countryside show that boy, that "wee Hal", so many things beyond all hope of speech or scratching plume, in that time when Henry was old enough to wander through it, yet young enough to wonder at it, Llacheu at his side. Sometimes along their childish adventures, Llacheu seemed to play at the role of Hal's first page; but often enough he seemed his far wiser adviser, a Merlin to his Arthur—though as the proud grandson of John of Gaunt, Henry would never have consciously admitted such a notion. Though there was no thought of his ever becoming king in those days—his father Henry of Bolingbroke had yet to storm the country and usurp King Richard's throne—young Henry of Monmouth, as then "wee Hal" was also called, well knew his noble lineage within the Lancastrian House.

Yet the odd, dark-eyed Gwentian lad knew the land so well, was so much a part of it, and it of him, that trees seemed to sigh and whisper respects over his head, the undergrowth parting before him, stones seeming to rise like hungry fish before his feet to assist his passage across cold brooks, and the old stone-walled ruins of the longdead seemed suddenly peopled again, full of circles of drifting whisperers, like perfect clouds stirred up to show themselves reflections in a pool until then undisturbed beneath their skies.

Often, in that last fine summer before Henry's mother died and a new, itinerant life began for him, the two boys explored those enchanted greenwoods together, climbing slopes to descend through sweet-scented meadows, tripping through shallows of the Monnow all clad in dim, blue mists, hefting with them sticks sharpened into spears or swords or walking staves; assailing lazy sheep that in their minds became enemy battalions; slipping out of the sight of scowling plough-men to hide behind hayricks, or in hedgebote commons where they seemed to see each singular ray of yellow light divided from its sunny brethren; creeping silent through dusky brakes amidst the hunching shadows of dwarf oaks whose roots rose up from the mould-scented earth like Scyllas arisen from sleep, and where darker shadows slunk just out of direct sight, leaving blood-freezing tracks behind on the leaf-strewn floor of the forest, as if some enormous and cloven-footed thing had walked before them there, on two legs, like a man; in their fancies the boys could see such panic-impregnating horrors far more clearly than they ever did glimpse them with their eyes, the tracks in truth so faint and uncertain in the dry wood.

All that time, through those briefly endless summer days, pretending themselves on perilous quests through long-unconquered lands, now seemed more than fond memories to the fading sovereign; they seemed to have been a prelude—preparation for some otherwise unknowable journey. He had, once, thought all of it a part of his journey toward manhood, and through the rest of this life, and perhaps somewhat it was . . . but had it not been something more as well? This life had been so brief, and the glow in the world had been gone, nigh forgotten, for some time . . . but then this man, this room . . .

"I knew thee as a child."

"Didst thou?" laughed the stranger. "Well, perad-venture many ages ago, though I would wager even very young thou wast one to crave for thy manhood too soon, striving to put away childish things before thy time was ripe to do so. Now that thou wouldst ready thy soul for passage, it would befit its flight to become as a child again."

A blanched Henry grew brighter. "That indeed was all the naïveté and foolishness of a child—my rush to bid goodbye that pleasant state of being, and career toward another—to this horrible, dreadful state! I have not thought of those times since so long ago eschewing them; now that I do, at the end of all my days, I see they were my finest! I remember the flying, changing sky over Monmouth, the red beam out from the emerald vault falling like a sword on the cold rippling waters of the Wye, the old stone bridge there, magisterial mountains surrounding, mist-strewn, the dark forests marching endlessly across them, and those foothills and stretches of pasture in the valleys where in full daylight the green—ah! Such green was there, with the *hwyl* of the wind sailing over those green seas—those holy hills of Wales! You do call it the *hwyl*, that way which thy people sing the Services?"

"We do. Moreover, it is the way of our people for singing our being. It speaks not just of the wind, nor merely the sail, but sings the wind *within* the sail."

"I recall it! Yes, I should swear that land was greener than any other I ever have seen, or perhaps was it that I was so green then, that springing boy?"

"Who came to be King of our Summer Land."

"Even so, yet he left it all to perish in a place never meant to be his home, his winter come too soon, as though it sought the wrong solstice." Henry sighed heavily. "But you became a priest at the last?"

"*Non qui in ipsum*, but I would listen as one."

"And I would confess as a penitent." Henry was nearly weeping, suddenly flooded by memories of things he had forgotten through all these long years of intrigue and uprising since Agincourt, all of his striving for the final defeat of the Dauphin—although the latter had been far too cunning and wary to join Henry again in full battle and chance a second Agincourt. No, the coward had instead set about wooing away the Men of Troyes, and fracturing the alliances that treaty had provided. Many of those signatories wished nothing but to be allied to the winning side, one way or another—so that when Henry became too sick even to mount his warhorse—or when he was rushed through the land in a litter, the stench of the flux strong over him—then the Dauphin's lusty whispers met with eager ears and faithless. Henry urged his own trusted nobles to fight on in his absence, to secure if nothing else their rightful possession of Normandy; but knowing none of them to have such a spirit for command as his, what could he hope of them?

And what could he hope now for himself, or whither would his lost spirit go once gone?

Henry pulled himself more upright in the bed, so that breath could enter more easily. His voice grew consequently stronger, as did the memories from that fateful autumn of 1415.

"Throughout my reign, the wisest and most eminent of the clergy were retained at my right hand—there to advise, and to minister unto me. I was most devout; in our straits before Agincourt I three times attended the Mass. I harkened to the words of the priests, voiced faithfully my Hours and devotions, and sought the Lord's firm guidance over my government always. How can it be that I am left with such grave doubts as to what vistas should soon stretch before me, in that moment when all my breath is spent?" The king closed his eyes, shuddering. Then he opened them to look again on his strange confessor. "I have seen many strange things in this life, in unanticipated glimpses beyond the Veil of

Death—things of which my priests have, I am certain, only the scantest understanding.

"Thou knowest the story of our coming to France? How we sailed into the bay of the Seine, and marched the three miles inland to Harfleur? We invested a month with the siege, our legs sunk in the swamps around Seine and Lézarde, my knights in time grown weary, hungry, sickly. At the last we did prevail, but I began to fear for my mind in those days . . .

"In the night, in the camp, when as was my wont in fits of endless restlessness, I wandered the camp, warming my hands at the fires of my men, and talking with them, striving to build up their courage even as we strove every day with breaking down the western walls of Harfleur. They always knew me, those good men, by my scars—for I did not wear a crown or kingly robes whilst on campaign; those I kept in our baggage train.

"It was marvellous strange . . . there were nights wherein I could clearly overhear portions of conversations about our camp, but some of that chatter seemed most out of joint. It happened throughout the campaign, but I remember its start in the last of the warm nights, in sight of the walls of Harfleur before she was taken. A foetid fog had risen from the Seine, like an apparition; in it mingled the scents of meat cooking, as broth caught up in a cold rag, and voices of the men were displaced in the mist. I could hear them speaking together in the low firelight—sometimes the rough, rolling-barrel brogue of boys from the north country, sometimes strut-and-glut glots out of London, or even the vibrant, twining, musical talk of the Gwentian bowmen who so much outnumbered all the rest. Yet were there times, and that night one, when from the dim shapes of figures in the firelight floated voices speaking what I gradually found to be Latin, though it had a quality I did not recognize—assuredly it was not the language of any canons I ever heard, whether Italianate or ultramontane. No, in sooth its speakers were far too at ease with the tongue; it came from them as a first language, fluently, commandingly, the accents galloping from their mouths as nimble-limbed warhorses. At first, they did discourse most casually; but then of a sudden there arose a tumult out of farther darknesses. Then did they hasten to their feet, and in spite of the mist I say forsooth it seemed their trappings were most out of place. Their armour was sparse, and the swords worn on their right hips shorter than those of our knights. They bore rectangular shields as thick as the palm of a man, the coverings of hide or canvas embossed by metal at the centre and emblazoned with the emblem of a bull, *statant*. In the right hand did they heft two iron-tipped javelins. Voices rose in gruff readiness at the alarum, and then more forms rushed past me, stirring my soul both with terror and yet a kind of passion to join with them in some grand unending battle, and burning anew now to force myself therewith upon that coy and stubborn city. I took to my feet behind them in the dark, mud and water plashing high as I followed. One was amongst them who trailed his brilliant scarlet cloak—"

"Paludamentum."

"What sayest thou?"

"Thy pardon, my Liege. Do say on."

"I could see that cloak, that flowing crimson *paludamentum* as thou sayest, floating before me in all the billowing mist, and I did follow behind it, and the voice of him who wore it. He turned back toward us again and again, and it seemed his eyes met not just the eyes of those shady forms all about me but did also look into mine own, even as he urged us forward, bidding us flood *canalis in muros Bibracte*—the breach in the walls of Bibract! That man was bare-headed, and he seemed in the dimness to have savage, wild hair—until I could see that what he wore around his temples was a crown of leafy laurel! Even then, were I little sure of whom I saw, whose sight did ice my blood, his legionaries hailed him by name, and the name in full as I heard it with further acclamations of allegiance was 'Imperator Noster, Gaius Yooly-us Kaisar!' Then on into the darkness went we, my voice echoing his urgency, and mine own men stirring from their tents and following, and long before Dawn lit her fires behind the far side of that city we made an early day to blaze with the red-blooming fires of war!

"I saw them again at night, many days after, when we had left Harfleur far behind. My men were much sicker, exhausted with the marching, many of them reeking and suffering by the bloody flux, slowly dying on that winding way toward the Nord, to Calais—"

"The Harrying of the Nord," his companion proclaimed it.

Henry smiled wistfully. "No, not then. That night we were trapped on the southern bank of the Samara[1], whilst the French resistance, well-rested, well-fed and far outnumbering, hounded us on the northern side of the river, guarding for many leagues against any possible passage across. Our meat and corn were dwindling, and the nights far colder; the chill of that night seemed for me even deeper, sharper, when again I heard those ancient voices, their whispering warning: '*The corn is*

---

1 The River Somme.

*low, Imperator, and the Helvetii close on our heels. They seek
to entrap us before we can reach our supplies.'* As I caught
those bodiless words I could see between the trees, in
the swaying greys and blacks of nighttime, fearsome
barbaric faces flanked by dirty locks as soiled gold or
tarnished bronze or as rust-bitten iron; those strange
German faces so long not alive, looking out on us, the
grim grins behind their beards that I felt as well behind
our own backs as we marched through those dark,
cloud-shrouded days that rained betimes on our un-
sheltered shoulders . . . and I knew we had a hard battle
before us."

"Aye—in the fields and the woods by glorious
Agincourt."

"Yea—a day not even Death could hope to cheat me
of remembering.

"The French held us in contempt for our archers—
they had fought amongst themselves for the honour of
the *avant-garde*, for the greater chance to meet our own
nobles in chivalric combat. Thus they resented being
'murdered', as they thought it, by low-born men without name, face or title. What they little understood was
that it was I; those bowmen were brothers of my birth-
land; their deeds were mine, done at my command; it
was thus *my* hand that struck the Frenchmen down.
They fell not to lowborn men of any land—they fell to
me!"

"Thou art indeed the head of the body, Sire," said
his companion. "With English arms and Gwentian fingers didst thou seize thy day."

Henry nodded, his eyes scintillating, seeing again
the flashes of steel and the terrible raining of the arrows.
"The battle lines were drawn before dawn lit low on the
grey-browed horizon, and then I saw them there with us,

in our ranks—those men in their ancient armour! I had gazed upward from the roadway, beyond our knights and toward the woodlands which flanked those new-ploughed fields, where our archers had planted a thicket of sharpened stakes in the ground facing outward to check the charges of the enemy's mounted knights. The bowmen waited there in the dusky gloom, and amidst them were other forms, moving behind them in those woods set ablaze by the autumn, yet nary a noise did their movements make in all the dead leaves.

"When the battle was over, I came away from the field and sought the Duke of Orleans, who had taken to his bed, and would eat or drink nothing for his sorrow. 'Why dost thou not eat nor drink, cousin?' I asked him, and petulantly he said to me, 'I wish to fast.' I then advised him, 'Cousin, make good cheer. It is God who hath disposed of the victory, and who hath punished the French.' 'I believe it is so,' he told me. 'My men were struck with more than terror, for many have told how they saw before them terrible angels who strode about as soldiers, girded in unfamiliar array, and having horsehair plumes in the crests of their helmets; those Death Angels, the men say, did advance amidst the archers when they left behind their quivers to charge down upon our men-at-arms whilst they did struggle to stand where they were fallen in the fresh-furrowed mud of that field. Alas, how many a knight didst struggle to raise himself from the muddy ground, only to be hacked and battered down, some pressed beneath hooves or their comrades' fallen bodies, or even drowning in the muddy water trapped inside their own helmets? When thine archers advanced, those marvellous allies of thine came with them; the heads of strange steel javelins were discovered in the bodies of some of my knightly countrymen, yet there were no shafts upon them, for as we could tell the spear points were mounted to their shafts by a feebler linkage of lead; the softer metal broke asunder upon impact, leaving the steel embedded in the flesh of a dying man who could have no hope of hurling it back! What inscrutable methods do you English employ in war! I have not seen the like on any field of battle!' 'Nor have I,' I then confessed, at which words the Duke shivered beneath his bedclothes."

"There are men long interred, m'Lord, whose deeds still echo about the Earth," Henry's companion replied, no longer smiling; yet still there was a warmth about his mouth and brow. Beyond the window, the light fell longer. Harvest carts began to trundle out from the fields below, and the sun started to touch and torch the western horizon.

Henry still burned with memory. "Thou speakest truth, as this memory tells me: for I witnessed the legionaries once more after the battle, before darkness fell again. A reconnaissance of French raiders from a nearby village plundered our baggage waggons, stealing even my crown from its guard, for which cause I ordered the massacre of all prisoners taken. My men were so greedy for ransom that they hesitated, questioning me, but I commanded the captives' immediate execution. Then, in the midst of all chaos and blood, I heard the voices again. I remember what some of them were saying, and know they trod those roads in times long past, and that their baggage waggons too were raided! They were crying out that the Belgae and Atrebates attacked the baggage train, and again it seemed there were javelins hurled into Gallic aggressors by hands neither Anglic nor alive." Henry paused, a cloud across his brow. "Thou dost not think me mad, that I say I saw all these things with waking eyes?"

"Nay, Sire; I know thy mind wast sound."

"I will tell thee more. I dreamed a dream on that perilous journey, when I had lain myself to sleep before the plain of the Santerre, well before we had reached fateful Agincourt. We had been five days along the Samara, the French always checking us across the river, following with their far greater forces, and watching us starve. Many of my men burned with fever, neither able to eat nor drink, dying . . . I too was ill, and at last fell fitfully to sleep near that great tract through which by forced march we hastened on the next day, outstripping the French, to arrive at broken causeways near Bethencourt. These we repaired, and then we crossed the cold lazy water to gain a weary rest on the farther side.

"But it was in the night before that march that I dreamed a dream of that self-same plain—a dream most real, yet strangest of any I ever perceived, whether waking or asleep. Far across that plain I witnessed vast, scarring trenches, stretching far across the ravaged earth; the air too was filled with low dark clouds, clouds which shook with strangest thunders, or flashed with sudden fire. The ground would burst and be rent asunder, and yellow spectres floated over that wasted land where only twisted, spiralling hedges of metal grew. Out from that unnatural fog there lumbered dragons and beasts like no bestiary ever portrayed; they were grey or mayhap green, with long flat rolling feet, less like a war-engine's wheels than like the bellies of gargantuan graveworms, and these seemed unable to be stopped by any Earthly power, whilst out from the snouts in their swivelling heads they spat vicious and fiery Death. And down in those deep trenches and tunnels there were men, like you or I and yet too like none I have ever seen, asleep or awake, amongst the living or likely dead. And I heard some of those men singing a song, again in strange accents, and I could never forget their music, though I have spoken of it to no man before."

"Speak of it to me."

"My voice is weak, but I might strive to sing thee it. Let me try . . ." And Henry strained his weak, dying voice to sing that song yet long unwritten:

> "Keep the homefires burning
> While your hearts are yearning;
> Though your lads are far away
> They dream of home.
> There's a silver lining
> Through the dark clouds shining;
> Turn the dark clouds inside out
> Till the boys come Home.

"I know not the meaning of that song, or that dream, but I know those are our children I saw, far after here, in that Hell . . .

"*Dic mihi, Confessor* . . . was it I laid the road out that brought them there? What is it I have done by this life?"

His companion tendered no answers, and again Henry slumped in the bed, paler than ever, his eyes gazing low, glazing over. At last he looked up again with one final troubled question.

"I have confessed far more to you than to any other—more than my sins, more than my hopes of understanding . . . To what place is this coming darkness taking me?"

The glow was fading, nearly gone. The stranger lay his hand on the king's slumping shoulder.

"What should appear behind thine eyes, my King, if I were to tell thee, 'Home'?"

King Henry smiled even as he said it, his eyes already glowing with the sunsets of skies much farther west than those in the place of his final breaths; his eyes seemed like those of a child again, a very young child, before manly ambitions polluted his thoughts, when the wild and unpeopled lands all around him were still so full of wonder. On the hills, between trees growing blue with the dusk, with the sky behind them full of the melting gold of sunset, fauns and dryads, satyrs and nymphs appeared, but they seemed no longer sinister, no more the wicked and misshapen things he misremembered them being, the tracks they'd left behind but traces of an innocent and too-soon interrupted frolic. It was not they who had grown misshapen, nor they now who changed; but Henry indeed was made like a child again, and they were made of his being—there—and of the earth and the air, wood and streams and stones and sun; and they seemed there to welcome him home.

The embers of this vision receded slowly, until all the glow was gone. The man in the room closed the king's eyes, and then the room was dark and cold. And empty.

CHAMELEON IS TO PEACOCK AS SALAMANDER IS TO PHOENIX

Daniel Corrick

"Open my eyes and look around
Colours and concepts that confound"
—The Chameleons, 'View from a Hill'

For today, tomorrow and one day further a large, tiled chamber serves as an impromptu exhibit hall showcasing a select array of paintings and drawings. Their creators bring them here out of desire for financial gain, for the satisfaction of personal vanity and perhaps in the hope that they will form an interface between the worlds that lie within them and that which is inhabited by other people. Clutching wine glasses, people in attention-seeking attire walk up and down the length of the room past these paper windows onto artificial heavens and hells. For all the forced camaraderie the atmosphere here is one of tension: self-consciousness, envy and exasperation each vie with genuine interest in the minds of the attendees.

Out of the seventeen artists exhibiting here one stands out against the rest. Across his pages veiled maidens twist with ophidian grace, wars are fought between legions in scaled armour, lords and ladies dance in an impossible masquerade and solitary figures bow before alien sunsets. All these works are distinguished from the others not so much by the sub-

He had travelled down into the West End that day for
lunch with acquaintances wishing to commission a series of designs for use on promotional posters and their
website. The meeting itself had been an awkward af-
fair which left him feeling embarrassed and angry with
himself: the clients—a couple who ran the bi-monthly
"No More Tears" club night—had wanted six pictures
instead of the five they had initially agreed on for the
chosen price, and Vincent did not think it wise either
from a financial or political perspective to refuse them.
It was also clear that they had no idea of the time-scales
involved, so much so that most of the meal was taken
up explaining to the female side of the operation that
(despite her constant assurances of his being "so bril-
liantly talented") even if he put aside prior commis-
sions it just wasn't possible to have them all done in
two months' time.

Afterwards, not wanting to fight his way through
the crowds at Piccadilly Circus and at any rate without
the funds to allow guilt-free shopping, he had found
himself wandering along the edge of Regent's Park.
Above, the sky was clear, with that faint, indigo haze
which comes with summer; about the roads there was
a sweet moist smell in the air, the perfume of breath-
ing plant life. Magpies chattered in the trees beside the
road. He walked along the pavements with no destina-
tion in mind; as Colette did not return from her day job
at the market till 4:00 he had no reason to hurry back to
their flat and could afford to linger about town.

182

Eventually he came to an art gallery he sometimes visited. The Bormann Young Gallery was a squat, three-storey building constructed in an almost Cubist style, each of its wings finished in polished grey brick which shone in the sun. Though its permanent contents were architectural drawings and models, it sometimes featured temporary exhibits on quirky or grotesque topics which appealed to City counter-culture types and the more cerebral hipster. The board outside listed its current installation as "Fires of Life: A Journey into the Alchemical Mind". Vincent went in without further thought, the clear view of bronze, glass and sparkling brick impressing itself more on his mind than any thought of the exhibit.

The gallery building was largely empty; aside from the bored-looking Anglo-Indian receptionist who pressed a visitor's pass on him with little more than a nod he encountered no one in the central foyer, and on the upper floors found only a couple of students preoccupied in photographing one another in front of cases and a thickset official making notes on an iPad in a corner chair. He passed back and forth along the length of the room, momentarily preoccupied with the sound of his boots upon the polished floor and the way the sun beams catching him from all sides through the full-length windows and skylights cast reflections of his approaching footfall in the black and white tiles. This wide expanse of light and emptiness, coupled with the carefully set-out displays, gave the air of a building which was not officially open to the public, or of a filmset before the shooting began. Vincent felt glad he'd come here today; the slightly sealed-off, clinical atmosphere made the place seem a degree removed from the rest of London and its usual concerns.

The exhibit itself consisted of a selection of manuscripts displayed in glass cases over several floors and a final room filled with ornate-looking glassware—alembics and retorts and crucibles—where a wall-mounted television played a looping feature explaining the purpose of the alchemist's quest, interspersed with shots of precious metals in molten and solid states. The manuscript paraphernalia interested him the most, though this interest was superficial; aside from general dull curiosity he felt an almost bittersweet tug of "professional" envy at the artists and scribes who were once given the freedom to work with such high-quality materials, to lay red and gold caresses on glossy, enduring vellum and to have the end results of their labour, both imaginative and physical, guarded by heavy leather-bound volumes not seen outside the treasure houses of nations and their nobles.

Vincent paused, a little angry with himself at this illicit flight of self-pity. His own life had by no means taken a bad course. For over half of his thirty-five years he had devoted his time to what he really wanted to do, that is, draftsmanship and illustration. A course at Bournemouth and then one at Goldsmiths, paid for by supportive parents, had led to a part-time career producing album artwork and interiors for alternative magazines, supplemented by the occasional self-released comic. Later, when he had gained more exposure in the scene, he had gone on to collaborate with several larger names in a project which had almost been picked up for animation by an Italian studio. Although this failed, the connections he'd made had been invaluable, and within the space of eight months his first solo graphic novel had been accepted by a subsidiary of McMillan, to be published three years later to limited but not insubstantial critical acclaim. The years of practice and repetition, his style compressed and reshaped by the demands of varied work, had bought him a competence with the pen that he could have only dreamed of as a teenager. More than competence, it had also bought him consistency; whereas in his student days he would torture himself with the impossibly fine line-work and the minutiae of half a thousand pigments, he now worked in a much smoother, more accessible style that allowed him to produce drawings of the same quality within a commercially viable timescale. It was this stylistic evolution which served as the key to the door of financial viability. At present he had several publishers interested in further full-length works and was much in demand for stand-alone tattoo images; so much so that several respected musicians in the grime metal scene sported crystalline spiders and demonic machines originating from his pen upon their skins. The work had also brought him into contact with much of the London night-life scene, in particular burlesque and cabaret, a milieu in which he had met his current partner, Colette.

As he moved along the row of cases he wondered what the ancient scribes and calligraphers had thought of the subject matter they were illustrating. Had they believed its promises, had they even cared?

Most of the illustrations were crudely stylised in that archaic way which made it hard for modern man to gauge with what seriousness their creators took them to represent reality. Despite most of them originating in the 15th century at the earliest, they had more in common with the contents of medieval bestiaries than with Da Vinci. Many of them displayed a single animal in some act or pose symbolising an occult operation of the Master Work. In one, a black toad squatted in the middle of a flame; in another stood a white pelican with rosy breast; a third showed a green lion, its body made of foliage, devouring a sleeping sun; a particularly large specimen, a manuscript sheet nearly three feet across, held a crowned peacock with its colourful tail feathers unfurled behind it like a banner, each of the colours of the rainbow there marked out by a Greek character.

Vincent smiled to himself sadly. It was no good; the sight of the vellum manuscripts just reminded him of the unfinished storyboards awaiting him in this studio back at home.

He found himself thinking about Colette. He re-membered her as he'd left her the other morning sitting up in bed, the ivory flesh of her feet and calves show-ing through a fold in the violet dressing gown, her face already tastefully decorated with powder and carefully applied eyeliner (although she seldom wore the face paint and ornate glitters of her stage persona in private, Vincent couldn't recall ever seeing her without some make-up). This fading afterimage blended in his mind with those in the collage of show photographs she kept around the white dresser in their flat, a growing shrine to her own success. People always remarked on what a perfect partner she was for him: confident, darkly eye-catching and a talented performer in her own right, a model, lover and muse. And it was an impression both parties were keen to foster. From soon after their rela-tionship began he had taken to using her as the model in the life-drawing classes he was sometimes asked to give at the Strange Temptations Ball, which meant that not only his art but also the work of others, the devel-opment of which he had guided, inherited aspects of her form. She was unspokenly presented as a source of visual inspiration, and Colette took to this role with studied ease, accompanying him to publishing events in costumes just baroque enough to remind people of her cabaret stardom, and being careful to drop timely references to Vincent's art whenever the aesthetics behind her dress and performances were discussed. Every phrase she uttered, every party she attended, every public friendship she cultivated and every topic she claimed interest in was a reflexive move to fit the two of them more neatly into the Soho art scene that surrounded them. This was all done without thinking, as if movement towards that goal was as natural to her as breath. He'd almost come to believe that she really was a person who, because she had no extraneous questions beyond the concerns of her career and social life, existed free from doubt. He should envy that, he told himself, at the same time dimly wondering why he didn't.

For some reason these thoughts extinguished any limited interest the exhibit had held and Vincent made his out way out and back onto Regent's Park.

There was perhaps nothing for it but to return to the flat. He stood outside, unwilling to make a decision. Guilt at the thought of avoiding work conflicted with guilt about wasting the chance to spend time in something close to nature; the day's beauty was pleasantly distracting, a soporific to break down the neat partitioning of time.

As he observed the moist green light filter through the lime foliage he became conscious of a movement nearer to the ground by the low wall which separated the rows of ornamental bushes off from the pavement; he looked down and saw the being which was to have such an effect on his career and life as an artist.

It was a chameleon, a large specimen about two feet long including its coiled tail. Its thick, gnarled body was opalescent in hue, flecked with scales of larger sizes as of precious stones set in a fabric of woven beads. Along its back ran a ridged crest similar in appearance to a row of newly emerged milk teeth. A band of metallic purple marked out its neck joint, above which sat the heavy, helmet-shaped skull sporting a delicate pair of twisted coral horns. The lids of its protuberant, globular eyes were ornamented with a spiralling golden pattern which made the black spherical pupils look even more dark and remote.

Vincent was transfixed, both by the sudden appearance of the creature and by the aesthetic bounty the sight of it presented. Its shape, colours and contours were so rich in visual possibility, like discovering a whole trove of paintings one had never known existed from a favourite artist. Something about it was so stylistically familiar (he must have been remembering a drawing of this species of chameleon he'd seen on a book or album cover) as to make his heart quiver with nostalgia: when younger Vincent had loved that style, that incredibly intricate detail and line-work, and would have spent hours trying to capture it with pen and ink or paint, lovingly adding details for each scale and fantastic whorl of pigment.

The chameleon picked its way through the bush cover slowly and with delicate purpose, its pale body contrasting with the spiky black-green leaves and dark soil. As he looked more closely he noticed how its colouring seemed to shimmer at a slight depth beneath the scales, as if the surface of its hide were translucent, a covering for the ever shifting silvery-pink mother-of-pearl haze. It evidently felt no need to deploy the camouflage abilities its kind was famous for; in fact it seemed totally unfazed by his presence, occasionally turning its eyes in his direction when he made a move but otherwise paying the human no heed. Vincent had the impression that he could remain watching it all day and it would not do a thing. His surprise at the creature's appearance gave way to joy as if in seeing it he was being permitted some cosmic favour.

When Vincent attempted to point out the creature to a passer-by, a dog walker, the man just peered at him with mute incomprehension and walked on.

He turned to watching for what felt like an indulgently long time before the practical regions of his mind made themselves heard. It must have escaped from the Zoo or from a private collection in one of the large houses; although the weather was hardly cold, England was probably not the place for a tropical creature such as this, and if it roamed free here there was a chance of it getting hit by a car. With a strange reluctance Vincent decided he ought to find one of the guards or go back into the gallery and ask the receptionist if she might be able to call someone affiliated with the zoo.

He had turned and thus was now facing the opposite direction to where he had been looking. Across the road there ran a spear-topped fence beyond which the wide lawns of the parkland could be seen. But there, at its foot, right at the spot which formed the centre of his visual perspective, was the chameleon again. It hadn't visibly moved into the area for there was no way he could have missed it crawling from the left or right side, those at the edges of his vision; it just seemed to emerge from the scene as if the entire three-dimensional backdrop were a fine film momentarily laid over it. That it still retained its original pigment suggested no trick of colour-changing was available.

Vincent re-orientated himself once more and looked along the sweep of the pavement, only to have the chameleon appear again in the same fashion as before beside a lamp post. When he came within a few feet it was as it had been before, a concrete and exotic anomaly on the London street.

He looked up. This time it was in the garden of a house, its dusty-silver body standing out against the rich green of the lawn.

The summer breezes twisted and whirled the folds of the artist's coat as he stood there, hands outstretched, wrenching his gaze from location to location, each time to be confronted with the same sight. It wouldn't change; wherever he looked for more than ten seconds the chameleon appeared, melting into sight out of the background some distance away. He shook his head from side to side vigorously as if to dislodge some speck of brightly coloured dust that had caught in his eyes. On high window ledges; on the gravel beside parked cars; surrounded by thorn, flower and tree; on the tarmac of the road; beside palatial columns; in front of painted walls and on the steps of great houses, Vincent saw the chameleon anew, his very vision caught up in some daylight dream. Surreality gave way to panic and he began to run, at the same time focusing on the palms of his outstretched hands so he wouldn't have to risk facing the sight of it for another second, and another and another . . .

He slowed as this panic quickly gave way to a brittle, laughing sense of absurdity, in which he could abandon all responsibility for action, whatever (for how could he know?) that might be, and even feel little excited bursts of humour. He couldn't do anything so he would just do as he had been doing before. A rational explanation would present itself to him eventually, but not now.

On his walk down to the Tube he didn't see the chameleon, but as soon as he entered the crowd there it was again, growing visible wherever the throng of people parted wide enough to allow a visible gap. He experienced a sudden, almost loving fear that it would be trampled, crushed beneath the feet of some office worker, but whatever power hid it from the gaze of others also seemed to protect it from physical contact with them.

He watched it for nearly an hour on the journey home, as it walked delicately back and forth before the outstretched legs of passengers, its fantastic eyes occasionally swivelling upwards at the flick of a newspaper or the turn of a page. Every few stops Vincent tried to draw another party's attention to it, not by name but merely by pointing and exclaiming in convivial tones, "Look at that", again to find not one person admitted to noticing the creature, or anything out of the ordinary.

It was waiting for him in the flat too. When Colette returned he made nervous conversation about the unreasonable demands and wheedling nepotism of the No More Tears couple, all the while following her gaze intently with his own. She gave no sign of noticing anything out of the ordinary. The reptile itself paid her no heed, as little interested in its surroundings as it had been in the park.

Over the course of their evening meal he dropped multiple passing references to chameleons into the conversation, none of which met with any flicker of recognition or increased animation on the woman's part. As for her own mood and concerns, Colette was the same

as ever: she would not be staying the night; she had
a mock photo-shoot with her newest outfit and would
thus need to prepare and depart by 8:00. For some reason awareness of this deadline grated on him and added a further sense of urgency to his initial desire to con-
vince another of his bizarre situation. That she couldn't
see the chameleon was one thing; that she didn't even
notice he was upset nettled him. Wasn't the encroaching
departure emblematic of their relationship, two neatly
maintained flowering paths running parallel to one another and only crossing at designated intervals?

When he finally attempted to tell her, the two of
them were in his bedroom, he seated on the edge of the
bed and her in front of the dressing table mirror carefully twining an array of pins into her dark hair. Down
beside her, merely a foot away, lurked the powdered-
silver form of the reptile.

"It's a chameleon. It's meant to blend in; that's the
point of them isn't it."

"I can see it wherever I look!"

"You've taken too many drugs"

"No, I haven't taken anything."

"Then you haven't taken enough drugs," she answered, her dark eyes sparkling with mischief.

"Listen Colette, I'm being serious here," said Vincent,
at which the French girl only laughed.

"Perhaps you are under attack from a witch," replied
Colette, who, since a fellow performer had taken part in
a seminar at Treadwells, affected to earnestly believe in
such things. Several body jewels were now attached to
her perfectly smooth face.

"I am being serious. I see the creature every moment
when I look up; I'm seeing it right now—there down
by the side of the dresser. It's not unpleasant; in fact, it,

the chameleon, is one of the most beautiful things I've ever seen, but I am seeing it, the only one seeing it, and that's really—you know—terrifying me. Do you think I'm losing my mind or something?"

She answered again without turning her head.

"If you really are seeing things, unusual colours or lights and stuff, you should see an optician as soon as you can tomorrow. It will probably stop anyway once you've slept. Let your chameleon slip back into the dreams from which all beautiful things come," she answered, emphasising her accent for theatrical effect on the last line: "Until then enjoy the free trip."

The chameleon did not vanish with the coming of morning. It was there when Vincent awoke, fading into view amongst the familiar objects of the room. Half-clothed and still fogged with sleep, he walked slowly in silence about the empty flat, watching it appear at every turn: now by the door, now on the kitchen counter, now by a stack of prints and now by Colette's wardrobe. His attempts to ignore it proved futile; even beyond its fantastic method of appearance, something in its form had the power to draw his mind back to it. When he tried to shower he found its presence in the small, white-tiled chamber so diverting that he temporarily lost all awareness of what he was doing, and, no longer conscious of the spray wetting his face, gave himself up to contemplation of the creature, tracing familiar patterns in the curve of its spiral tail and glimpsing old inspirations in its prism of scales, drawn always deeper to the visceral question of the connection between the life that shone in that pearly skin and his own.

For some reason, perhaps a lingering sense of resentment towards his partner, Vincent told no one of his phantasm and sought neither doctor nor optician. Instead, he put all his mental energy into trying to accept the chameleon as part of his visual background. Colette gave no sign of perceiving any change in his behaviour; in her mind she noticed that her lover was preoccupied and moody but put this down to the fact that pre-pub and digital editing work had meant that he was unable to pursue any fresh drawings.

Vincent kept this up for several days and was very pleased with himself. He told himself that he'd grown used to the chameleon, that he'd almost come to like its presence. It accompanied him on walks and to meals with friends, an attractive enigma following beside him like a familiar spirit. He could superimpose it on any scene he wished—a Cheshire chameleon. As an experiment he tried leaving out potential food items for it—slugs, cockroaches, butterflies he'd netted from the lavender bush on a neighbour's balcony—but these scattered offerings inspired no interest in the reptile, which merely watched his labours with indifference from beneath its mauve, vortex-patterned eyelids. No matter, that only meant the creature required no attention on his part, beyond the idle leisure time he might wish to give in admiring its fantastic jewelled form.

By the end of the third day this pretence of enjoyment began to pall. Its presence was a constant, niggling strain on his mind; an unanswerable question wherever he looked. Its way of inserting itself into a scene in violation both of the laws of perception and space infuriated him, and others couldn't have failed to notice a change in his demeanour, increased agitation and quick sideways glances when he thought no

194

one was looking. By now they must be wondering what was the matter with him (at present this concern was not a problem, it even showed kindness, but if things continued this way people would begin to drift away from him). He went to bed, so tired as to feel almost inebriated, and indifferent to Colette's kisses.

He spent the fourth day wandering lost through the streets of Bloomsbury, hoping against hope that some solution or at least potential explanation for this mystery would come to him either from within or from without. Hours spent with the iPhone search engine sitting on the steps of the British Museum brought up chameleons as spies, as the ghosts of the unbaptised in Mediterranean folklore, as the herald of life eternal in Bantu dream-time, as a vital component of love potions in the Arab world . . . in short, all and nothing . . . He was thrown into a frenzy of excitement for a couple of hours when he met a young Rastafarian busking in Trafalgar Square who claimed also to be able to see the reptile, only to realise the colourfully dressed woman was humouring him in an attempt to get him to share whatever drug she imagined him to be on.

On the morning of the third day he suddenly grew hysterically angry. Why would people not see it, why wouldn't they admit to seeing it; why wouldn't artists, children and animal-lovers take advantage of this fantastic, bizarre scenario—one guaranteed to become an internet sensation—to observe and interact with that gorgeous animal whilst it still crawled free? After all, they would pay good money to see such a creature in a cage or glass tank . . . It was so unfair . . . The whole thing was a lie, a fucking lie. He knew the chameleon wasn't real; didn't his resistance to just picking it up and moving it away prove that? Everyone saw chameleons; it was a private thing one didn't talk about, like masturbation . . . Or perhaps there was no such thing as a chameleon and everyone was just pretending; the entire population of London was in conspiracy against him; the chameleon was the first visual symptom of an incipient brain tumour that the God in whom he did not believe had chosen to afflict him with . . .

Alone in the flat he laughed until hot tears came to his eye, then suddenly felt very foolish and virulently angry with himself.

He subsequently ignored the creature for a whole afternoon, only to sink into a brooding gloom come evening and thence spend hours staring at it, his finger-tips flexing rhythmically with every movement it made. He wanted people to see the chameleon, not only to validate the testimony of both mind and senses, but also so they might appreciate its fascinating, intricate beauty, a beauty which at present was locked away from the rest of the world by the walls of his own skull.

That night Colette gave a performance in her new costume of black glass and magpie feathers.

The beginning of the next week brought Vincent back into his studio. The location, coupled with anticipation of the work ahead, fired him with a strange defiance. This room was, in virtue of its contents, a concrete biography, a record of his personal development more apposite and revealing than any which could be culled from document or recollection; what it held told of happy memories of art school and murals painted with his then girlfriend, nostalgia for freedom stretching into a different kind of life, one of routine success in which he made a name for himself, a darkly promising persona in the Soho night scene, and developed a trademark style to go with it. It would be strange having the chameleon observing him; ever since he'd begun to earn a living from his penmanship he had been accustomed to working in absolute solitude.

The design he planned to embark on today was destined for use on the first of the No More Tears posters. It was to be of a swan maiden, an impossibly waif-like figure shown from head to bust with sweeping arch-angelic wings unfurling from her shoulders and a delicate carnival mask of the same stylised feathers. So far he'd only completed a rough contour drawing, scarcely more than a series of quick pen flicks on the wide A3 sheet. At this point, only a couple of sketches beyond the draft-pad stage, many illustrators still preferred to use an artist's pencil, but he chose to move directly to ink, as the stark, clean line better suited his quick, street-wise style.

He positioned himself at a desk, the manuscript board propped up in front of him, the windows through which could be seen a smear of green foliage to his right, and the door behind. The chameleon was not visible but he could feel its presence a few feet away on the table covered with loose sheets (he could not resist a quick glance sideways which proved his suspicion correct). Vincent took up his pen and began to work.

The first task would be going over the tips of the wings adding in a diagonal stroke for each individual point; this aspect of the image would require more detailing than he was ordinarily wont to employ in his drawings. Moments passed with him carefully repeating the same action.

When Vincent looked up momentarily he noticed a tremor in the corner of his vision, a faint hazy burst of colour akin to that which migraine sufferers experience.

The chameleon moved a little way towards him in silence. Its colouring had altered in some subtle fashion: the silvery scales had acquired a certain sheen, or else the light was catching its body in a singularly unpleasant way.

Vincent returned his attention to the drawing. It was at this point a radical change came over the creature.

Whereas before it had always been that pearlescent silver, now its body shone and rippled with a hundred terrible colours, bilious and unbearable to look upon. Thick, livid yellows and dirty scarlets, shades of mustard gas and bad blood, smears of leaden blue like poison and the greys of fever visions, billowed out across the coat of scales, boiling and coagulating into further shades, each band of colouring merging into the next in such a way that it pained and confused the eye of the watcher. From the tip of its coiled tail to the filigreed horns upon its head, the chameleon had become a kaleidoscope of nightmarish intensity; only the jet pits of its eyes remained the same, oblivious to the visual corruption playing out across its body.

Vincent retched, his shock upon seeing it change overwhelmed by physical pain and revulsion. The sight of it lit a fire in his skull more invasively agonising than the worst headache, for with the pain there came a deep, visceral sense of disgust directed towards himself as much as to the chameleon. He wanted to vomit, to purge himself of whatever this taint was. His eyes watered and there was a burning sensation of bile in the back of his throat.

He tore his gaze away from the chameleon only to have it reappear like a blotch of acid eating through the canvas of reality. In panic, with his eyes closed, Vincent stumbled his way out of the studio and into the bedroom, there to throw himself on the bed and bury his face in the pillow.

Going round in his mind was the thought that he would be faced with that sight forever. Beyond the pain it was also the ugliest, most shameful thing he had ever witnessed; if he had to face it every waking hour he would go mad or suffer a fit. He lay like this for what seemed like hours before nervous exhaustion drove him into a sickly, fitful sleep.

Upon coming to, he found with great relief that the chameleon had returned to something like its normal shading. There was still a suggestion of pollution in those metallic pale scales; the silver was no longer pure; it had that faint, hinted-poisonous look of lead or pewter. By the end of the day this too had receded and the mother-of-pearl colouring was once again clean.

From that moment Vincent had entered into a new stage of his torment. Whenever he attempted to work, that nightmarish transformation occurred anew, assaulting his eyes and throwing him into paroxysms of physical and moral loathing. Twice he tried without taking his eyes from the paper, making an effort to turn his vision into a white tunnel, but the concentration required to do so was counterproductive; it made giving himself over to the picture virtually impossible, and, besides, for a period of a few hours afterwards he would still be haunted by the sight of that creature in a blaze of toxic colours. Physical disgust at the sight was accompanied by guilt at knowing that he was somehow responsible for such a transformation.

Long hours of weariness found him in the studio once more, surrounded by the drooping paper rags and picture sheets that had once formed the basis of his career. Pens and other writing implements lay scattered across the tables threatening to spill onto the floor; an album full of draft sketches had come open spilling its contents: on one such sheet a pen cartridge had burst, the spilt ink forming a flower-shaped puddle which erased the head of a dying mermaid. Outside the sky was clouded; it was that bright white cloud of summer that seemed to flicker like video static, adding a faint, grainy texture to the surface of objects as if it eroded them with its touch.

There was no way forward if he could not work. It would be more than the end of a career; it would mean the end of an entire lifestyle, both for him and his partner. Gone would be the delicate public choreography of artist and model. All those years spent developing and mastering a consistent style, of artistic evolution under the pressure of worldly demands leading to his independence, would mean nothing. He may as well have been blind . . .

It was then an idea entered his mind, a very simple idea, one which he was surprised had not come to him when all this had begun. He could kill the chameleon, crush it and dismember it, reduce it to a pile of carrion muddying its silver hide with blood, and so at last rid himself of this curse. Others could not reach it, but he knew he could—it existed only for him, thus was his to kill. The thought of snuffing out the life that stared from behind those psychedelic eyes awoke some hidden appetite; it inspired more passion in him than Colette ever did, replacing the fatigue that suffused his bloodstream with a boiling nervous energy.

From a cupboard he fetched an implement, a small hammer. As he moved across the room he could feel its weight, the temperature of the wood, the smoothness of its lacquered handle in his palm, and he fancied too he could taste the tang of iron within his mouth, lustful and bitter.

The chameleon looked up; it seemed unafraid, tilting its crusted skull from side to side as Vincent stood over it with the weapon ready.

His rage died just as quickly as it had kindled, opening a vacuum within his consciousness, just as the passing of a flame reveals the depths of the empty hearth. Seldom before had he been so acutely conscious of how Man's freedom positions him between innumerable worlds: that sense of existential vertigo, of the dizzying abyss of choices and outcomes. He could bring that hunk of metal down—there was no external impediment, nothing holding him back; he was free to destroy the creature forever. And yet morally he couldn't. He realised then with a certainty which transcended reasoning that if he were to do so he would be doing something so terrible that it would irrevocably mark him off from the rest of humanity, that its effects would taint the future. For the first time in his life Vincent believed in Sin.

Weeks passed and Vincent slumped under the enervation of defeat. The same day seemed to repeat itself, only with less detail each time. His work, his plans, had stalled. At first giving excuses to clients provided some occupation, but he soon lost energy for this and met their enquiries with muted indifference. Colette assumed his sudden inertia was due to depression and recommended half-jokingly that he either try mindfulness or take more coke (in her own mind she congratulated herself on being understanding and standing by him).

A muted, rainy afternoon found the artist once again collapsed in a chair in the studio, head in hand, staring at the withering of his career and life's desire as encapsulated by the disused room. What had once been a living autobiography had now became a kind of psychic tomb, the portfolios and unfinished drawings grave goods to accompany the soul of a for-a-time Soho art star into the underworld of fading history. In front of him was the same sheet of paper, bare of all but the swan girl outline he'd started back before it all began.

His constant reptilian follower rested itself on the windowsill beside him, its turreted eyes observing the watery world outside with indifference.

Vincent felt a surge of affection. It wasn't the creature's fault that it changed so hideously when he gave form to his ideas; something in his work or his creativity triggered that reaction. Just as the creature of camouflage is obliged by instinct to take on the shades of its background, so the phantasmal chameleon was attuned to some hidden deformity of his artistic nature which manifested in these drawings. He was the one deserving of blame and guilt, the guilt of inflicting such monstrous changes on it.

The creature moved forward again, stretching out and flexing one of its clawed feet.

Vincent returned to the whiteness in front of him and quickly traced a few lines on the blank sheet. It was a movement devoid of conscious intention, as spontaneous as birdsong, yet once he started he found he could not stop—soon he had traced a complete outline of the bent limb.

A sudden change came about the creature, but of a different nature this time. Whereas before the creature's skin had taken on a palate of corruption, it now blossomed with shades of unimaginable tenderness. Each scale was as of an opal softly glowing as curling rainbows and iridescences of forgotten dreams played beneath its surface of pale milky fire. These wonders flickered away almost as quickly as they had appeared.

This new sight pierced Vincent with an emotion which was half anticipation and half nostalgia. In haste he turned his attention to the unfinished swan maiden and began tracing a delicate spiral scale design on the curve of her check beneath the left eye. The ink employed was black but in his mind's eye he saw the patterning completed in many colours, a brush of a butterfly's wing on his lady's face. He executed this design at panicked speed for fear that he would lose his grasp of those patterns even as he strove to capture them, but his mind retained them as clearly as it did the memory of his first moments of love.

As he worked, that beautiful alteration spread over the chameleon again, only this time brighter and more vivid.

In the days that followed, Vincent divided his time between rapt contemplation of the mesmeric patterns becoming visible on the chameleon's skin and feverish work with pen and manuscript. He began dozens of sketches incorporating or inspired by some aspect of the chameleon's form—a smudge of pigment on its back became a shadowy orchid, the curl of its horns the backs of a lunar mountain range, its jagged crest the columns of an avenue in a drowned city. Impossibly slender figures danced beyond scaly veils, a spiky-haired nude bore psychedelic whorls on her nipples and pudenda . . . Gone was the old, sensible method of beginning with outlines in pencil sketch; Vincent worked with whatever colour called to him, blending one into another to capture that labyrinthine complexity, only giving them solidity with black lines at the finish. His efforts were rewarded with further revelations of colour and shape. Whereas before they had quickly faded into silvery oblivion, they now remained permanent, altering only in their increasing complexity. The creature's whole body was a palimpsest of dimly familiar signatures and arabesques and his was the task of deciphering that fantastic script.

It was everything, he thought: it was the shapes in the crawling yellow ivy that used to grow over the windowsill of the Limehouse place where they'd lived as students, it was the metallic blue-violet they had used for the background of their wall painting, it was the angular form of the hawk tattoo he had designed for a roommate's sister, it was happy memories of art school and murals painted with his then girlfriend, it was early sketches he'd done to his favourite albums trying to turn their sound into colour, it was shapes in the clouds picked out through a haze of weed smoke, it was tomorrow's azure, nostalgia white and romance gold; it was warmth, beauty, freedom and joy.

Throughout his labours the chameleon flamed with heart-aching beauty, its stained-glass body shining out with celestial lustre, casting radiances and drawing rich tapestries for the eye to drown in. The outlines of its body blurred as if in a heat haze.

If only another could partake in this, recognise it as he did, then between Vincent and that person there would be a meaningful exchange, infinitesimal in the cosmic scheme of things but as intimate as love and as precious. Without his activities, though, it would all remain across an unbridgeable divide; it was his calling to make these beings and vistas of dream visible to others, as he had somehow known since the beginning. He strove harder with his designs, delving deeper and deeper into what showed itself.

No longer did Vincent have to look to his phantasmal companion for inspiration, for the duality between it and the page was breaking down. Ideas flowed directly from mind to paper. Those patterns put down by the pen upon the white sheets appeared mirrored in the chameleon's own markings. Both equalled the visions coming from within him. And then, as he finished putting the final touches on his last work of the day, a cloudscape of mosaic complexity, Vincent lifted his gaze and took in the contents of the room laid out before him; for a moment both pictures and creature appeared more vividly, standing out against the scene, and then with a final blur of colour the chameleon faded from view, leaving the material world forever.

As the first day of the showing draws to a close the attendees find themselves returning to these works again and again, unsure how to react to them, their own ambitions and interests momentarily numbed. Some are enthused by them, some angered by them; all agree that they have some quality which sets them apart from the other artworks. Today, at least, none will claim possession of them, for the artist himself cannot be found amongst the crowd. When the place closes, these pictures will remain there still, doorways into a realm of infinite form and colour.

AMEN

Quentin S. Crisp

I am Hewelet. Surely these, my very thoughts, are heard, like heartbeats—universally and in some breathless dreadfulness of secrecy—heard and judged. And this is the uttermost crisis of uncertainty, that might become anything. It seems to me that I am being led towards a terrible cloud of the unknown that writhes with darkness and silver fire, and I do not know either what that darkness or that fire portends.

The great fear that long made sore this little heart battened on me unspoken; unspeakable, it could not be hidden. A worm moved beneath my skin and, I thought, the very skin of the world. Things, at last, crowded upon me. I could not vanquish them. A shadow fell. Or else my shadow turned on me and overcame me. I was carried from under it to a chamber. When understanding came to me, I was given a task.

The hand of my guide, as strong and cold as a blade, showed me the book on which I was to work, bound with a fantastical bivalve shell of carbuncled silver and gold. I was commanded: I would write, decorate and illuminate the final page; the most important page since it was the culmination, as it were, the legislation and enactment, of all the book contained. However, that final page required a single word only: Amen.

Such was my task.

Without further explanation, I was left alone to it. I had given my life to manuscript, to the inking of word in flesh. The final page of this book, verso, was smooth and voluptuously white—the flesh side of the page. Perhaps it was supposed that I needed little instruction, but the creamy void of this abertive vellum and the freedom I had been given, twinned to an imperative, made me dizzy and hesitant for some moments.

First, anyway, I would rule the page with lead point and carve my quill. I had been furnished for this task with all the materials and tools I could want. The desk was an ordered treasury of pigments—lapis lazuli, malachite, saffron—of gum arabic, gypsum, gold leaf and powdered gold, virgin quills sand-baked but still uncut, of dogs' teeth for burnishing, gall nuts and hens' eggs, tools to cut, to scrape and to grind with, and pestles and bowls to mix in.

Orientating myself by these things, I began to plot my course. In my mind I saw the letters upon the page. They would be large, with the height of five lines of normal text and more for the initial. I ruled accordingly, guiding my lines by the prick marks at the edge of the page. Then, thinking of what would come next, I realised how ungathered, still, were my wits. It would not be easy to work on a book already bound, especially with no design prepared to work from.

I sat back in fresh hesitation and perplexity. This would take both boldness and minutest care, and with each moment that passed I grew more anxious at the difficulty. Was there not, perhaps, something I had overlooked? Might I find help in my surroundings?

I looked up from the desk and to the chamber. A nameless apprehension, I realised, had kept my eyes lowered until then. Beeswax candles, diffusing a sweet, clean scent with their virgin glow, illuminated in patches the shelves that lined the wall. The chamber was circular, as if occupying one entire floor of a tower. From the little I remembered of how I had come here, I reflected this could not be the case. There were no windows and no other door than that through which I had been led. A word was carved into the door's stone lintel: Purgatorio. Yes, I had seen the same word on the lintel on the opposite side, coming in. Considering this desk and the paraphernalia it held, I might have expected, instead, "scriptorium", but, after all, some materials were lacking. I needed something on which to sketch out my design before I committed it to the page as I had been commissioned.

So I began to explore the chamber, feeling lost in its strangeness as I might be in the empty immensity of a desert. I found many curious things, more curious still for being kept in one place together. Some of the objects made me recall things I had read in books on alchemy, yet they were not themselves the things I had seen or found described in any such books, and I could not name them. I began to think, as I picked up one thing and then another, that I was only the most recent of unnumbered visitors who had all been led to this chamber and given tasks of various kinds, and what I examined now, in their absence, were the products of their labour.

I do not know why, but I paused a long time, with difficult emotions, when I came to a spoon carved ornately in wood. There were flowers in it and interlacing patterns, whittled with a homely hand but a sure one. It must have been a keepsake of some kind. I could not help being sensible of the movements of hand that had shaped this, and of the life that had moved the hand. It was as if that person had only lately quit this chamber, as if I might hope to catch the echo of his feet upon descending stairs. Near the end of the handle, carved into what looked like a scrolling pennant, was the name, "Arlette."

Whatever the allure of this mystery, I decided it was a distraction from my purpose. I searched among the books that also were kept in this place. None had the blank pages I needed. Then I took one from the shelves and, opening it, found it was a copy of *De consolation philosophiae*, the golden book of Boethius' last days. I turned the pages and my eye fell upon a passage by chance.

> *Hae sunt enim quae infructuosis affectuum spinis uberem fructibus rationis segetum necant hominumque mentes assuefaciunt morbo, non liberant.*

My eye shifted to the initial and I read the whole passage. I read, and with Boethius' image of the thorns I thought of the parable of the scattered seed and of how some seed fell among thorns. I could not doubt this was what Boethius had had in mind, and again I admired the rooted profundity of the old texts that none but a philologist might discern. But I was disquieted at what I understood, and I turned quickly to the back of the book. To my surprise, I found there what I needed — two unstained leaves — and I took the book to the desk and cut out the unused pages.

How strangely that reading of Boethius had affected me. I sat at the desk but again I could not begin my task. I was thinking of the dreadful circumstances under which Boethius had written his last book, and I thought, too, of the content of that tome. In my chest there fluttered a peculiar foreboding as well as a queer and tremulous equivocation of hope.

My mind was full of seeds and thorns.

Seeds and thorns . . . *He who sets his hand to the plough and looks back . . .*

I saw young shoots breaking through the surface of the earth, from darkness into light. An idea came to me that was not a single idea but an image of living brilliance seeming to answer with boldness, hope and truth all the fears that circled me. It was a fecund image, as the earth must be where the good seed falls. I would render it in line and colour and make it brilliant in fact with the gold that had been provided for me like a sign of grace.

I sketched out the design on one of the spare pages I had cut out from Boethius. It needed little correction and I knew by the faithfulness of my hand to what was in my head that in this image I had captured truth. I was impatient to transfer it to the page for which I had been tasked, but I steadied myself. First, between the lead-point lines I had drawn there to guide me, I executed, in firm curves, the "m". Remembering what I had read of the secret import of letters, I thought of "mem" and the Holy Name of God. The "m" I rendered first that I might work against its constraint with the initial "A". Usually, I would have completed the "e" and the "n" too, before starting on the "A", but, after all, I felt the image of that initial inside me as a glittering inspiration and I feared that if I waited, my mind would lose its hold on something so effulgent and wondrous. Therefore, immediately I finished the "m", I began work on the initial.

I have often been engrossed in a design, so that I am as much contained in my mental world as a snail is in its shell. That was especially true on this occasion. The lines scratched with quill on vellum, straight, curved, spiralling, seemed to harmonise so closely with time that they became time itself, and keeping pace with time's inner convolutions, I did not know that it passed.

Line by line, the image formed. The "A" stood in a furrowed field as a storehouse for grain. Below it, a wingéd ox drew the steady blade of a plough. The figure of a man led the ox by one horn with his right hand, casting grain behind him with his left. Farther back, crops were already sprouting from the freshly turned sod.

It was finished. I sighed with relief and pride at my accomplishment. Now I only had to gild and to colour it.

However, it was at this precise interval that a strange light fell through the window of my mind, and I could not decide whether what it showed there was truth or illusion. Looking to the pots of pigment and gold, suddenly, and with a shrinking perplexity greater than before, I understood—or, as it seemed, remembered, with some full-bosomed wave of memory—the purpose of my task. It was to praise God, yes; to praise in a way worthy of God, with this gold, this lapis lazuli, this malachite, the very glories of the Earth that God made. And yet I must take no pride in my work, nor delight in gold because it was gold, but only because its lustre might serve to glorify God. And so I was stricken with fear and perplexity. If I did less than my best, how could I do work worthy of God? Yet how could I do my best without pride to tell me I was equal to the task? The first is acedia, the sin of the coward who dare not love God; the second is the sin of Lucifer, who loves himself as God.

The story and the struggle of my life stood plainly before me and I knew what great and unspeakable things were at stake. With my recognition of the purpose of my task, I remembered how closely this thread of dilemma was woven into my very soul. All the belovéd tools and materials of manuscript and illumination, as dear to me as my own hands, my own eyes, my own heart, appeared suddenly a subtle snare, as if I saw these bright objects in a nightmare and their usual brilliance, with which, on parchment, I might make in deathless image the plumes of a peacock, had now a refracted meaning, their attraction malign that revealed the malignancy of my heart. And all the time, this question writhed in my clutches like a snake: Can this be truth? Truth is light, yet this light—oh, my soul!—casts a shadow.

Was the evil already in the design I had accomplished—if so, in what part, and how?—or might it yet be avoided? A trembling fear forbade me to start anew; I had no choice but to go on. I would apply gold and pigment in faith, like a petition. I selected the first flake of gold, for the right horn of the ox. I laid it in place, smoothed it flat against the vellum, scratched away the excess so that it filled the outline only. So began the illumination and the colouring. Again I was engrossed, but this time without the flowing confidence I had felt when inking the lines; this time it was as if I crawled a stone-flagged floor on hands and knees towards the throne of God, and judgement. Yet where I crawled, I left colour.

Then this, too, was finished. Gold glittered against bistre. Deep red and blue formed an infinity of rich mystery like excellent drapery. White doves perched upon the bejewelled granary of the "A". The design was complete, a perfect, visual fantasm, it seemed to me, of a spiritual conception. Strangely, I saw no answer in this perfection to the question of whether I had failed of succeeded in my task. I only observed a kind of joy in the image, in its perfection and chromatic vibrancy at the same time as in a certain formal and balancing solemnity. The latter was fitting, of course; joy must not become intemperance.

Two letters remained, the "e" and the "n". I paused, and for a moment I felt more like myself than I had since coming to this chamber. I had strange thoughts. I should not say "strange", perhaps. They were familiar but inexpressible. They belonged nowhere at all, and I was not sure why I had them now, except that they felt to me of the same fabric as the oldest thoughts I had ever had—sighing and commonplace and local and free and vast as infant ignorance—and perhaps this was the last time I would think such thoughts. Anyway, it was time for me to finish my task.

The "e" was executed without error or unsteadiness. The "n" was about to be completed in the same way, when it occurred to me, for some reason, that the downward stroke at the end could not stop at the line I had ruled. I sank quickly past the line and I began to scribble, spontaneously, something that had not been in the design. I had started it almost without thinking, and yet, in truth, I had thought. I had thought, "It will go badly for me if I spoil, in these last moments, the page on which I am to be examined." And in the instant I thought that, the extended downward line and the scribble became inevitable. My quill, with a kind of fatal ease and swiftness, as if this were the very outpouring of my soul, a mere spilling of ink in some disastrous grace, traced the lines of impious babooneries, absurd gargoyles, gurning and bounding. At their centre was the image of a spider, lowering itself on a thread from the "n", its abdomen bulbous and its rabbit-eyed, grinning head solemnly bearded and crowned with thorns.

I had scribbled my own doom. I reflected on it with the eyes of a draughtsman and extended thin legs on a hideous web.

Well, and what was this for? I did not know. Only, I had felt like it very much, and then, when I did it, it was as if I confessed my whole life. And here it was, a mere impertinence on the page. And yet, I hoped that someone might see this unexpected thing and smile, divining the secret thought of a stranger; smile, or anyway, something of that sort.

All was still and silent. It seemed I was alone and yet had time. I could take my knife and scrape away these drolleries. It even seemed a folly that I let them remain. I contemplated, but found I could not make the decision to erase the images with which I had finished the work. I sighed and turned my eyes to the jars of pigment once more and raised my quill to set about colouring the spider and its retinue of demons. How placidly I worked now, my hand seemingly charmed in its passage across the vellum.

When this, too, was done, I laid down the quill with a feeling of emptiness as if, indeed, I could do no more.

I thought again of the spoon and the unknown person who had carved it and a cavernous wordlessness echoed within me. Then began a palpitation of miscellaneous feelings harnessed in mutual disharmony, as if royal musicians, banded together to celebrate the completion of the Tower of Babel, had begun to play the moment God had struck the tower, scattered the people and confused their speech.

The door to the chamber swung open, its heavy creak one more instrument in this Babylonian orchestra. There appeared beneath its lintel the guide who had brought me here, with eyes of fire, wings of glorious smoke and face of crystal beauty. His hand fell upon the completed page and fire sprang up, consuming it.

Then I was taken through the door and into the darkness. Beyond the darkness, drawing closer, is a vast bank of cloud whose scrolling folds are all illuminated with gold and silver flame.

XYSCHATON
(ACHRONOLOGY MIX)

James Champagne

"What is the death of the body, after all, compared
with the unbearable death of youth?"
—Yukio Mishima, *Forbidden Colours*

Topology 22: The Tumultuous Upsurge
(Come Clean!)

As the Coil composition sibilated hypnotically within my head like a stoned ectoparasite, Z watched the
floor-to-ceiling windows on the walls of my bedroom
begin to extend themselves horizontally into the horizon, like Morrison Timeworms, or human beings when
seen through a 4th-dimensional Leng-Space lens, and
at the same time my bedroom began to duplicate itself
like a malfunctioning Universal Constructor (or, alternately, a von Neumann clanking replicator machine),
and while it seemed to extend backwards into time it
was as if Z was being pulled *away* from it, so that Z saw
multiple versions of myself seated naked in my time
machine pulling away from me so that it seemed to extend backwards in time it was as if Z was being pulled
away from it so that Z saw multiple versions of myself
seated naked in my time machine pulling away from

me so thatitseemedtoextendbackwardsintimeitwasas-
ifZwasbeingpulledawayfromitsothatZsawmultiplev-
ersionsofmyselfseatednakedinmytimemachinepulling-
awayfromme me from away pulling machine time my
in naked seated myself of versions multiple Z saw that
so it from away pulled being was Z if as was it time
in backwards extend and then as reality fell apart in
oecumenic disintegration (calling to mind the Natalie
Portman and Mila Kunis *Black Swan* club scene delirium) Z became aware of eldritch beings surrounding
me in a surrealistic circinate manner, but Z was unable to look at these beings directly, was only able to
see them in quick glimpses at the periphery of my vision, at the corners of my eyes, and trying to describe
them in fourth-dimensional vernacular is perhaps a
fool's errand, but in some ways they reminded me of a
hallucinatory hypnogogic animated version of a Jarry
woodcut (I'm thinking specifically of the one that appears right before the start of the "Autoclete" chapter
in Jarry's book *Black Minutes of Memorial Sand*, which il-
lustrates an early depiction of Jarry's Palotin creations:
here, jack-in-the-box-like creatures with pointy conical
hats, oversized manga-style eyes, stupidly frozen grins
on their mask-like faces, and accordion-shaped bodies), and Z watched as these queer creatures stretched
themselves upwards and downwards with their odd
accordion bodies, and they were moving their arms
and hands in an abnormal Elisa Lam-ish fashion, as if
they were trying to communicate to me via some sort
of supermundane sign language, and as their hands
moved Z could see the afterimages of their hands trailing behind them, like slugs leaving trails of ichor in the
æther, and they then shapeshifted into beings that bore
a most startling resemblance to the Hobart globster sea

218

monster of 1962: large, amorphous lumps of mirror-like flesh covered with gills and roynish hair, and flickering across the surfaces of their bodies Z could see recreations of scenes from the past triggered by relict memories of things that Z had read in books, historical events that, for whatever reason, had intaglioed themselves into my mind, and Z saw Colin Wilson, aged 17, standing before the reagent shelves at his analytical chemistry class during the long, thermogenic summer of 1947, back when he was working as a lowly lab assistant, and in his hands he's holding a bottle of hydrocyanic acid, and he's thinking about committing suicide by drinking it, is visualising it burning a hole in his throat as it sizzles down his oesophagus—here, in this etiolated state of mind, not even the anodynal work of George Bernard Shaw may save him—and then Z saw Neil Andrew Megson with his friends Spydee and Little Baz in a flat in Solihull in 1967, conducting a séance with a wineglass and the alphabet, and Z watch as they get into contact with a spirit that identifies itself as Mebar, who tells them, "Move a fin and the world turns," then suddenly everything went dark all around me, and Z was all alone in my cardboard box, floating in a tenebrous abysm of deep time and gelid nothingness, and my SkullSong v.2.3 biochip audio player was evidently malfunctioning as it had switched off from playing Coil to a new song, the eerie untitled second side of Maurizio Bianchi's 1982 *Regel* LP, and then in the center of this necrotic tabula rasa, past the ramparts and towers outside of time known as Dantour (where, in the Library of Ectoplasmus, the Klippoth Congress convenes amidst the shattered shells, and the Salamander Children circle jerk and hiss hymns to the Cancer Axis like "Kim Kardashian's *Rolling Stone* boobs are our power animal"), Z saw a familiar sight.

Topology 2: Calling on Vanished Faces

But enough about mutilated chicken feet. To get back to my original point, in which Z argued that boy worshippers have a greater appreciation of the Tragic. One could also make the claim that boy worshippers in Legion are tragic figures, in that the source of their emotional and erotic fixation is by its very nature ephemeral: the Holy Grail of hebephilia is utterly transient, a spectral cup for spectral fingers. The hebephile wants to freeze time, to preserve the youthful beauty of their sexual desires in amber, but this is truly a Sisyphean wish: their masturbatory fantasies are in fact biochemical threnodies. To give just a few examples, consider the Australian pop singer and YouTube sensation Troye Sivan, who achieved some degree of popularity around the years 2015-2016. To be sure, he was alluring back then (though at the time in which I'm writing this, which is the year 2036, obviously his good looks have faded), but go back and watch his earlier videos, like the one he uploaded to YouTube in November of 2007, where, at the age of 13, he recorded himself singing a cover version of the song "Tell Me Why." He looks (and sounds) utterly ambrosial in it. Or look at Isaac Hempstead-Wright, who portrayed the character Bran Stark on the old TV show *Game of Thrones*. In season 1, he was almost stunningly beautiful, truly a sexy little boy, but in the later seasons, after the cancer of puberty hit, well . . . still handsome in his own way, but something was missing, some essential spark had gone out. And the less said about the Finn Wolfhard Decline of 2021 (or, even more tragically, the exterior deterioration of the once stunningly beautiful William Franklyn-Miller) the better. All of this goes to confirm my theory that every grown man is a walking haunted house, with the ghost in question being his lost youthful form. Z could sum it up in the form of an apothegm: all men undergo two deaths, the first (and more poignant) one being the passing of their boyhood design.

Topology 3: The Fanged Illusion

Many schools of Buddhist thought claim that all of what we think of as reality is actually an illusion. But what they don't tell you is that the illusion has teeth, and that when it bites you, it hurts. Of all the various indignities our minds and bodies undergo during the courses of our lives in this march to the Bardo of Suffering, Z think the very worst thing is what time does to our physical appearance. I've already provided a few examples of boys who have been tainted by time, but Z could just as easily look at a photograph of myself, then gaze into a mirror in the present day, to be reminded of the truth of my heuristic mentations. Z truly was a beautiful boy, looking almost like a dead ringer for the actor Julian Mohn (otherwise known as Leonardo). Z had a flawless, angelically attractive face and long, light-brown hair that could almost be characterised as girly (another confession: few things titillate me more than 11-14-year-old boys with long girly hair). Yet Z look in the mirror now, as a man in his forties, and Z realise that Z look like a cross between Bob Balaban (as he appeared in his guest star role as Phoebe Buffay's dad in the prehistoric American TV sitcom *Friends*) and a raddled Dalton from the old JRPG *Chrono Trigger*, just without the camp eyepatch. To go into further detail, Z have a round, clean-shaven, oddly cherubic-looking face (still angelic, but now the spavined visage of a fallen angel), a large and somewhat creased forehead, vulturine eyebrows, long, light-brown hair that flows down to my shoulders, and a thin mouth. My best feature is clearly my eyes, which are framed behind a pair of old-fashioned bifocals: these eyes are dark-brown flecked with yellow, suggesting Nibelungen gold buried in some long-lost dwarven cavern. Z should also mention that I'm not what could be considered tall by any stretch of the imagination, though at the same time it would be a mistake to think of me as a gnome: I'm actually 5 feet and five inches. Oh, and my blood type is "B." As for my voice, the best way Z can describe it is as sounding quite a bit like that of the Algeria Touchshriek character from David Bowie's 1995 album *1. Outside: The diary of Nathan Adler or the art-ritual murder of Baby Grace Blue: A non-linear Gothic Drama Hyper-cycle.*

Topology 23: Boy Ocean (Narcissupocalypse)

Z could now see the planet Earth in its entirety, only it no longer resembled any satellite photograph of the planet that Z had ever seen in my life (how it was possible that Z was surviving in outer space in a mere cardboard box was another story entirely). What Z mean is that the planet looked completely white, as if its collective landmasses and oceans had frozen over. Initially, as my time machine approached the atmosphere of the planet, and Z could see that the continents and oceans were glazed with an alabaster coating, Z assumed that the planet had undergone some sort of drastic ice age.

But as I got closer to the planet's surface, Z perceived that this white surface was moving, or perhaps *writhing* was the better word. It was when Z had arrived about 20 to 30 feet over the surface that Z could finally see what it was that covered the planet in greater detail: Z saw that it was *myself*, as a 12-year-old boy, only *multiplied*, billions of times, so that billions upon billions of naked clones of my 12-year-old self utterly quilted the macrocosm, occupying all available free space. It was like gazing down into a schoolboy snake pit, and Z could see that all of the clones of my young self were wriggling against each other's bodies, licking and kissing and masturbating and fucking: an eternal orgy of preadolescent skin. All the cities of Man were gone, crushed under the weight of the blanket of boys, and there were obscene mountains made of boyflesh as far as the eye could see. Oceans that had once upon a time contained all the waters of the Earth were now gone, replaced instead by an ocean of boys. Staring out at this teknon panoply, Z marveled at the Perfection Z saw before me, and wondered to what Empyrean realm Z had been taken, for surely this must be Paradise.

Topology 12: The Geochronmechane

It was then Z first began to study the art and writings of the American artist and architect Paul Laffoley (1935-2015), who was the sole member of the Massachusetts-based think tank known as the Boston Visionary Cell. Best known for his intricately detailed and large-scale paintings that explored various subjects such as UFOs, alchemy, the Qabalah, and the occult, Laffoley had also been obsessed with the idea of time travel. In the mid-

1970's, Laffoley not only created a theory for time travel (which was this: "If you can control and amplify pre- and retro-cognition, pre-perception of the future and retro-perception of the past into an exaggerated form, that you will then fulfil the definition of time travel as Wells presents it in his novel," with Wells being a reference to H.G. Wells), but he also conceived of a device known as the Levogyre. In 1990, Laffoley created a new painting known as *Geochronmechane: The Time Machine from the Earth*, which provides an illustration of just what such a time-travel machine might look like. According to Laffoley, the machine uses an Orgone motor both to control and amplify the phenomena of psychokinesis, while the Levogyre is used to disconnect the time machine from the eight motions of the universe, using a complicated system of gimbals, space-time dilation, meta-energy and chakras. Z spent many hours carefully studying this work of art but eventually came to the conclusion that what Laffoley was articulating was simply beyond my ken. There were lots of references in the painting to the Chronpuknozone, cause-effect modules, time-antennas, wormholes, nootemporal and eotemporal levels, and of course, the Chakra-Pendula-Time-Oscillator, and while Z understood some of the basic concepts informing Laffoley's designs (to use but one example, my extensive readings into the pioneering work of Wilhelm Reich had left me well aware of the concept of Orgone energy), at the same time Z could not understand how this complex amalgamation of theories could combine to create a functioning time machine. Still, Laffoley's painting sent me down another theoretical promenade, when Z noticed, running along the bottom of the painting, a list of names of the artists, writers and thinkers that had inspired Laffoley's time machine. Some of these names included H.G. Wells, R. Buckminster Fuller, and, most importantly for my researches, the infamous French Symbolist and Pataphysician, Alfred Jarry (demiurge of the scatological 1896 play *Ubu Roi*), that biological precursor to the Dada/Surrealist/Futurist movements of the 20th century.

Topology 20: Time Machine Go!

My mind thus made up, Z first set my music player to begin playing track 3 off Coil's 1998 album *Time Machines* ("5-Methoxy-N, N-Dimethyltryptamine: (5-MeO-DMT"), and then (following a brief prayer to Doogu, otherwise known as The Blob, whom the Lemurian [problematical Weird Fiction terminological reference redaction] informs us is the Cyclic Chronodemon of Splitting-Waters), Z took a hit on the pipe, while with my other hand Z threw down the lever, thus activating the time machine, and then before I knew it:

Topology 16: The Z Explanation

A brief digression: I'm sure that some of you, by this point, are curious as to why I've been replacing the word "I" with the letter "Z." Perhaps you're under the impression that Z am simply being twee and precocious, or that Z have employed this strategy to make this story more difficult to read/understand. But Z can assure you that it is no mere postmodern pretension, but instead is simply force of habit, or respondent conditioning. Once again, this is something that may be traced back to my employment with HydraData. You see, when I'm at work, my corporate masters prefer that all HydraData employees substitute the letter "Z" in place of the word "I" when referring to ourselves, in an attempt to further depersonalise us: we are even encouraged to cut our arms with a razor blade should we accidentally refer to ourselves using the letter "I" (obviously one of the company higher-ups was familiar with Master Therion's *Liber III vel Jugorum*: "(c) Avoid using the pronouns and adjectives of the first person; use a paraphrase . . . On each occasion that thou art betrayed into saying that thou art sworn to avoid, cut thyself sharply upon the wrists or forearm with a razor, even as thou shouldst beat a disobedient dog. Feareth not the Unicorn the claws and teeth of the Lion?"). As one can imagine, this workplace practice eventually spilled over into my real life, and has thus now become a Pavlonian acquired behavior. Luckily, the use of the word "I'm" carries no such negative taboo (ditto for "I'll," "I've," and so on).

Topology 24: Jump!

Suddenly Z understood what had happened. Z had obviously accidentally gone into the future rather than the past, and what was before me now was the Earth to be. The phenomenon of XY ecophagy that Z was now a witness to was obviously the end result of my mad experiment with time: my younger haecceity self-replicating uncontrollably, until it quickly overwhelmed Earth's environment, wiping out all other life: a hebephiliacal variation on Eric Drexler's "grey goo" doomsday scenario. Faced with this knowledge, Z came to the only natural conclusion. First, Z mentally ordered my SkullSong audio biochip to begin playing an appropriate song (Fad Gadget's "Jump"). Z then leapt out of my time machine and a second later Z was plummeting away from the still-hovering cardboard box, with the boy ocean beneath me rising up to swallow me whole, their arms reaching up to me in benediction.

Topology 8: Alien Existence

One of the reasons why I'm so prone to anxiety is not only am Z a boy worshipper and an aesthete of the transitory (a sexual preference that can still provoke the odious obloquy of an anile society, even in 2036), at the same time Z couldn't act on my urges because I'm an *ethical* boy worshipper. Unlike many boy worshippers out there, Z don't really think that the objects of my affection are emotionally and physically equipped to be used in the manner intended by their would-be paramours and admirers (obviously, there are exceptions: Z have known a small number of gay acquaintances who, as teenagers, had fantasised about being seduced and fucked by older men). This then was my situation: Z wanted to fuck boys but at the same time my ethics forbade it. Metaphorically Z felt like Odysseus and his crew traversing the Strait of Messina, with Scylla on one side of me and Charybdis on the other: Z was between the proverbial Devil and the Deep Blue Sea.

Topology 13: The Pataphysical College

Seeing Jarry's name fingered a memory in my mind, a memory in which Z had purchased one of his books many, many years ago, the name of this book being

Alfred Jarry: Adventures in Pataphysics: Collected Works I (Atlas Press, 2001). Z vaguely recalled an essay in this book revolving around time travel, so Z promptly found the book in my archives and sure enough, my memory was ultraprecise. The essay was entitled "Commentary & Instructions for the Practical Construction of the Time Machine," and it first appeared in the 110th issue of *Mercure de France* (February 1899). Written by Jarry under the pseudonym of Dr. Faustroll, the essay gives a set of instructions as to how one can erect a time machine: apparently it involves a lot of spring balances, fly-wheels, gyrostats, ratchet-boxes, camshafts, bevel gears, and chains of quartz wire, among other things. There is also a lot of windy theorising on the concept of time travel, with jargon-heavy references to the "Luminiferous Ether" and "Riemannian spaces" that Z didn't entirely understand. The problem was, Z wasn't entirely sure that Jarry understood what he was talking about either. In any event, this proved to be another dead end (the same went for my re-reading of "The Mayan Caper" chapter from William S. Burroughs' novel *The Soft Machine*, though the theoretical implications of Burroughs' Lemurian insurgency in the occult time war with the One God Universe made for interesting bedtime reading).

Topology 6: Eater of Dreams

The dispiriting nature of my work environment was matched by the dispiriting nature of my work itself. HydraData was a highly competitive entertainment content provider determined to corner the market and wipe out all of their competitors. Most of the divisions that made up the company were tasked with creating entertainment, but not all of them followed such lofty pursuits. One of the shadier divisions at HydraData, the one that Z worked in, was officially known as the Creative Disillusionment Division; unofficially, it was known as the "Eater of Dreams." Those of us who worked in this division were tasked with seeking out various blogs and other social media platforms, keeping an eye out for any works of art created by impressionable young people, said works of art being everything from songs, to poetry, to videos, and so forth. In the opinion of HydraData, these young people were potential future competitors, and forthwith their artistic dreams had to be squashed before they could develop further. Once we found such a young person, we would then embark on a merciless campaign against their work, mocking them and their creations using a variety of aliases and pseudonyms. 90% of the time we succeeded in causing them to give up their life's dream, and in some cases we left our victims so emotionally devastated that they took their own lives (which usually resulted in big fat bonuses and promotions for all involved). As Z said, dispiriting work.

Topology 9: Grayve Times

Z also had to contend with another dilemma, namely, my aversion to the modern times in which Z found myself existing. It was becoming increasingly difficult to ignore the grim news that surrounded our reality like a malignant purple cloud. For example, the rise of the nihilistic death cult known as the 99,942 Children of the Atrophied World Serpent (yes, they had exactly 99,942 members), who worshipped the incoming near-Earth asteroid known as 99942 Apophis (so-named after the ancient Egyptian deity Apep, enemy of Ma'at, also known as the Uncreator and most often symbolised as a hydra-like mass of serpents: one of His nicknames was "Lord of Chaos"). Then there were all of the news stories of the plights of those citizens who had, in an attempt to escape the so-called Tyranny of Biology, made the decision to undergo the augmentation process: harrowing tales of Neuropozyne dependency and rejection psychosis, the kind of lurid stories that those with transhumanist agendas pretended didn't exist. That flyer Z had seen on the wall announcing the Grayve Times rave at UnderNet.245.91.003 (no doubt some kind of morbid gathering being organized by Rhizosigil propagandists, Yettuk cultists, Amnion cosplayers and Omarian Hive-Mind fetishists). Even the popular music of the day offers my soul no sustenance. At the time of which Z am writing, the #1 song in the USA is "Praise the Mutilated Sky" by the ultra-chic MeMeVid superstar Nigel Semen-Cornflakes (his real name).

Topology 11: Fringe

Now that Z had a goal to motivate myself with, my life was suddenly flooded with meaning again, and free of all crippling hebetude Z threw myself into this new project with as much zeal as Z could muster. My course of action was clear: Z needed to build a time machine. Obviously, such a thing is easier said than done. Before Z could set about building such a contraption, Z realized that Z would first need to study the concept of time travel itself in great detail, for once Z had grasped the mechanics behind the process, than Z would be able to create a fully functioning device. In this regard Z decided to shun the conventional books on the subject and instead turn to the less trodden paths of fringe science, outsider art and renegade literature: the Old Science. Keep in mind, as the CCRU once observed, "Everything interesting happens on the periphery." The fruits of this research Z will now share below.

Topology 1: Prolegomenon:
a Monody for Preterite æons (tell the others)

Z would asseverate, with the utmost sincerity, that the typical boy worshipper has a greater grasp for the aesthetics of tragedy than anything that you could extract from the festering Folios of that most overrated Bard of Avon. In this matter Z speak from a position of experience, being a theoretical boy worshipper myself (Z use the word "theoretical" because I've never actually carried out the vice itself, not counting within the cozy Mauve Zone confines of my skull). Oh, don't mistake me for your average garden variety paedophile: that overused word can't even be applied in classification to myself, as my own particular perversion could best be categorised as narcissistic hebephilia, which is a sexual attraction in adults towards children aged 11-14 that bear a resemblance to oneself at that age: pubescents and early adolescents, in other words. For whatever reason, I've just always felt a sexual attraction towards boys of that age, though it's not as if I'm in love with *all* boys of that age group. I'm very picky and particular about what Z like and dislike, being of discriminating taste (to be more exact, Z am primarily sexually interested in boys who looked exactly like Z did at that age, which kind of narrows the field). Z will admit that Z even find the word "BOY" itself sexually exciting, and there have been occasions where just seeing the word on a printed page has been enough to give me a considerable erection. To break it down using the analytic process, the letter "B" resembles a pair of spatulated buttocks as seen from above (assuming that the buttocks are of Kardashianesque dimensions), whereas the letter "O" is a proxy for the asshole itself. Z suppose you could say that the letter "Y" resembles the footprint left behind by a two-toed chicken, and while one may wonder what possible sexual connotation *that* image could have, Z would like to point out that the day on which Z experienced my first genuine ejaculatory experience was also the day that my parents got me my first pet, a chicken that had suffered some sort of mutilation to the effect that it only had two toes on each foot rather than the standard four: therefore, in the twisted neuronic labyrinths of my mind, I've come to associate mutilated chicken feet with the discovery and function of the orgasm.

Topology 4: The Cancer of Caducity

What I'm getting at here is this: that time is *evil*. Z wish Z could claim that this is an autochthonous cerebration on my part, but obviously others have come to this same conclusion. Certainly Dr. Leroy Jekyll elucidated as much in the so-called "Xith Notebooks" left behind to his family following his disappearance back in 1973, and the researches conducted by Dr. Adam Kadmon

into the recherché belief systems of fabled Atlantis reveals that even in the Elder World, others were aware
of the malignant nature of Time. Not that any of this
helped me in the least, for though Z knew the name
of my enemy, there was no way in which Z could vanquish it . . . after all, how can you battle a dimension?

Topology 21: Worship the Glitch (Axsys-Crash)

$C1/24F7: A5 10   LDA $10 [$00:0010]   A:0000
X:1000 Y:0003 D:0000
DB:7E S:15C7 P:envmxdIZC
$C1/24F9: 0A   ASL A   A:417F X:1000
Y:0003 D:0000
DB:7E S:15C7 P:envmxdIzC
$C1/24FA: 0A   ASL A   A:82FE X:1000
Y:0003 D:0000
DB:7E S:15C7 P:eNvmxdIzc
$C1/24FB: 18   CLC   A:05FC X:1000
Y:0003 D:0000
DB:7E S:15C7 P:envmxdIzC
$C1/24FC: 65 10   ADC $10 [$00:0010]   A:05FC
X:1000 Y:0003 D:0000
DB:7E S:15C7 P:envmxdIzc
$C1/24FE: AA   TAX   A:477B X:1000
Y:0003 D:0000
DB:7E S:15C7 P:envmxdIzc
$C1/24FF: BF 02 70 D2 LDA $D27002,X [$D2:B77D]
A:477B X:477B Y:0003 D:0000
DB:7E S:15C7 P:envmxdIzc

My name is Dr. Gemini Philotanus (what few friends I have call me 'Gem' for short). By day, Z work as a Dirty Word Specialist for the HydraData Corporation, which maintains its worldwide headquarters in the city Z currently reside in. As far as day jobs go, it could be classified as dispiriting, uninspiring work. The headquarters of the HydraData Corporation were located at the blighted borderland of the city, on a sabulous industrial park, and consisted of a number of sterile office buildings that were interconnected by an intricate network of skywalks (a useless bit of esoteric trivia: when viewed from above using Google Maps, the buildings resembled the Goetic seal of Malthus). My own office is situated in one of the outermost of the buildings. Though office isn't quite the right word, as it is essentially just one cubicle among many other cubicles in a large room that Z cohabit with many of my fellow corporate drones. Each of these cubicles contained a desk that was an identical workstation with its neighbours; they each held the same type of holo-computer terminal, 4D printer, and so on. The room itself was large and rectangular, and its eastern and western walls were lined with large pennons, the fronts of which were decorated with JPGs blown up to gigantic proportions, these JPGs being screenshots taken from the 1974 film adaptation of F. Scott Fitzgerald's novel *The Great Gatsby*, the image that of the famous dilapidated billboard from the film, displaying the sinister bespectacled always-watching eyes of Dr. T.J. Eckleburg. Just as those artificial, almost God-like eyes had silently observed the actions of the characters in both the film and novel, so it felt they also watched over us at HydraData at all times. And yet despite this paranoiac strain of thought, at the same time Z found it oddly comforting that one of the mysterious, never-seen head honchos of HydraData was apparently a big fan of the Robert Redford *Great Gatsby*. It gave them a slight bit of personality, made them feel less like Robbe-Grillet bloodless abstractions. But my coworkers and Z certainly felt like Robbe-Grillet bloodless abstractions, and it didn't help matters that we were all forced to wear identical clothing while on the clock, the clothing in this case being mauve-colored jumpsuits with the HydraData logo embossed on the front, this logo resembling the old Throbbing Gristle lightning bolt logo, just with a stylised serpentine face at the pointy tip. What I'm trying to get across here is that the HydraData Corporation was the very personification of abstract corporate horror.

Topology 15: Thinking Inside the Box

Finally, after researching and mentally dissecting all of these diverse conjectures and theories on the subject of time travel, Z came to the conclusion that perhaps the best way to solve a complex problem was through the simplest solution. So Z decided to employ the DIY *Calvin & Hobbes* route: Z found a cardboard box (one that was large enough that Z could comfortably sit inside in), wrote the words "Time Machine" on the side with a big, felt, black magic marker, then fashioned a crude dial system on the interior surface of the box (writing in a number of years around this dial, including the year that Z hoped to travel back to, which was 2004, the year in which Z was 12). The final touch was the implementation of a lever that would serve as the primary activation mechanism. Z then set about procuring for myself an extremely powerful synthetic psychedelic tryptamine (often employed by Nemirion Physicists to "Open the Gates") which was currently the trendy such hallucinogen of that year, the name of this drug being entitled "Mindphaser" (yes, a reference to the Whitehouse debut album *Birthdeath Experience*, though you've probably never heard of it).

Topology 19: Abstract Nympho

With some alarm, Z realised that ruminating on these ethical qualms was causing a decrease in my libido. To replenish my diminishing sexual energy, Z closed my eyes and visualised how Z hoped the events of my time travel expedition would unfold. The date Z had selected to return to was November 17th, 2004. Why that particular date? Simply because my parents had left me alone at home that night for a few hours to attend some kind of parent-teacher conference (ironically, the subject matter of this conference was protecting your children from sexual predators). It just so happened that Z still had a set of keys to my old house from way back when. According to my diary from that year, on the evening of November 17th, 2004, Z had taken a shower at 7 PM, then spent the next few hours in my bedroom playing the video game *Metal Gear Solid 3: Snake Eater* (which had been released that very day; Z had purchased my copy of it that same afternoon), while awaiting for my parents to return home. Upon arriving back in 2004, my plan involved me using the keys to enter the house, at the exact moment that my younger self would be taking a shower. Z would then sneak up the stairs (as stealthily as an under-aged rent boy seeking the flat of a British MP in Dolphin Square at Pimlico), enter my old bedroom, and hide in the closet, where I (ah, forgive this slip on my part, but Z must break off this narrative for the nonce to get a razor blade to mark my arm with . . . okay, back again), where Z would then wait for my younger self to finish his shower. When my younger self would return to the bedroom, Z would wait for myself to begin playing his (Z mean, my) video game. What with the TV facing the closet, this meant that my younger self would have his (Z mean, mine . . . fuck, this is getting confusing) back turned to the closet. Z would then sneak out of the closet and use a rag (remember, the cum-stained rag) doused in chloroform to render my younger self unconscious. Z would then use my handcuffs and bondage restraints to pinion my younger self into immobility. And after all that was done, then Z could finally have my way with . . . well, me. Z wasn't sure how things would proceed from that point on, but Z had some ideas for things that Z wished to try out: Z pictured myself gripping the top of my head with one hand while plunging my cock into my mouth, over and over again. And then, at the critical moment, Z saw myself ejaculating all over my face (it would be crucial to have music playing inside my skull during the violation: one song I had in mind as an appropriate rape soundtrack was Robert Ashley's "Purposeful Slow Lady Afternoon" off his 1979 album *Automatic Writing*). Obviously Z was tempted by the idea of sodomising myself and decorating the interior of my own youthful bowels with semen, but Z didn't want to run the risk of damaging that orifice. After all, my younger self would have to live with the pain, and Z didn't want him to suffer too much (remember that I'm an *ethical* Urning).

Of course, Z had to make sure that Z finished having my way with myself before Z woke up, and Z would also have to make sure that Z had cleaned my younger self off (away, incriminating spilth!) and also that Z had managed to leave the premises before Z had woken up as well, because Z didn't want my younger self to have any traumatic memories associated with this event (and what could be more traumatic than a memory of being fucked by one's future self?). The great thing about this scenario was that if this experiment of mine actually worked, and if Z managed to go back into the past, rape myself, then return to the present day, there was really nothing stopping me from repeating the experiment, over and over again, on a weekly or even daily basis if need be, until the end of time: Nietzsche's Eternal Recurrence taken to a pornographic extreme.

Topology 10: Persistence is All

In light of all this, Z began seeking a roborant to my existential crisis. This involved a lot of reading, and much time spent in meditation: Z lost count of how many hours Z spent meditating naked in the centre of my bedroom, in the lotus position, listening to the song "Anthem of the Trinity" off Terry Riley's classic 1980 album *Shri Camel* on loop inside my skull over and over again. Finally, after much thought and meditation, one day the solution to all of my problems came to me in a stereotypical "Eureka" moment. Like many great scientific or philosophical discoveries, it came during a twinkling of routine, everyday banality: Z was in my bathroom, jerking off (or "copulating with the Atmosphere" as Zos would have it described) while staring at a photograph of myself at the age of 12 (something I did at least once a week; as I've said, Z was very cute at that age), and at the moment of ejaculation, when my mind voided itself, the idea came to me just as Z was coming, like a chthonian muse ascending up from the Charonian stairway of my subconscious. Why not build a time machine for the express purpose of going back in time so that Z could fuck myself as a younger man? It was a win-win situation for me: on one hand I'd finally be able to achieve my lifelong dream of fucking a boy, and on the other hand, technically, Z wouldn't be doing anything wrong because I'd literally be fucking myself. One could almost argue that it was nothing more than a highly advanced form of masturbation, really.

Topology 17: The Rites of Zom

Finally, the crepuscular hour of my grand experiment had arrived. Before embarking on my expedition Z was seated in the armchair of my study, bereft of habiliments, my erect penis gripped firmly in my hand, and as Z stroked myself Z had my eyes closed and Z was listening to music on my SkullSong v.2.3 biochip audio player (the song currently playing within the interior of my head was "Mu" by Sun Ra, off his *Atlantis* album). Contrary to what you might be thinking, Z was not masturbating to relieve any tension, but rather to build up some of the requisite sexual energy to power my time machine, as instructed by Bertiaux (it was also for this reason that Z stopped masturbating before reaching the climacteric moment, as Z did not want the energy to go to waste). Once a satisfactory amount of sexual puissance had been built up, Z rose from my seat and exited my study, walking down the hall to my bedroom, my cock pointing the way like a dowser's wand. In the centre of my bedroom (and pointed in a north-west direction) rested my time-travel machine, the outer surface of which Z had decorated with witchy-looking sigils and voudon vévés. Most of these glyphs had been drawn using paint and ink, but a few had been consecrated with mine own semen. Resting at the back of the box's interior was a small bag containing a number of necessary items for the upcoming Frolic: my drug kit, a bathrobe, a cum-stained rag and a bottle of chloroform, handcuffs, an S&M-style ball and gag, and various documents to identify myself should Z run afoul of the law. Z climbed into the box, and then, while readying my dose of Mindphaser, Z instructed my SkullSong biochip to start playing a new song: "Witness the Spread of the Dream" off the Cut Hands album *Black Mamba*. Over a soundscape consisting of a sinister and hypnotic drone, an eerily emotionless female voice began robotically reading off a sequence of numbers: 51, 24, 26, 11 (this was followed by some very cryptic lyrics). Once my hit of Mindphaser was ready, Z next checked the numogram time-map to make sure it was set at the appropriate date, and Z saw that it was: 2004. Everything was ready.

Topology 7: *En rade*

Anyway, every day after work Z would take the Musk Hyperloop to get back to my house, which was located on the opposite edge of the city. Stepping through the front doors of my house and entering my demesne was always one of the highlights of my day, as Z have always viewed my habitat as a Huysmansian haven from a hostile world, and after hours spent in the banal and antiseptic warrens of HydraData, it was a relief to find myself surrounded in an environment that Z had especially designed to match my aesthetic standards. A few of my prized possessions include a framed publicity poster for the 1964 French film *Les amitiés particulières* (*This Special Friendship*), which was itself an adaptation of a novel written by the notorious boy fucker and libertine Roger Peyrefitte: this poster was a photograph of the then 12-year-old Didier Haudepin, who played an altar boy in the film, and in this photograph the super sexy Haudepin was playing peekaboo like a shameless little slut. There were numerous framed Pierre Joubert prints, including one depicting Neptune as a teenage boy. In the nautical painting I speak of, this teenage Neptune is riding atop a large (and oddly jovial-looking) seahorse-type creature, and he is utterly naked, his genitals tastefully hidden from sight: on his head the boy (who has long blonde hair) is wearing a golden crown, and with his right hand he is holding a trident, while his left hand clutches the reins of his mount. In the waves surrounding the boy-god are assorted blue- and green-skinned undines and mermaids (for the record, Z have also often jerked off to one of Joubert's *Jungle Book* illustrations, which depicts the Mowgli character butt naked and seen from behind, his glorious mouth-watering ass on full display, knife in hand as he confronts a pack of wolves whose fur is stained with blood). And who could forget to mention one of my favourite works of art produced in the 21st century, an untitled collage by Michael Salerno (of Kiddiepunk fame) from his 2016 Firestarters series: the upper half of the artwork is a photograph of a house on fire, with smoke looming above the roof and great tongues of flame unfurling from the windows. A jagged white rip runs erratically through the centre of this collage, and on the bottom half of the artwork is the head and upper torso of a beautiful boy (as seen from a side profile). This shirtless boy is lying flat on his back, with his eyes closed, while his mouth is open and his tongue is extending upwards. Seeing as he's posed directly beneath the largest of the flaming windows above, the overall effect is that it makes it look as if the boy is licking the flames in a delirium of phlegethonian ecstasy. As Z said, a most impressive work of art. But by far my most prized possession was the very pair of tight white briefs so erotically worn by the then-12-year-old Zachary Gordon during the infamous "running around in only his underwear" scene from the 2010 film production of the 2011 film *Diary of a Wimpy Kid: Rodrick Rules*: Z kept these framed up on the wall and stored behind glass, and Z treated them with the same veneration that a Christian would treat the Shroud of Turin. Oh, it would be remiss of me not to mention my beloved book collection as well. Shelf after shelf housing some of my all-time favorite books, including Tony Duvert's *Strange Landscapes*, *The Boyish Muse* by Straton of Sardis, my collection of vintage *Destroyer* magazines, the Penguin Classics 3-in-1 edition of Peter Sotos' novels *Index*, *Lazy* and *Tick*, and also Phil Slackmeyer's epic World War II memoir *Hell in Triplicate: A Company Clerk Remembers* (Z mention that latter title just so you don't operate under the impression that I'm a complete pervert in every way, shape and form; Z do have other interests aside from boys, collecting sea glass being another). To make a long story short, my home was my haven, and Z would often like to whittle away the hours taking in the beauty of my plutonian pretties while blasting Terry

Riley and John Cale's song "The Church of Anthrax" on my deluxe cochlear implants (like most people these days, Z now essentially have an MP3 Player biochip installed inside my head that lets me play music directly into my inner ears, thus bypassing the need for clunky headphones or anachronistic earbuds: the technical name for this audio biochip is SkullSong v.2.3).

Topology 14: Arachnid Lycanthropy

The next book Z consulted was Michael Bertiaux's *The Voudon Gnostic Workbook* (to be exact, the ultra-rare and equally ultra-expensive first edition put out by Magickal Childe, Inc. in 1988, not the more easily available second edition published by Weiser Books in 2007 or, for that matter, the even more easily available third edition issued by Star Venom Press in 2028). The book is divided into four parts, the first of which is entitled "Voudoo Energies," and it was here that Z found the information Z needed, in chapter 2, lesson 1a: "Lessons on the 'Points-Chauds': Le Temple-Des-Houdeaux." But Z found Bertiaux's writing very hard to follow, so Z ended up turning to David Beth's slim but venomous volume *Voudon Gnosis*, which had been published by the Scarlet Imprint in 2008 (my own copy was numbered 302 of 555, and it was personally autographed and inscribed to me by the author himself). In this book Beth looks at the Le Temple Des Houdeuax lessons described in Bertiaux's book and explains them in a somewhat more lucid manner. As far as Z could tell, this was how the time-travel operation is conducted: first, one sits at a Voudon altar in a room that is only illuminated by either candles or natural light. The time traveler concentrates, then opens the Gates to the world of the Voudon spirits. The time traveler proceeds to raise sexual energy by "any means necessary," and once this energy has been raised they then "enter" (in a mental or imaginative sense) the Temple Des Houdeaux (which is, again, a mental construct or projection). The time traveler than visualises himself (or herself or itself or noself) as a were-spider with eight legs (to better frighten off the bad-UFOs and sex vampires), these eight legs corresponding to Bertiaux's eight directions of space. The time traveler then concentrates on the "leg" (or direction) that corresponds to the time period in which they wish to explore. Visualising the guardian of that direction, they proceed to mentally "draw" that guardian's vévé as a way of establishing contact with them. Once this contact has been established, the time traveler can then project themselves through that sigil and begin exploring the selected time period. So if one wished to travel to the past of the Earth, they would utilise the northwest strand of the web, which was under the domain of the lwa Mystere Araignee, otherwise known as the Mother Spider of Scorpio (conversely, activating the south or southwest strand would take one to the Earth's future, the world of Oerg-8: a sexo-magickal culture of erotic schedules controlled by perverted servo-mechanisms powered by neo-orgonomic energy matrices: beware the siren's call of the System and the Monitor).

Topology 25: Drowning in Beauty

Z cannot claimed that Z landed with a splash because the mass that broke my fall was not made up of water, but of boyflesh. For a moment, Z floated atop that "ocean" of naked boys, boys who looked exactly as Z did back when Z was twelve, and Z smiled the first authentic and gratified smile that Z had ever smiled in my entire life. Then Z was sucked beneath the surface, as by quicksand, and in seconds Z was plummeting down through that sea of naked boys, unable to breathe. It was like being ingurgitated by a monolithic blastosphere, and during this process the ending of David Bowie's song "Time" was ironically looping within my skull. And yet the smile remained on my face the entire duration, all the way down that fantastic death abyss. Saikaku once famously wrote that "Making love to boys is like the sleep of a wolf under a flower whose petals are falling." But in my dying moments, as my last breaths were sponged up by that ocean of pubescent flesh, I received the primal revelation: to make love to a boy is to drown in beauty.

Topology 18: Astral Disaster

Before taking my first hit of Mindphaser, Z hesitated, the pipe held immobile before my lips. On some level Z was aware that what Z was about to do was, in so many ways, utterly unprecedented. That evening Z was going to not only be violating the laws of science (through the perversion of time travel), but also the laws of Nature (through my intention of literally fucking myself). Like Huysmans' Durtal character in *Là-Bas*, Z was about to create a new vice, and how many men can lay claim to such a thing these jaded days? Yet Z was aware that these violations could have catastrophic effects on the world at large, not only on a physical but also a psychic level. If my experiment went wrong, it had the potential of unhinging Time itself, could even permanently destroy the very conception of beeline chronology and linear perception. This was something that Z needed to think long and hard about: these ethical breaches and the ramifications that could result from them, and what it might all entail for the future of my species. Never mind the danger of attracting the prurient interest of Anthropol (themselves unwitting agents of the Archons of the Architectonic Order of the Eschaton). Was the risk worth it? Should the rest of humanity suffer for my orotund surquedry? Was my desire to fuck myself as a boy capable of knocking Time out of joint, thus creating a reality where there were no true beginnings and no true endings? Yet perhaps this act of calendric secessionism was the key to my salvation, the one and only way in which Z could triumph against Time, my eternal foe; for is not the hourglass a prison pinioning the soul of a dreaming desert, something screaming to be smashed so that its noble captive can be liberated from its shackles? You know how to swallow darling. Let's see you do it!

Come on honey . . .

"If there is one thing you can say with computerized certainty about any sexual feeling it is this: it is a repetition of a previously experienced sexual feeling.

Pleasure is the repetition of past pleasure. So someone who is attracted to small boys is simply attempting to travel back in time and re-experience his own past pleasure."

—William S. Burroughs

ABOUT THE AUTHORS

Avalon Brantley is the author of the collections *Transcensience* and *Descended Suns Resuscitate*, as well as *Aornos*, a mind-staged hallucinatory tragedy in the classical vein, set in Greece during the Archaic Period. Avalon Brantley passed away on March 5, 2017. Her posthumous novel, *The House of Silence*, was released by Zagava in 2017.

James Champagne is the author of the collections *Grimoire: A Compendium of Neo-Goth Narratives* (2012) and *Autopsy of an Eldritch City: Ten Tales of Strange & Unproductive Thinking* (2015), both published by Rebel Satori Press. He has also written two novels, *Confusion* (self-published, 2006) and *Harlem Smoke* (forthcoming). His work has appeared in the anthologies *Userlands: New Fiction Writers From the Blogging Underground*, *Mighty in Sorrow: a Tribute to Current 93 & David Tibet*, and *Marked to Die: A Tribute to Mark Samuels*. He was born in 1980 and lives in Rhode Island.

Brendan Connell was born in Santa Fe, New Mexico, in 1970. His works of fiction include *Unpleasant Tales* (Eibonvale Press, 2013), *The Architect* (PS Publishing, 2012), *Lives of Notorious Cooks* (Chômu Press, 2012), *Miss*

Homicide Plays the Flute (Eibonvale Press, 2013), *Jottings from a Far Away Place* (Snuggly Books, 2015), and *Cannibals of West Papua* (Zagava, 2015).

Daniel Corrick is a writer and philosopher living in London. For several years he ran Hieroglyphic Press and, with Mark Samuels, co-edited the journal *Sacrum Regnum*. He is interested in literature dealing with themes of transcendence and the connection between beauty and the supernatural. Since an early childhood encounter with dogmatic short-furred weasels, he stands for the nullity of politics, black glittery things and the absolute triumph of the modal perfection argument.

Quentin S. Crisp was born in 1972, in North Devon, U.K. He studied Japanese at Durham University and graduated in the year 2000. From 2001 to 2003, he did research in Japanese literature, on a Monbushô Scholarship, at Kyôto University. He has had fiction and poetry published by Tartarus Press, PS Publishing, Eibonvale Press, Snuggly Books and others. He currently resides in Bexleyheath, is editor for Chômu Press and is studying for an MA in philosophy at Birkbeck College.

Colin Insole lives in Lymington, on the edge of the New Forest in England. He has contributed to a number of anthologies, including tribute volumes to Bruno Schulz, William Blake and Emil Cioran. His novella 'Bluebells I'll Gather' was recently published in 'Darkly Haunting' by Sarob Press. Colin's first collection of stories, *Elegies and Requiems*, was published by Side Real Press (Newcastle upon Tyne) in 2013.

Justin Isis has lived in Tokyo for close to ten years. His collections include *I Wonder What Human Flesh Tastes Like* (2011) and *Welcome to the Arms Race* (2016) from Chômu Press, and the forthcoming *Pleasant Tales II* from Snuggly Books, as well as the poetry collection *Divorce Procedures For the Hairdressers of a Metallic and Inconstant Goddess* (2016). He has previously edited Chômu Press's *Dadaoism* anthology (2012), and *Marked to Die: A Tribute to Mark Samuels* (Snuggly Books). His stories have appeared in *Postscripts* and a number of anthologies.

Damian Murphy is the author of *The Imperishable Sacraments*, *Seduction of the Golden Pheasant*, and *Abyssinia*, among other collections and novellas. His work has been published on the Mount Abraxas, Les Éditions de L'Oubli, and L'Homme Récent imprints of Ex Occidente Press, in Bucharest, and by Zagava Books, in Dusseldorf. His latest collection, published by Snuggly Books in September of 2017, and the first to be offered in a paperback edition, is entitled *Daughters of Apostasy*. He was born and lives in Seattle, Washington.

Yarrow Paisley lives in Western Massachusetts. His fiction appears in a number of publications, among them *Dadaoism* from Chômu Press, *Strange Tales V* from Tartarus Press, and *Marked to Die: A Tribute to Mark Samuels* from Snuggly Books. His Snuggly Slim is called *Mendicant City*. His collection *I, No Other* is available from Whiskey Tit.

Ursula Pflug is the author of the novels *Green Music*, *The Alphabet Stones*, *Motion Sickness* (a flash novel illustrated by SK Dyment); the YA novella *Mountain* and the story collections *After the Fires* and *Harvesting the Moon*.

She edited the anthologies *They Have To Take You In* and *Playground of Lost Toys* (with Colleen Anderson). Her award winning short fiction and essays have appeared in Lightspeed, Fantasy, Strange Horizons, Postscripts, Leviathan, LCRW, Now Magazine, Bamboo Ridge, NYRSF, Great Jones Street and others. Her short stories have been taught in universities in Canada and India, and she has collaborated extensively on multimedia projects.

Colby Smith is a native of West Virginia. His flash fiction has been published in AntipodeanSF and ZeroFLASH. He is currently working towards a BA in Geology, as well as minors in paleontology and English, at Ohio University.

D.P. Watt lives between Scotland and England in an otherworldly, misty borderland. His collection of short stories *An Emporium of Automata* was reprinted by Eibonvale Press in early 2013 and his second collection, *The Phantasmagorical Imperative and Other Fabrications*, was published in 2014 with Egaeus Press and is now available in a paperback edition. His third collection *Almost Insentient, Almost Divine* was published in 2016 by Undertow Publications and was nominated for a Shirley Jackson Award. You can find him at The Interlude House: www.theinterludehouse.co.uk.

A PARTIAL LIST OF SNUGGLY BOOKS

LÉON BLOY *The Tarantulas' Parlor and Other Unkind Tales*

S. HENRY BERTHOUD *Misanthropic Tales*

FÉLICIEN CHAMPSAUR *The Latin Orgy*

FÉLICIEN CHAMPSAUR *The Emerald Princess and Other Decadent Fantasies*

BRENDAN CONNELL *Metrophilias*

QUENTIN S. CRISP *Blue on Blue*

LADY DILKE *The Outcast Spirit and Other Stories*

BERIT ELLINGSEN *Vessel and Solsvart*

EDMOND AND JULES DE GONCOURT *Manette Salomon*

RHYS HUGHES *Cloud Farming in Wales*

JUSTIN ISIS *Divorce Procedures for the Hairdressers of a Metallic and Inconstant Goddess*

VICTOR JOLY *The Unknown Collaborator and Other Legendary Tales*

BERNARD LAZARE *The Mirror of Legends*

JEAN LORRAIN *Masks in the Tapestry*

JEAN LORRAIN *Nightmares of an Ether-Drinker*

JEAN LORRAIN *The Soul-Drinker and Other Decadent Fantasies*

CAMILLE MAUCLAIR *The Frail Soul and Other Stories*

CATULLE MENDÈS *Bluebirds*

LUIS DE MIRANDA *Who Killed the Poet?*

OCTAVE MIRBEAU *The Death of Balzac*

DAMIAN MURPHY *Daughters of Apostasy*

KRISTINE ONG MUSLIM *Butterfly Dream*

YARROW PAISLEY *Mendicant City*

URSULA PFLUG *Down From*

DAVID RIX *A Suite in Four Windows*

FREDERICK ROLFE *An Ossuary of the North Lagoon and Other Stories*

JASON ROLFE *An Archive of Human Nonsense*

BRIAN STABLEFORD *Spirits of the Vasty Deep*

BRIAN STABLEFORD (editor) *Decadence and Symbolism: A Showcase Anthology*

TOADHOUSE *Gone Fishing with Samy Rosenstock*